What Reviewers Say About Bold Strokes Books

"With its expected unexpected twists, ~~~~~~~~ dose of humor, *Blind Curves* is a very ~~~~~~~~ guessing." – *Bay Windows*

"In a succinct film style narrative, with s~~~~~~~~ driven plot, and crisp dialogue worthy of ~~~~~~~~ and Rivers novels are ... an engaging Hollywood mystery ... series." – *Midwest Book Review*

Force of Nature "...is filled with nonstop, fast paced action. Tornadoes, raging fire blazes, heroic and daring rescues... Baldwin does a fine job of describing the fast-paced scenes and inspiring the reader to keep on turning the pages." – *L-word.comLiterature*

In the Jude Devine mystery series the "...characters seem fully capable of walking away from the particulars of whodunit and engaging the reader in other aspects of their lives." – *Lambda Book Report*

Mine "...weaves a tale of yearning, love, lust, and conflict resolution ... a believable plot, with strong characters in a charming setting." – *JustAboutWrite*

"While these two women struggle with their issues, there is some very, very hot sex. If you enjoy complex characters and passionate sex scenes, you'll love *Wild Abandon*." – *MegaScene*

"*Course of Action* is a romance ... populated with a host of captivating and amiable characters. The glimpses into the lifestyles of the rich and beautiful people are rather like guilty pleasures ... a most satisfying and entertaining reading experience." – *Midwest Book Review*

The Clinic is "...a spellbinding novel." – *JustAboutWrite*

"*Unexpected Sparks* lived up to its promise and was thoroughly enjoyable ... Dartt did a lovely job at building the relationship between Kate and Nikki." – *Lambda Book Report*

"*Sequestered Hearts* ... is everything a romance should be. It is teeming with longing, heartbreak, and of course, love. As pure romances go, it is one of the best in print today." – *L-word.comLiterature*

"*The Exile and the Sorcerer* is a mesmerizing read, a tour-de-force packed with adventure, ordeals, complex twists and turns, and the internal introspection of appealing characters." – *Midwest Book Review*

The Spanish Pearl is "...both science fiction and romance in this adventurous tale ... A most entertaining read, with a sequel already in the works. Hot, hot, hot!" – *Minnesota Literature*

"A deliciously sexy thriller ... *Dark Valentine* is funny, scary, and very realistic. The story is tightly written and keeps the reader gripped to the exciting end." – *JustAbout Write*

"*Punk Like Me* ... is different. It is engaging. It is life-affirming. Frankly, it is genius. This is a rare book in that it has a soul; one that is laid bare for all to see." – *JustAboutWrite*

"*Chance* is not a novel about the music industry; it is about a woman discovering herself as she muddles through all the trappings of fame." – *Midwest Book Review*

Sweet Creek "... is sublimely in tune with the times." – *Q-Syndicate*

"*Forever Found* ... neatly combines hot sex scenes, humor, engaging characters, and an exciting story." – *MegaScene*

Shield of Justice is a "...well-plotted...lovely romance...I couldn't turn the pages fast enough!" – Ann Bannon, author of *The Beebo Brinker Chronicles*

The 100th Generation is "...filled with ancient myths, Egyptian gods and goddesses, legends, and, most wonderfully, it contains the lesbian equivalent of Indiana Jones living and working in modern Egypt." – *Just About Write*

Sword of the Guardian is "...a terrific adventure, coming of age story, a romance, and tale of courtly intrigue, attempted assassination, and gender confusion ... a rollicking fun book and a must-read for those who enjoy courtly light fantasy in a medieval-seeming time." – *Midwest Book Review*

"*Of Drag Kings and the Wheel of Fate*'s lush rush of a romance incorporates reincarnation, a grounded transman and his peppy daughter, and the dark moods of a troubled witch—wonderful homage to Leslie Feinberg's classic gender-bending novel, *Stone Butch Blues*." – *Q-Syndicate*

In *Running with the Wind* "...the discussions of the nature of sex, love, power, and sexuality are insightful and represent a welcome voice from the view of late-20-something characters today." – *Midwest Book Review*

"Rich in character portrayal, *The Devil Inside* is an unusual, unpredictable, and thought-provoking love story that will have the reader questioning the definition of right and wrong long after she finishes the book." – *JustAboutWrite*

Wall of Silence "...is perfectly plotted and has a very real voice and consistently accurate tone, which is not always the case with lesbian mysteries." – *Midwest Book Review*

Romantic
INTERLUDES 1: DISCOVERY

Visit us at www.boldstrokesbooks.com

Romantic

INTERLUDES 1: DISCOVERY

edited by

RADCLY*f*FE and
STACIA SEAMAN

2008

ROMANTIC INTERLUDES 1: DISCOVERY

ISBN 10: 1-60282-027-9
ISBN 13: 978-1-60282-027-2

THIS TRADE PAPERBACK ORIGINAL IS PUBLISHED BY
BOLD STROKES BOOKS, INC.
NEW YORK, USA

FIRST EDITION: SEPTEMBER 2008

CREDITS
EDITORS: RADCLYFFE AND STACIA SEAMAN
PRODUCTION DESIGN: STACIA SEAMAN
COVER ART: BARB KIWAK (WWW.KIWAK.COM)
COVER DESIGN BY SHERI (GRAPHICARTIST2020@HOTMAIL.COM)

CONTENTS

INTRODUCTION

It's really very simple. Romance—the act, the emotion, the quest for, and the celebration of—is one of the quintessential human experiences. Infinite in form, universal, and unique, romance embodies all that is good, noble, and honorable about the human condition. In the short stories contained in this anthology, the Bold Strokes authors explore romance with the same challenging, provocative, sensual, and erotic power that is the signature of our novels. Romance—as you've never lived it before.

Radcly*f*fe 2008

Romance brings out the best in all of us. From the boundless optimism of new love, to the rediscovery of something feared to be lost, to the deep appreciation of a cherished partner, to the transition from couple into family—with all of the new obstacles and emotions that entails, these stories explore the spectrum of women loving women. Joyful, rejuvenating, erotic—this is romance at its finest.

Stacia Seaman 2008

Born and raised in upstate New York, ERIN DUTTON now lives in beautiful middle Tennessee where she works in the 9-1-1 system. In her free time she enjoys reading, movies, and playing golf.

She is the author of three novels, *Sequestered Hearts, Fully Involved*, and *A Place to Rest*. She's currently working on a Matinee romance, *Designed for Love*, which will be published in November 2008. She is also a contributor to the anthology *Erotic Interludes 5: Road Games*.

FINDING MY MUSE
ERIN DUTTON

*S**he traced her tongue along the arch of one slender foot.*
Alex leaned over my shoulder and read aloud, then paused and said, "That's hot, Cote. Where do you come up with this stuff?"

I shrugged, unable to explain where the words came from. I'd been writing the stories in my head in one form or another for most of my life. That fact that it had eventually evolved into a career as a romance novelist was an added bonus.

"I'm serious. Your books sell like hotcakes." I cringed at the cliché. "Women lap this shit up."

I laughed. "You're such a romantic."

Her look of offense was obviously feigned. "Hey, I can be romantic. Just because I'm not as hopeless as you."

"Ha. You? Romantic? Sweetie, I don't think opening the bedroom door for a woman counts as romance."

"How can you keep churning it out?" Alex straightened and stepped away. "Especially since I can't remember the last time you had a date, let alone sex."

Her assessment was a bit too close to the truth for me. Normally, I would have asserted that my single status was by choice, but with Alex there was no point in pretending. She'd been my closest friend for ten years, starting when I used to date her cousin, and there was little I could put past her.

"How do you know I haven't had sex?"

"Because you'd have told me."

She was right, I would have. But I got defensive anyway. I spun around in my chair and pinned her with an accusing look. "Well, just because you can get it whenever and wherever, doesn't mean the rest of us can."

"You're an attractive woman. If you'd put yourself out there you could meet someone."

"Even if I wanted to, I don't have time. I've got to have this draft done in two weeks." I clung to a familiar excuse instead of admitting that since I'd gained those extra ten pounds, I didn't feel so attractive anymore.

She shoved a hand through hair as dark as midnight and so thick it immediately fell back onto her forehead. "Why do I bother?"

Because I knew she didn't expect a response, I turned back to my computer and resumed typing.

❖

"Damn it, this scene is not working," I muttered, my voice muffled by the pencil clenched in my teeth. Though I'd been working exclusively on my computer for years, I still liked the feel of a pencil in my hand. I twirled it while considering ideas and, when typing, I tucked it behind my ear.

Idly, I spun my chair around, resisting the urge to give up for the night. The more frustrated I got, the less chance I would sort out the problem with my latest sex scene. From my desk in the small dining room that I'd converted to an office, I could see the living room. The sofa, soft fleece blanket, and television were calling my name. Turning away, I forced my attention to the manuscript and within minutes I was typing again.

A knock at the door interrupted what little momentum I'd had going. After dropping the pencil on the desk, I stood. When I opened the door, I couldn't contain a gasp. Alex was stunning in a perfectly tailored black tuxedo sans tie. A jacket cut to fit her broad shoulders and narrow waist covered a starched white shirt left open at the collar. Features that I'd been looking at for years suddenly seemed more striking. Angular cheekbones slashed beneath dramatic gray eyes. I'd never fully appreciated her strong jaw and full, sensuous lips.

"What is this, Cote?" She gestured to my sweatpants and threadbare tee. "It's Friday night." Shaking her head, she shouldered her way past me. "Good thing I came to rescue you."

"Hey," I protested before following her to the living room. While certainly not a fashion statement, my sweats were my most comfortable pair. My face was free of makeup and I'd pulled my long brown hair into a sloppy ponytail. Over the years, Alex had seen me at my worst, and I'd never been self-conscious about my appearance. But now with her looking so incredible, I just felt frumpy.

"I promised Laura I would go to her fund-raiser tonight for gay and lesbian victims of domestic violence, and my date got sick. You know I hate to go to these things alone. So go put on your party dress."

Our friend Laura had tried to rope me into the fund-raiser as well but I'd begged off, saying I had too much work to do. Alex settled on one end of my leather sofa, propped an ankle on the opposite knee, and gave me an expectant look.

"I have a lot of work to do."

"You can take one night off. Go get dressed."

"As you so delicately pointed out, it's not a matter of just throwing on a dress." I crossed my arms uncomfortably.

She shrugged. "So we'll be fashionably late." When I didn't move she adopted her most charming smile, lifting one side of her mouth higher than the other and drawing her eyebrows together slightly. "Don't make me go alone. I'd really love the pleasure of your company."

I'd been a victim of her persuasive efforts before. "You know that Romeo shit doesn't work on me."

"Please, Cote. Go put on that black number that makes your breasts look perky and come with me."

I sighed, knowing she'd keep asking until I relented. "Okay, but I'm not rushing."

She grinned and picked up the television remote. "I'll wait."

Grumbling, I headed for my bedroom, but she was already engrossed in a documentary about dromedary camels and wouldn't hear me complaining anyway.

As I passed through the bedroom, I pulled the black dress from the closet. With the right bra, it did display my breasts nicely. But I hesitated, thinking instead about the red one I'd bought at Neiman Marcus months before and hadn't had an occasion to wear. After replacing the black one, I reached to the back of the closet.

The V-neck was so deep that the cap sleeves threatened to slip off the ends of the hanger. The bodice was snug but beneath the bust it flowed loosely to just above the knee and would disguise the extra weight on my hips and thighs. Or so I'd optimistically convinced myself when I'd splurged on the dress. And it would go perfectly with those strappy black heels I never got to wear.

I took my time in the shower and afterward, applying floral scented lotion before slipping into the dress. Standing in the middle of my bedroom, I nearly gave in to my panicked desire to take the dress off. The plunging neckline left absolutely no room for a bra and revealed far more skin and cleavage than I was comfortable with. But it did fit perfectly, accentuating the right curves and hiding the others. Besides, it was too late to return it, and who knew when I would get a chance to wear it again. As a reclusive author, my social calendar wasn't exactly bursting with cocktail parties.

I studied my image as I applied makeup and found myself thinking about Alex, sitting out there looking stunning. The eye shadow I chose was meant to enhance my green eyes, and the mascara promised volume and thickness. I wondered if she would notice. Of course she wouldn't. I was her friend, a pal, and she was only here because her date got sick.

I made her wait fifteen more minutes before I returned to the living room. Stuffing my keys in the small black clutch, I touched her shoulder as I passed.

"Ready?"

She turned off the television. "Sure, I…"

I was at the door before I realized she hadn't followed and she wasn't speaking anymore.

"Alex?" When I turned, she was staring at me.

"You…ah, nothing. You look…um, I mean…"

I'd never seen her struggle so much to get something out. "What's wrong, hot stuff?" I teased.

"That's not the black dress," she nearly stuttered.

"No. I thought I'd surprise you." My normally confident friend was flustered, a seal of approval for the dress.

She trailed her eyes over my body and I felt my chest and neck flush as her gaze lingered on the exposed curve of my breasts. Then she cleared her throat and visibly brought her reaction under control.

She moved close to me and took my hand. "You look beautiful. Shall we?"

She led me to the street, still wet from the day's rain. Her silver Saab was parked a block away beneath the orange glow of a street lamp. As we walked I wrapped my arms around myself to ward off the slight chill.

"Do you want my jacket?" She stopped, already slipping it off her shoulders.

"No. I'm fine." I grabbed her lapels and pulled the jacket back around her. Not wanting to wrinkle it, I smoothed the fine fabric over her chest. Her familiar musky cologne had never brought this flutter to my stomach. "Really."

"I don't mind."

"I'm fine. Let's go."

She put her arm around me and tucked me against her side for warmth as we walked the half block to the car. She opened the passenger door, then, when I was settled, circled the car and slid behind the wheel.

"What kind of crowd is it tonight?" I asked as she steered into traffic.

"Rich people who don't know what else to do with their money, no doubt."

"So, your circle of friends?" Despite the obscene fortune Alex's family had amassed, she was the most unassuming person I'd ever met. She'd worked hard and had earned her place in law school, then built her practice on her own merit. Still, I couldn't resist the opportunity to tease her about her snooty peers.

"Hey, Laura is your friend, too."

Laura, Alex's ex, was the chair of the fund-raising committee for tonight's event. She was Alex's opposite, embracing her trust-fund status. If you were in her circle, Laura could be a best friend, but she was also quick to judge and a bit of a snob.

"Is she still with Olivia?"

"Yeah, they're going strong. And I take full credit for that." She glanced over, and in the dim interior of the car, the amusement shone in her eyes.

"Is that how it works? You get credit because they got together while both were commiserating over how you broke their hearts."

"Yes." She turned into the U-shaped drive in front of the Palisades Hotel. "Here we are."

She tossed the keys to the valet as she jumped out of the car and hurried around to open my door.

"My, my, your manners are showing tonight," I purred as I grasped the offered elbow.

"I'm trying to salvage my reputation."

"Why? I already know you're a player."

"Yeah. I never could get anything over on you." Her smile appeared forced and at odds with the flash of disappointment in her eyes.

As we entered the hotel, she guided me into a crowd of people headed for the ballroom. Inside, she barely seemed to notice the crystal chandeliers refracting light throughout the room or the dozens of tuxedoed waiters circulating trays of champagne and canapés. She was comfortable among the men and women in formal wear. On the arms of many of those handsome women in exquisitely cut suits were women in all manner of gowns and jewelry.

A cluster of musicians in one corner provided a string accompaniment to the din of conversation. Alex leaned close, her hand warm against the back of my shoulder.

"Would you like a drink?"

"Yes, please."

"I'll be right back." Ignoring several passing waiters, she headed for the bar. Champagne made Alex sick. I knew she'd come back with a glass of Zinfandel for me and a Highland Park for her.

"Why, Cote, what a pleasure."

I turned at the lilting voice behind me to find a tall brunette, who looked gorgeous in a deep blue sheath, accompanied by an equally statuesque blonde. These were the type of beautiful women Alex usually got involved with, and suddenly I felt ridiculous for thinking she would notice me just because I put on a new dress.

"Olivia. Laura." I accepted Laura's half-embrace and glanced around the room with admiration. "Everything looks perfect."

"Well, it's for a good cause. I thought you were otherwise engaged this evening."

"She was," Alex said as she handed me a glass. "I kidnapped her."

"Alex's date is ill."

"Well, then, how convenient that you could fill in," Olivia said, though her eyes were on Alex.

"Yeah, lucky for me." Grinning, Alex wrapped an arm around my waist and pulled me tightly to her side.

Olivia's eyes narrowed and she draped a hand on Laura's shoulder. "Darling, you really should continue greeting your guests."

"Thank you both for coming," Laura said with a smile before following Olivia toward a group of newcomers.

I elbowed Alex gently. "That's not very nice."

"*She's* not very nice," Alex countered quietly. "The woman burned half my clothes."

"But next time you'll get all of your stuff from a woman's house before you dump her, won't you?"

"I'm done with all that." She paused to sip her scotch. "I'm ready to settle down."

I laughed. "You?"

"Really, Cote. I'm not getting any younger. I need to start thinking about who I want to grow old with." Her eyes were dark, almost slate, and intent on my face as if she was gauging my reaction.

"I didn't realize you thought about stuff like that. Sometimes it seems like you're only interested in having a good time."

"I probably deserve that." Her wounded expression made me feel guilty. "You're the one who's always telling me the women I date are too shallow and I deserve more."

"And I still think so. What about tonight's date?"

She stroked her fingertips down the outside of my arm. "Tonight's companion is a gorgeous brunette in a smokin' red dress, who is definitely way too good for me."

I drained the rest of my wine and blamed the heat creeping up my neck on the alcohol. "I meant your original date."

"Ah, you wouldn't have approved."

"Vapid blonde?" I guessed and she nodded guiltily.

"But that's enough talk about my failures." She took my empty glass, set it on a nearby table, and extended her hand. "Dance with me."

Laying my hand in hers, I let her lead me to the small dance floor already populated by several couples. She stepped close, and despite my heels, she was still several inches taller. I draped an arm across the top of her shoulder, letting my fingers rest against the side of her neck, and when she pressed her other hand to the small of my back, I felt the warmth through the silk of my dress.

We'd danced together before, but never had I been so aware of the breadth of her shoulders, her firm thighs brushing mine, or the commanding way she guided me around the floor.

I noticed more than one envious stare in our direction. "Every woman in the room is trying to figure out how to get me out of the way so they can have a crack at you."

She scanned the room slowly. "Actually, you've got that wrong. All eyes are on you, or more specifically, that dress. The femmes are wondering where you got it and if they would look this great in it. And the butches are imagining what they would do to get you out of it."

Trying for cool, I slowly raised an eyebrow. "Present company included."

Her quick blush was charming, but to her credit she kept her composure. "Sweetheart, I already know how to get you out of it."

Did she hear my heart thumping against my ribs? "Really?"

She pressed her palm harder against my back, bringing our bodies flush, and I imagined I could feel her nipples through our clothes. Her mouth next to my ear, she said, "All I have to do is bring you a pint of Cherry Garcia and a sappy chick flick and you'll be out of that dress and into your flannel pajamas in no time."

I slapped a hand lightly against her shoulder and pushed her back, restoring the space between us. "Very funny." The flash of disappointment was surprising. We had flirted before, but until tonight I'd never felt let down at the inevitable reminder that we were nothing more than *buddies*.

She laughed and tugged me close again. "Are you having a good time?"

"I couldn't have written it better."

We moved together in silence for several more minutes before I felt her sigh.

"Something wrong?"

She was quiet for so long I started to worry, but when I would have pulled back to look at her, she held me tight.

"I have a confession," she whispered against my temple. "My date didn't get sick."

"What?" Now I did draw back and found embarrassed amusement on her face.

"I told her I had a family emergency and couldn't make it."

"Why?"

When she took a deep breath, I suddenly got nervous about her response. "Because I knew if I came here with her, I would spend the entire night wishing she was you."

If I were the swooning type, that definitely would have been the place for it. I stared at her, trying to comprehend what I'd just heard. At some point we'd both stopped dancing and now just stood in the middle of the floor with our arms around each other.

"Why didn't you say anything?"

"You're my best friend and I would never want to screw that up. Besides, I didn't think you'd take me seriously, given my reputation."

"So what changed?"

"I couldn't face another stupid fund-raiser with some random woman. And then when I saw you in that dress—you were so beautiful. Sometimes when I look at you, I forget to breathe." Alex smiled shyly. "Does that sound corny?"

It did. But I liked it.

"Didn't you notice that I kept finding reasons to touch you?" Tentatively, she stroked my cheek as if still afraid I would reject her. We'd touched each other often, in many ways, through the course of our friendship, but this was the first such reverent caress. "And I'll admit, your crack about me not being romantic stung a bit. So tonight, I wanted to prove you wrong."

She'd opened a few doors, brought me a drink, and danced with me as if I were Cinderella. Taken separately, none of these things was terribly original. But standing amid the fairy tale with my dashing escort, I was swept away.

Alex wanted me, I could see that clearly in her gaze, and it made my heart race. The only thing stronger than that desire was the love that had been the foundation of our friendship for years. And as I watched, it grew and deepened, forged like the strongest steel in her gray eyes.

Ironically, while I spent hours a day trying to figure out how to put a new twist on the same old story, she had made that old story perfect, simply by being Alex.

My mind was still spinning her words around, but my body was already reacting. My nipples tightened and when I flexed my thighs to relieve the ache between them, the muscles in Alex's jumped in response. I framed her face in my hands and studied her for a moment, seeing the visage of my friend as if for the first time.

"Cote, please say some—"

I slid my hands to the back of her neck and pressed my lips to hers. Silky soft, the hair at her nape curled around my fingers. She opened to me, freely allowing my exploration of her mouth. Fingers dug into my hips and one of us moaned. Her body was taut beneath my hands and vibrating like a bowstring pulled too far.

"You're shaking. What's wrong?" I held her tighter as if I could stop her trembling.

"You make me nervous."

"Me? Why?"

"Because. It's *you*."

I smiled and kissed her neck. "I'm no different than anyone else."

"Yes. You are. You're special."

"I get that you respect me, but," I took her hand and pressed it to my chest so she could feel my heart pounding, "you don't need to put me on a pedestal. I'm flesh and blood."

She raised an eyebrow. "Ah, yes. You are."

Her palm against the bare skin between my breasts, she slipped her fingers under the edge of my neckline. When she brushed against my nipple, I gasped as pleasure chased through me. She circled over it again and again, making me wet. Her slow smile let me know that her confidence had returned, surging back to restore the swagger in her hips as we began dancing again.

But she wasn't the only one who could tease. Steering her toward the darkened edge of the dance floor, I swept my hand inside her jacket and when I cupped her breast, felt her sharply indrawn breath.

Throbbing with need for her, I murmured, "Alex, if you've made a sufficient appearance at this event, I could use your help with something."

"Hmm?"

"When you came to my house earlier, I was working on a scene that was giving me some trouble." Under her jacket I tugged her shirttail free so I could touch her skin. "So I thought maybe you could come home with me and help me work out some of the—kinks."

"Kinks, huh?" She took my mouth aggressively, her tongue sweeping inside my mouth, and sucked my lower lip. Lifting my hand from her breast, she squeezed it and led me toward the door. "I've definitely got some ideas for you."

MEGHAN O'BRIEN is a twenty-nine-year-old software developer who lives in Northern California with her partner Angie, their son, three cats, and one dog. A native of Royal Oak, Michigan, she is thoroughly enjoying the weather in her new locale.

Meghan is the author of two previous novels, *Infinite Loop* and *The Three*, and of *Thirteen Hours* (Bold Strokes Books, May 2008). She has had selections included in the BSB anthologies *Erotic Interludes 2: Stolen Moments*, *Erotic Interludes 3: Lessons in Love*, *Erotic Interludes 4: Extreme Passions*, and *Erotic Interludes 5: Road Games*. Meghan is extremely excited to have joined the Bold Strokes family and plans to continue writing for as long as humanly possible. Look for her new Ebook version of *The Three* from Bold Strokes Books in 2008.

SEEING KATE
MEGHAN O'BRIEN

L eah quietly unlocked the front door to their new house and crept inside. Kate's car was parked in the driveway, two hours before she was supposed to be home from work. Of course, *she* was home early, too, since her hard drive had crashed and graphic design was a lot less feasible without the benefit of technology.

She hoped like hell Kate hadn't come down with something. Getting sick on a Friday afternoon would be a tragedy, especially when they were both looking forward to the weekend and all they could accomplish on their home projects list. Maybe Kate was napping— they'd spent a lot of late nights working on the house recently.

Leah climbed the stairs as quietly as she could. If Kate really was sleeping, she wanted nothing more than to take off her clothes and slip in bed beside her. Even after ten years together, the feeling of skin on skin with Kate was enough to make the rest of Leah's world disappear. And she desperately needed the escape right now. She was tired, and greedy for the chance to relax with her partner. Smiling at the thought of surprising Kate with a midafternoon cuddle, Leah opened the bedroom door and stepped inside.

Kate was in bed, but she wasn't napping. Leah stared for a moment before understanding what she had interrupted. Sprawled naked on the comforter, Kate had her legs spread wide and one arm thrown over her face. Her other hand worked sensuously between her thighs. Clearly she hadn't heard Leah's entrance, because she never faltered in her self-pleasuring and kept her eyes covered, thrusting her hips into her hand.

Shocked, and hit with a warm wash of arousal at the unexpected sight, Leah hesitated, uncertain what to do. Kate never masturbated in front of her, and Leah suspected that being discovered like this might embarrass her. But could she just walk out of the room and pretend like she never saw Kate touching herself? Should she offer to help?

Frozen in place, Leah was almost glad when Kate took the decision out of her hands. As though sensing Leah's presence in the room, she uncovered her face and turned toward the door. For a moment Kate stared blankly, then she gasped, quickly pulling the comforter over her body.

"Hey," Leah said softly, offering an apologetic smile. Her heartbeat picked up at Kate's obvious distress. "It's just me."

"Hey." Kate clutched covers over her bare breasts. She sounded slightly out of breath. "I'm sorry, I wasn't expecting—"

"No, I'm sorry. I didn't mean to barge in on you, sweetheart. I thought you might be sleeping, so I was trying to be quiet."

Kate's face was fiery red and she couldn't seem to meet Leah's eyes. "I needed some mental health time, so I told my boss I was leaving at noon."

"My laptop died," Leah said.

"Oh. I'm sorry."

They fell into awkward silence as Leah tried to decide how to proceed. Kate was clearly uncomfortable, and that was the last thing Leah wanted. Crossing to the bed, she sat down and leaned in to plant a gentle kiss on Kate's neck.

"Don't be embarrassed," Leah murmured. "You looked beautiful."

"I'm sorry, I…didn't want you to see me like that."

"Why not?" Leah asked, perplexed. They had always been very sexually open with one another, and Kate sounded far more upset than she could understand. "How many times have I seen you naked, honey? Or made you come?"

"You're right, I know." Kate's eyes filled, and her lower lip trembled slightly. "I'm sorry, it's silly."

Leah sat back on the bed and studied her partner, feeling her stomach turn over at her obvious embarrassment. There was something Kate wasn't saying. Uneasy about Kate's reluctance to share what was wrong, Leah murmured, "I know you masturbate. I hope you realize that I'm not immune to that particular temptation, either."

Kate looked like she wished she were somewhere else. "I know that."

"Tell me what you're thinking, darling." Leah stroked a finger across Kate's jawline, trying to bring her back. "Since when are you embarrassed about sex?"

"I'm not embarrassed about sex," Kate mumbled.

"You seem pretty embarrassed about something."

"I'm fine." Taking a measured breath, Kate smiled and scooted to the side, still under the blankets. "How about you get in here and we take that nap?"

A shiver crawled down Leah's spine. What could be so terrible that Kate couldn't talk about it? They had been together too long for this.

"Katie?" Leah asked tentatively. "Please talk to me. You're making me worry that something is really wrong."

Kate exhaled, and Leah could see it all over her face, that she was waging some kind of internal battle. After a moment, she straightened and met Leah's eyes. "I feel awkward because we haven't made love in a while, and I wasn't sure how you would feel about me…you know."

"How did you think I might feel?" Leah's throat went dry when a startling thought occurred to her. "Guilty?"

"I don't know," Kate said quietly. She broke their gaze, looking toward the window, which let in broad stripes of late-afternoon sunshine. "Weird, or something."

"Has it really been that long since we made love?" Leah searched her memory and found she couldn't remember exactly when the last time was. Surely within the past few weeks. That didn't seem so bad, given how busy they were.

"A couple months," Kate said quietly. "Almost three."

"I can't believe that." Leah felt a sense of dread. How could she have not noticed something like a three-month lapse? "It can't possibly have been that long."

"On my birthday."

"Oh," Leah whispered. That was right. After a birthday dinner at Kate's favorite restaurant, they came home and made slow, sweet love. It had been wonderful, and as Kate pointed out, it happened almost three months ago. "Wow."

"It's not that big a deal," Kate said softly. "I was just…in a mood today. I thought I would scratch my itch before you got home."

Leah studied Kate's face, troubled by how cautiously she tried to brush off her observation about their sex life. Kate was obviously keeping track of something Leah hadn't even noticed. And that meant Kate's discomfort was her own damn fault.

"Why didn't you say anything?" Frustrated and guilty, Leah knew her tone was accusatory. "I wasn't not having sex with you on purpose."

Kate's eyes flashed with alarm. "Honey, I don't want to upset you."

"You're not upsetting me." The denial sounded ridiculous, and Leah stopped, trying to rein in her emotions. In a marginally calmer tone, she repeated, "I'm not upset. I just don't understand why you didn't say something sooner."

"I just figured that if you didn't want to make love—"

"It's not that I didn't want to." Leah knew she was lashing out at Kate for something that wasn't her fault, but she just felt so damned ashamed. "I just…didn't think about it."

"And I didn't want to push you."

Leah blinked back hot tears and swiped at her eyes with the back of her hand. "That's not pushing me. It's talking to me about how you're feeling."

"I'm sorry I didn't say anything," Kate said in a shaky voice. "But I didn't want you to have sex with me just because I asked you to."

The comment hit Leah like a punch in the stomach. How could she have neglected Kate for so long that she could even think that? "You're my partner. My best friend. Sex with you could never just be about fulfilling some kind of duty."

"I believe you, but I was trying to respect your limits, too."

"You should never be afraid to ask for what you need." Leah watched Kate's throat work, and finally met her gaze. "I want you to be happy."

"I am." Kate caressed Leah's shoulder and grinned a little. "Masturbating doesn't make me unhappy. There are worse ways to spend an afternoon."

Leah almost smiled, but she was still too focused on her obvious failure. "I feel like a complete asshole. I really had no idea that I'd been ignoring you like that."

"You've been stressed out. I understand, darling. I really do." Kate took Leah's hand in both of hers, letting the comforter fall down to pool around her waist. "I keep telling myself that we're just so busy. I figured that was what was going on."

"What else would it be?" Leah tried to meet Kate's gaze but got distracted by the sight of her pale skin, the dark pink of her nipples. So different from her own brown skin and even darker brown nipples.

"It was hard not to worry that maybe it had something to do with me."

"That I wasn't interested in sex because I didn't want you?"

"Yeah," Kate whispered.

"Don't I always tell you how beautiful you are? How brilliant, how funny?" Leah touched Kate every day, cuddled her every night. She thought she was doing everything right. How could Kate not know? "I love you. I'm crazy about you, still."

"Even though?" Kate said, cracking a smile at their familiar refrain.

"Even though."

Kate brought Leah's hand to her lips and kissed her knuckles. "I love you, too. And I do know you love me. Really."

"You've been worrying about this a lot?" Leah hated to think that Kate could have kept this a secret from her, this fear she carried around. How terrible that Leah had been too busy to notice.

"A little bit."

"Well, I'm glad my laptop died." Leah squeezed Kate's hands. "Because we needed to talk."

Kate seemed to notice for the first time that her comforter had fallen, and she gathered it back up. Leah watched the bashful gesture with a profound pang of regret. She reached out and stopped Kate's hand before she could cover her breasts.

"Don't," Leah whispered. "Please."

"Sorry." Kate left herself uncovered, but a deep flush rose on her chest. "How about I go wash up and then we can cuddle?"

Leah nodded, studying Kate as she crawled out of bed. As her partner strode naked toward the bathroom, Leah found herself paying attention in a way she hadn't in a while. Kate really was a beautiful woman. Leah's breathing hitched as she watched the rolling of her hips and the gorgeous fullness of her ass. She knew from experience that

Kate's creamy skin was silky smooth and that her curves fit perfectly against her when they curled up in bed. Now that she was taking the time to notice, she felt like she was falling in love all over again.

Kate wasn't the same skinny little girl Leah met all those years ago, for damn sure. Ten years older, maybe twenty pounds heavier, she had never looked sexier in her life. Leah felt an almost overwhelming rush of desire, breathless and dizzying. She was an idiot for letting herself forget, for even one moment, that words weren't always enough. She needed to show Kate what she was feeling.

Leah rose to take off her clothes. Funny how she could see Kate every day without really *seeing* her. There was a time when Leah's every moment was filled with an intense physical need for her lover, but somewhere along the line, everyday life began to intrude more and more.

"I'm an idiot sometimes," Leah called out. Naked now, she stood facing the bathroom, talking over the sound of the faucet. "I do realize that."

The stream of water cut off. "Stop." Kate came into the bedroom in a T-shirt that came to mid-thigh. As she walked, the hem rode up slightly, revealing just a hint of the dark curls between her thighs. "You're just fine."

When Kate smiled, the corners of her eyes crinkled slightly, testament to a generous life lived in good humor. Leah smiled back. Ten years she had been the recipient of those smiles. That she had stopped marveling at each and every one tore at her heart.

"No, I *am* an idiot." Leah met Kate's eyes, willing her to see the sincerity of her next words. "And you're breathtaking."

Kate slowed, looking uncomfortable as she folded her arms over her stomach. "Thanks."

Leah caught Kate's hand and tugged her forward. "I mean it, Katie. You're more beautiful every day."

"Honey, you don't have to prove you're attracted to me," Kate said softly. "I really do know."

"I'm not trying to prove anything. I'm looking at you and telling you what I see."

Leah brought Kate's hand to her lips and kissed the knuckles softly. Kate's lower lip trembled, and when she sat on the bed, Leah enfolded her in her arms.

"I love you, Leah," Kate whispered. "I've really missed you. A lot."

Leah buried her face in Kate's neck, inhaling deeply. Such a familiar smell, so soothing, and in this moment, also utterly inflaming. All the love she felt for Kate welled up in her chest, a wave of emotion so strong it was almost painful, and she exhaled shakily. Those feelings of love flared into lust, and Leah held on tighter, swept away by the intensity of her sudden need.

Brushing her lips against Kate's throat, she mumbled, "I love you, too. And I want you. Badly."

"Sweetheart—"

Leah could tell Kate was worried that she was acting out of pity, or a sense of obligation. But pity was the last thing on her mind, and the only obligation she felt was to satisfy the intense, crippling hunger she felt for the woman in her arms. Shaking her head, Leah scraped her teeth over a jumping pulse point on Kate's throat.

"I want you," Leah repeated, grasping Kate's bare hips. "God damn it, how have I gone so long without having you?"

Kate's breath caught as Leah pushed her hands under her T-shirt, then slid them up over her bare sides. "Leah," she whispered, somewhere between protest and desire. "Are you sure…"

Leah shut her up by kissing her hard on the mouth. Kate groaned and immediately gripped Leah's upper arms with both hands, holding on tight. Deepening the kiss, Kate growled into Leah's mouth and crushed their bodies together in a desperate embrace.

They tumbled backward onto the bed, making out like the college kids they were when they first met. Licking at each other's mouths, hands roaming, they moaned their passion into the quiet of the afternoon. Leah's hands found Kate's heavy breasts beneath her T-shirt, and Kate slipped her fingers between Leah's thighs, caressing the soft skin close to the juncture. The gentle touch sent a jolt of pleasure through Leah.

"Remember that first weekend we spent together in college?" Leah asked breathlessly. She felt now like she did then, consumed by the mindless need to touch her lover. The stomach-twisting anticipation, the adrenaline that coursed through her body, took her right back to those first days as Kate's lover. "I was so sick by Sunday, and so sore."

"That's what happens when you go two whole days without

stopping to eat or sleep." Kate's nostrils flared as she palmed Leah's breasts. "God, I love your skin."

Watching Kate's pale fingers twist her dark, turgid nipples, Leah grimaced in pleasure-pain. "I want you more now than I did even then," she murmured. "And I want to take my time and show you exactly how much I love you." She moved Kate's hands from her breasts and tugged her close for a gentle kiss. "But we have to get rid of that T-shirt first."

Without a word, Kate pulled her T-shirt over her head, tossing it onto the floor. Leah moved in for another kiss and eased Kate back against the pillows. When she had Kate on her back, Leah settled on top of her, groaning her appreciation when soft thighs wrapped around her hips. Kate's wetness mingled with her own, sharpening her fierce need even further.

"I'll admit," Kate whispered in between kisses, "this *is* better than masturbating."

"Thank you." Leah smiled, grinding her hips into Kate, feeling a thrill of satisfaction when Kate arched her back and moaned. "We have the whole weekend in front of us, Katie, and I'm going to lick you for as long as you can stand it."

Kate cried out softly, her eyes beseeching. "I need you so badly, honey. I really do."

Leah kissed her way down Kate's throat to her chest, stopping to take one of her nipples between her lips and suck hard. She cradled Kate's other breast, rolling the nipple between her fingers.

"I was thinking about you earlier," Kate gasped. "About this."

Murmuring encouragement, Leah continued her trail of kisses over Kate's soft stomach, mumbling in appreciation when her lips found the damp, curly hairs between Kate's legs. "You smell so good," Leah growled, and pushed Kate's thighs apart. Her pussy was dripping wet, heavy and swollen. "And you're so fucking sexy."

Leah traced the very tip of her tongue along Kate's dark pink labia. Such a familiar taste, and so delicious. She pulled Kate open with her fingers and gently explored her opening with her mouth. Kate exhaled loudly, her fingers tangling in Leah's hair, keeping her in place.

Minutes passed. Leah meant what she said. They had all the time in the world right now, and she intended to spend that time worshiping her partner. At first she ignored Kate's clit entirely, eager to draw the pleasure out, to work her up and not let her come too fast. This was about showing Kate how much she loved her, and she wanted it to last.

Leah pressed her hands into Kate's inner thighs as she licked her, and smiled against her wetness when she felt Kate begin to tremble. She played her tongue over Kate lightly, focusing on the taste and feel of the hot flesh against her mouth, unconcerned about the orgasm she knew she would eventually cause. Leah would only make Kate come when she begged for it, and not a moment sooner. Until then, this act was a love letter to her partner, a message of how much she adored her.

Kate's breathing grew heavier, and she began to writhe beneath Leah's tender attention. Her clit hardened, throbbing against Leah's tongue, larger than Leah could ever remember. Thighs shaking, Kate gripped Leah's hair harder and pushed her hips into Leah's mouth.

"It hurts," Kate whimpered, thrusting her hips into Leah's face, still holding her head and grinding her clit against her lips and chin. "I need to come so bad it hurts, Leah. You're killing me."

Pulling away for a moment, Leah said, "I'm loving you."

"I can feel it. I love you, too."

Kate's voice wavered, and Leah heard the tears that had come to the front. She couldn't wait anymore. She pressed a single finger inside, whimpering at the exquisite tightness that surrounded her. Lowering her face, she covered Kate's pussy with her mouth and laved the engorged clit with her tongue. Three strokes and Kate dug her heels into the bed and lifted her hips, voice cracking as she cried out her release. Leah hung on to her thighs, keeping their contact, and lapped up the hot juices that seeped from around her finger. She could feel Kate contracting around her and she groaned at the answering flood of wetness between her own thighs.

Finally Kate collapsed onto the bed, gasping, and Leah crawled up to gather Kate into her arms. Still trembling, Kate wrapped her arms around Leah's shoulders.

"That was incredible," Kate choked out. "I can't remember the last time I came that hard."

"Me neither." Leah kissed her neck and pressed her hips against Kate's thigh, painfully turned on. "You are so fucking hot, Katie. You taste so good."

Kate pulled away and flipped Leah onto her stomach. The sudden rough handling took Leah by surprise and stoked her arousal even higher. She hugged her pillow and raised her hips into the air, opening herself to Kate, desperate for her touch.

And she wasn't made to wait. Kate thrust inside her quickly, rocking Leah forward against the bed. Crying out, Leah pushed back against Kate's fingers, greedy for more. She wasn't sure she had ever needed to come so badly in her life.

"I'll take my time later," Kate said with a groan, leaning over Leah's back, pumping into her hard. "Right now I need you to come on my hand."

Kate knew exactly how to touch her, precisely how to drive her wild. Leah gritted her teeth and held on, grunting at each stroke. Dense, burning pleasure formed deep in her belly, threatening to explode. When Kate slid her thumb up and pressed inside her anus, Leah was lost. Stiffening, she cried out hoarsely as her orgasm ripped through her.

"That's right, baby." Kate still thrust steadily. "Give me everything you have, darling."

Leah withstood the pleasure as long as she could, until her head swam and she was afraid she might pass out. Then she collapsed and closed her thighs. "I need a break," she said, voice faltering as the aftershocks of her release continued. "I'm sorry, I want to keep going. Just a minute, I swear. I just…I need to breathe."

Laughing, Kate settled next to her and slowly withdrew her fingers. She cradled Leah in a tight hug, so close that Leah could feel Kate's heart beating against her back. "We're not in college anymore, are we?"

"My stamina may have taken a hit in my old age," Leah conceded. "But you're better than ever."

Shifting to embrace Leah face-to-face, Kate smiled. "I needed that. Thank you."

Leah shook her head and kissed her. "Thank you. For putting up with me, even when I'm an idiot."

"You're not an idiot." Kate returned her kiss with a string of gentle pecks across the bridge of Leah's nose.

"Three months without that?" Leah captured Kate's mouth in a deeper kiss. When she drew back, she whispered, "Yes, I'm an idiot."

"Then I'm an idiot for not talking to you about it sooner."

"True enough," Leah said, smiling.

Kate pinched her on the hip, then reached around to grip her ass and pull her closer. "Nice."

"Just do me a favor, okay?" Leah looked deeply into Kate's warm brown eyes. "If I ever stop paying attention again, smack me across the back of the head. For real. Because I'll deserve it."

"Deal," Kate said shyly. She hid a yawn behind her hand, looking sheepish.

"You're right." Leah chuckled and tugged the comforter over their bodies. "We're not in college anymore."

"I think I'm ready for that nap now," Kate admitted. "I guess my days of nonstop sex are in the past."

"Mine, too," Leah said. "But the truth is, it was never as good then as it is now."

"It was pretty good, though." Kate grinned. "Excellent, in fact."

"It was. But I love you so much more now."

Kate cuddled close, sighing contentedly. "Me, too. And I'll love you even more when we wake up from this nap, believe it or not."

"And then?" Leah closed her eyes, smiling as she anticipated the answer.

"And then," Kate mumbled sleepily. "Round two. Ding ding."

Leah managed a giggle as she drifted off to sleep. She had a lot of lost time to make up.

MJ WILLAMZ grew up on California's Central Coast but now lives in Portland, Oregon, where writing is an integral part of her life. Since 2002, she's had over a dozen short stories accepted for publication, mostly erotica with a few romances thrown in for good measure. Her first published novel, *Shots Fired*, is due out in November from Bold Strokes Books.

Rediscovering Willow
MJ Williamz

The bright sun caressed my face, and the warm breeze lightly tousled my hair as I drove down the once-familiar streets of the town where I grew up. It had been four years since I was last there, but my BMW rental was on cruise control as I made my way to the grocery store.

My mother was dying. My brothers and I were in town, waiting for the inevitable. All of us together in one house, and nobody had bothered to stock the liquor cabinet. Hell, the fridge didn't even have a single beer in it.

Walking through the store, I heard someone yell, "Tawny Sue!"

My heart stopped. Tawny? That wasn't a common name.

"Whatever" came the reply, sounding like an insolent teen. Tawny couldn't be that old, could she? I did the math in my head. Yes, she could.

My stomach in knots, my heart in my throat, I followed the voices until I saw a very attractive woman and a teenage girl. The woman stood about five-feet-ten, with long brown hair that had a liberal dosing of gray throughout. She glanced at me, her emerald eyes registering no recognition.

"Willow?" My voice cracked as I said it.

She turned to me and smiled politely, still apparently unsure who I was.

"It's me, Remy."

"Oh, wow! I didn't know you were back in town."

"I'm not. I'm here because my mother's dying."

"Oh, Remy, I'm sorry to hear that."

"Thanks." I didn't want to talk about that. I didn't know what I wanted at that moment, but I knew I didn't want to talk about the woman who'd ragged on me incessantly over the last thirty-five years.

"But you're still here, huh?" I asked.

"Yeah. We moved back about ten years ago."

"Good for you," I said, not really understanding why anyone would move back to her hometown.

The silence was strained. I didn't want it to be. I wanted to have smooth lines to make her laugh. I wanted to hear her say my name again. I wanted to be able to make the awkwardness disappear. But I couldn't. My brain had short-circuited.

Before either of us could say anything, Tawny whined, "Mom."

"We need to get going," Willow said.

"Yeah. Me, too. Hey, Willow…I'm at my folks' house. Give me a call, okay? Maybe we can get together."

"I will, Remy. That would be great."

"Mom!"

"I'll talk to you soon, then," I said and walked off.

As I did, I heard Tawny say, "Who was that, Mom?"

She didn't remember me? I was her parent for two years. She was my little girl. But she wasn't even three when her mom and I split up. Logically, she couldn't have remembered me. But I didn't want to think logically. I didn't want to think at all.

Two days later, my mother was still hanging on and my brothers were driving me crazy with their pro-Bush propaganda. I was about to crawl out of my skin. Then the phone rang.

"Golden residence," I barked into the phone, easily slipping into the practices of my childhood.

"Is this Remy?" I could hear her voice quiver.

"Yeah, it's me. Is this Willow?" I hoped I didn't sound desperate.

"It is. How's your mom doing?"

"She's still the same. Hey, I wanted to say…I can't get over Tawny. She has grown into a beautiful young woman."

"With a not-so-beautiful teenage attitude."

"She looks just like you, Willow."

There was silence on the other end.

"So," I broke the awkwardness, "did you want to get together for a cup of coffee or something?"

"I'd like that."

As much as I wanted to beg her to let me come get her right then, I needed to keep some of my pride.

"How's tomorrow looking for you?"

"Tomorrow would be great."

"Excellent. I'll pick you up around ten?"

"Ten would be great."

She gave me directions to her house and we said our good-byes.

❖

At ten o'clock sharp, I pulled up in front of an old farmhouse just south of town. The fog had yet to burn off, and the idea of coffee with Willow warmed me in various ways.

"Where does one go for coffee around here?" I asked when she'd let me in and led me to her kitchen.

"Anywhere you want. You know, we have Starbucks here, too."

"You do?" I feigned surprise. "If I'd known that, I'd have moved back from Seattle."

"Sure you would. Seriously, Remy, is there any place you'd like to go? Anything you want to see?"

As much as I wanted to respond that any place would be wonderful as long as she was with me, I played it cool. "I'd really like to drive down to the beach. How does coffee with an oceanfront view sound?"

She hesitated briefly, and I wondered if I'd been too bold.

"Coffee on the beach sounds wonderful."

The drive started off with another uneasy void in conversation. I continued to wonder if she was really comfortable going to the beach with me. That was where we had spent much of our time when we were together.

I finally decided that the girl we once shared was probably the safest topic. "So Tawny's quite a handful, huh?"

She rolled her eyes. "You have no idea."

"Tell me," I said, and we relaxed into her telling horror stories and me laughing at her. I'd missed having a family. I was bummed to have missed the first broken heart, first detention, even all the teenage attitude. Well, maybe not *all* the teenage angst, but I really did wish I could have been there for her as she grew up.

The fog had started to burn off when we pulled up to the little coffee shop across from the pier in the beach town.

"You sure the coffee here's fit to drink?" I asked as I held the door open for her.

"You wanted coffee at the beach. Our choices are limited."

We sat sipping our coffee and catching up on our lives. We talked about some of the houses I'd renovated in Seattle. She seemed surprised that I owned my own company and had for five years. She had moved back to town so Tawny could grow up in a small community. She was also painting full time, and the Central Coast of California was the perfect backdrop for a landscape artist.

"So you've raised Tawny all by yourself?" I asked.

"Yep. It's been just the two of us."

"You never met anyone else, then?"

"Oh, I've dated a few women. But none of them seemed special enough to disrupt Tawny's life over."

I nodded.

"And you, Remy? Surely some woman got her hooks into you."

I shrugged. "I've been too focused on building my company. I haven't really had time for a relationship."

It was so easy to talk to her, so comfortable. Two hours later, the fog was completely gone and the weather was perfect for the beach—low seventies with a slight breeze.

"How about a walk on the pier?" I asked.

Her response was dead silence and again I wondered if I'd crossed a line. The end of the pier was where we'd shared our first kiss so many years before.

"Never mind. I shouldn't have asked."

"No, no. It's okay. I'm being ridiculous, I know."

"No, you're not," I said, instinctively reaching for her hand. "I don't mean to bring up painful memories."

She pulled her hand away, her eyes shimmering with tears. "The memories of the pier aren't painful, Remy."

I didn't say anything at first. Thoughts were racing in my head—could it be that she remembered our time together fondly? Did she ever think about me? About us? What would have happened if we'd stayed together? But I knew the answer to the last question. I was too heavily into partying when we'd been together. I was too immature to be a partner, much less a parent.

"How 'bout we just head back?" I asked, standing.

"No. Come on. Let's walk the pier."

We walked silently, each lost in our own thoughts. I was having serious fantasies, wishing I could be with Willow again, but I had no idea what she was thinking. Until we reached the end.

"You've grown up," she said matter-of-factly.

I just stared at her.

She turned and looked out over the water. "When we were together, all I ever wanted was for you to grow up."

The urge to touch her was overwhelming. I slid my hands into my pockets for safety. "And now?"

She moved closer to me and ran her hand over my jaw. Her touch, so new yet so familiar, seared. "And now you're all grown up and responsible and mature." Her hand dropped. "And you live a million miles away."

"But I'm here now, Willow. I'm right here right now."

"I have a life, Remy. A life without you. A lonely life, but it's a life. And here you are being everything I want in a partner, and I can't have you."

I placed my finger under her chin and tilted her face so I could look into her eyes. "Why shut me out? Why not explore these feelings? We're both feeling it. Let's see where this goes. Okay?"

Her eyes searched mine. "You can't be feeling what I feel."

"Oh, yes, I can. That and more," I said before lowering my mouth to hers. Our lips barely met, we were both so tentative. But the sparks from that brief passing heated me from head to toe. When the kiss ended, I rested my forehead on her shoulder.

"Please, Willow. Don't deny this. Don't walk away without seeing where it takes us."

"You're right," she said, taking my hand and leading me back to the car.

We kissed again, this time allowing our passion to flare. We were both breathless when the kiss ended. We drove back to the farmhouse in silence again, but this time, it was silent anticipation. Our fingers intertwined, but our thoughts were our own.

Just before we got there, Willow spoke. "We're doing the right thing, aren't we?"

"Nothing has ever been so right, baby."

When we got to the farmhouse, we were like two nervous kids on a first date.

"Can I get you something to drink?" she asked.

"No, thanks. I'm fine." I mustered up enough nerve to take her in my arms again.

"Are you okay?" I asked.

She nodded.

"Are you sure?"

"I'm as nervous as a virgin on her wedding night." She smiled. "I'm not even sure I remember how to do this."

"We can go slowly," I said before I claimed her mouth. It wasn't long before the passion flared again, and our kiss intensified.

She finally broke the kiss and led me to her bedroom. I looked at her queen-size sleigh bed and imagined sleeping there every night, waking up with her every morning. I drew her to me again and unbuttoned her sweater while I nibbled her neck.

Her bare skin quivered at my touch. As I kissed downward, I felt her body tremble. Concerned, I stood upright and pulled her tightly against me. The feel of her hardened nipples poking me through my T-shirt threatened to cloud my judgment, but I contained myself and simply held her.

"Are you okay?" I asked.

She nodded and whispered, "Never better."

I gently laid her on the bed and lowered myself next to her. I kissed her neck and sucked her earlobe while my hand teased her body. I itched to close my hand over a breast, but I needed to know she was ready. Her hand soon covered mine and guided me over to a waiting breast. She rolled me on top of her and our bodies melded as one. Our mouths fit together perfectly, tongues dancing together, lips hungrily devouring each other.

Soon our hands were roaming all over each other's bodies. In a tangle of arms and legs, we managed to get our clothes off, and finally we lay skin to skin. I was in awe of Willow's beauty. She was even more beautiful than she had been all those years earlier. I couldn't get enough of her. I touched, kissed, licked, and drank of every inch of her.

I was insatiable, as was she. The more I gave, the more she wanted. The more she wanted, the more I gave. I needed to meet her every need. I wanted to fill her up and leave her wanting more.

We made love until we were both completely spent. We lay, limbs entwined, relishing the simple pleasure of togetherness. I kissed her shoulder.

"I've missed you, baby."

"I've missed you, too. I just didn't realize how much."

"Life's not the same without you. It never has been."

"So now what?"

I propped myself up on an elbow and looked at her. I used my free hand to trace her body anew. "Now what, what?"

I saw fear in her eyes. "You know what I mean. You leave here and that's it?"

"No. No, no, no, no, no." I kissed her. "It's not like that. Besides, I'm not going back to Seattle anytime soon. Even after Mother passes, I'll be in town helping to get her affairs in order."

"Do you think you'll be able to spend time with me while you're here?"

"Yes. I will. If you want me to."

"I want you to so much it hurts."

"Okay. So it's decided. And who knows? I'm sure there are houses around here that need renovation, too, right?"

"Do you mean that?"

"Like I've never meant anything before."

I moved on top of her, needing to rediscover everything I once believed I'd lost for good.

LISA GIROLAMI has been in the entertainment industry since 1979. She holds a BA in Fine Art and an MS in Psychology. Previous jobs include ten years as production executive in the motion picture industry and another two decades producing and designing theme parks for Disney and Universal Studios. After six years as the director of creative development for a firm in Los Angeles, she has returned to Disney as a senior show producer. She's also a counselor at a mental health facility in Garden Grove. She also has two romance novels, *Love on Location* and *Run to Me*, both with Bold Strokes Books. She currently lives in Long Beach, California.

TOLUCA #9
LISA GIROLAMI

With one last heave, Sarah hoisted the crate of CDs up against her chest and started up the poolside stairs of the Toluca apartments, her new and unexplored residence in North Hollywood, California. A few children splashing in the pool and enjoying the summer sun displayed mild interest in her efforts as she hooked the screen door of apartment number nine with her foot and flung it open.

Sarah carefully stepped over the boxes that held the few meager belongings she had brought from a houseful back home. After setting the crate down next to five other crates of CDs, she picked up the small television from the floor. She placed it on one of the boxes, plugged it in, and turned it on. Since she'd left a week before, she'd felt the anxious ambience of her solitary life. In the motel rooms across the States, on her way toward her new life in California, she'd kept the televisions on to help cut through the stillness.

She checked the refrigerator. It was as empty as a desert well. *Dense brain*, she thought, *who did you think would have stocked it?* There was no girlfriend anymore. No roommates. This was it, pal. A one-bedroom apartment for one person. She raised her hand to her chest to quell the aching clutch that lodged there. It was the same clutch that had followed her out to California.

With a heavy sigh, she looked over at the paperwork that her new employer had sent. It needed to be filled out before she started her job on Monday, but as she listened to the sounds coming from the pool outside, she decided that for the moment, her stomach was more important than anything else. She scooped up her keys and went out the door to scout her neighborhood for grocery stores.

❖

"She's cute." Judy adjusted the top of her blue knit bikini.

"She certainly is." Shayna sipped her soda.

"Who's cute?" Caitlin joined her two friends and laid her towel out on the chaise closest to the pool.

"Toluca number nine." Shayna motioned toward the apartments on the other side of the pool. "She just left."

Judy gestured toward the street. "We've been watching her carry boxes upstairs. Got to be from out of state."

"Cut-off denim shorts." Shayna nodded, confirming Judy's suspicion. "And I think she's single."

Caitlin laughed. "All that from a few trips between the street and her apartment?"

Judy dramatically adjusted her sunglasses. "I'm a practiced observer of human nature."

Shayna leaned over and kissed Judy. "Yes, you are, baby."

"And I think she'd be just right for you, Cait."

"What makes you think that?"

"She's cute…"

"You already said that."

"And there hasn't been anyone that's piqued your interest in a long time."

Caitlin harrumphed. "There's a difference between my interest being piqued and actually *wanting* any piquing."

Judy and Shayna stared at her.

Caitlin grabbed the suntan lotion a little too forcefully and splurped coconut SPF 8 everywhere. "I just want to enjoy my summer without any drama."

Shayna shook her head, "Girl, you said that all through last spring and last winter, too."

❖

Sarah arrived back just before dusk. With an armful of grocery bags, she walked between her apartment and the Vineyard apartment next door. The Toluca and the Vineyard were two-story, ten-unit mirror images of each other. Facing inward, they shared a garden-encircled swimming pool. The same two women who were there when she left still sat in chaise chairs on the Vineyard side. They cuddled cozily and Sarah grinned a little shyly.

She made her way around potted plants, trying to see around her bags when, from the deep end of the pool, a cheerful voice called hello. Sarah shifted her bags to see a blond-haired woman lounging in the water. Her arms were crossed, resting on the edge of the pool.

"Hi." Sarah smiled, noticing that crystal drops of water dotted the woman's freckled shoulders.

"You're the new neighbor?"

Sarah nodded. "Drove in this afternoon." She held out her bags. "The cupboard was bare."

"Welcome! Where are you from?"

"Texas."

"I heard it's beautiful there." The blonde smiled up at her.

A voice from across the pool broke in. "Why don't you put those groceries away and come back and enjoy this incredible weather?"

"Those are my friends. And neighbors," the woman in the pool said.

Sarah hesitated, suddenly feeling dreadfully shy, and fumbled for a response. "Thanks, but I've got some work to do before Monday."

"I'm Caitlin Hill, by the way." Caitlin held up a hand in a pleasant wave and then crooked her thumb behind her. "I'm in Vineyard number two."

"Sarah Cavanaugh. Toluca number nine." A sudden rush zipped up her spine. *What a gorgeous woman she was!* She smiled again and turned to walk away, suddenly feeling excited and lonely at the same time.

❖

Caitlin watched Sarah climb the stairs. Sarah was shorter than she was. And a little thinner. The curls of her brown hair framed a face that was more natural and pretty than she was used to seeing at the bars in L.A. Just before Sarah disappeared into her apartment, she turned and looked right at Caitlin and smiled widely. Caitlin waved again, delightfully intrigued by the new neighbor. Having caught her infectious smile, Caitlin swam over to Judy and Shayna, who had been watching the encounter.

"We told you she was cute," Judy said.

"And single, I bet," Shayna added. "Didn't have many boxes. Her ex must have taken her for everything she had."

Caitlin laughed but had to disagree. She was more than cute. She was beautiful.

❖

Sarah got up early the next morning and unpacked her boxes. She set up her laptop and then took a mental inventory of the apartment. The kitchen was stocked with food and the bathroom had the essential toiletries. Except for a single futon, she didn't have any furniture, nor did she have extra sets of sheets, but she'd take care of those things once she got her first paycheck.

The Sunday morning sun brazenly beckoned Sarah as it blared through her blinds. It was just after eleven, so she decided to reward herself with a break. She changed into her swimsuit, grabbed her only towel, and headed down to the pool.

There were a few kids in the pool and some adults lying around the perimeter. Caitlin and her friends were not there, though, which produced a slight lump in her throat. Pondering the silliness of the feeling, Sarah settled into a chaise lounge by the deep end. She lay in the sun for an hour, feeling the warmth seep down into her bones. The suntan lotion she'd applied had worn off as she'd turned over and back a few times, so she decided to take a dip before reapplying.

The water instantly cooled her down when she dove in. She ran her hands along the bottom, feeling the cement's roughness before pushing herself back up. Breaking the surface, she immediately felt the sun's heat again and reveled in it. She could get used to this.

"Hey, Toluca number nine!" Sarah heard someone call as she was getting out of the pool.

Caitlin's two friends had arrived and were setting their towels down. "I'm Judy and this is Shayna," the taller one called from the other side. "Vineyard number seven."

"Sarah," she called back, over the splashing of some kids.

"Barbeque at eight. Right here." Judy indicated the pool. "Wanna come?"

She did. "Sure! What shall I bring?"

"Just a beverage and you. We have everything else." Judy and Shayna waved and then settled into their lounge chairs.

Sarah applied more lotion and lay back to soak up the early afternoon sun, happy for the first time in months.

Just after eight, Sarah moved her blinds aside and peered down at the pool. She counted about twenty or thirty women, some sitting in lounge chairs, others standing by three BBQs or sitting at the edge of the pool.

Nervous and excited about attending her first California party, Sarah took a deep breath. "Here you go."

Clutching her can of beer, she mingled with the crowd. Though she didn't know anyone, she was happy to be around what looked to be an all-lesbian party.

"That's quite a spectacular smile," a voice behind her said.

Sarah turned. "Caitlin! Hello!" She was thrilled that her first new California friend had come over to greet her.

"The smile?" Caitlin pressed with a warm smile of her own.

"It's been a long time since I've been around this many women."

"Yeah." Caitlin's expression grew somber. "I said the same thing when I was released from prison."

Sarah felt her throat clutch. "Prison?"

Caitlin laughed and then looked around the pool speculatively. "No. I was just joking. Although I can't vouch for absolutely everyone here at this party."

Sarah was amused, liking Caitlin's humor. "I'll keep that in mind."

"You look hungry. May I show you over to the barbeques?"

"That'd be great."

"What brings you here to the Toluca apartments, Sarah?" Caitlin asked when they sat down on the steps of the Vineland apartments overlooking the pool and party, just far enough away that the music would not impede their conversation.

"Starting a new life, I suppose," Sarah said. "I ended a bad relationship in Texas." She paused a moment and took in a deep breath. "And then I threw some things in my car and left."

"Wow. Just like that, huh? With nothing at the other end and you just showed up here? That's brave."

"Not that brave, I'm afraid. I already had a job lined up."

Caitlin laughed. "Well, still, it must have been difficult to leave everything behind."

Sarah took in Caitlin's face. The glow of the lights that lit the nearby palm trees illuminated her skin. A genuine warmth permeated Caitlin's words and Sarah felt it in her chest.

"It was hard, yes. But I'm glad I'm here."

"I'm glad you're here, too." Caitlin lifted her can to Sarah's and they clinked them together. "You'll like these apartments. Everyone here is pretty cool."

She's glad I'm here, too! Sarah savored the unexpected rush of pleasure for a second before asking, "How long have you lived here?"

"Almost five years. I work in Hollywood, just over the hill. I'm a financial advisor for a bank."

"So you're good with money?"

"Luckily, I take my own advice. I'm saving to purchase my first house in two more years."

"That's great, Caitlin."

"Well, the work is easy and I'm home by five o'clock every day, so I can't complain." Caitlin liked Sarah's energy. She was charming and personable and very easy to talk to. So many of the women she'd dated were caught up in themselves or their careers or who they knew. And Sarah was refreshingly not like that at all.

They easily fell into discussions of family and work, and Caitlin shared what she knew about the best places to eat in North Hollywood.

Their beer cans long empty, Caitlin motioned to the party. "I've been dominating your time tonight. I don't want to hog the newest guest."

"No." Sarah knew she'd responded a little too quickly. "This is nice. Right here."

Caitlin grinned and then scanned the crowd. "You'll eventually meet most of these women at some point. They either live here or are always visiting."

"I'm in no hurry. Besides, I'm batting a thousand right now."

"Batting a thousand?"

"My friends back home warned me about California. They said that as soon as I got here I needed to be careful because"—she counted on her fingers—"I'd be forced to smoke pot, I'd be called Tex, and I'd be teased about my accent." She smiled. "But so far with you, none of those have come true."

"I imagine that must have been nerve-wracking to think that those things could happen. I must say that I don't smoke pot, you certainly don't look like a Tex to me, and I think your accent's pretty cute, actually."

Sarah relaxed, feeling her tension drain away, owing it all to Caitlin. "Maybe it's the two beers I've had or maybe it's the great company. But you're easy to talk to."

"Thanks. So are you."

Well past midnight the party had dwindled down, and Sarah and Caitlin were helping Judy and Shayna gather up the discarded paper plates and empty cans. The last of the partygoers were jingling car keys and waving good-bye.

"We can handle the rest of the cleanup," Shayna told Caitlin and Sarah. "You two go relax somewhere."

"Come on," Caitlin said. "There's a patio table with our name on it."

❖

"...so there I was, carrying my fifth crate of CDs out to my car," Sarah recounted as she and Caitlin sat close enough that their knees touched. "Those CDs filled up more of my car than the rest of my belongings combined! But I was thinking to hell with her. And then I thought, ah crap! My ex has the CD player."

"Well, look at it this way," Caitlin said, "maybe you don't have anything to play them on yet, but those CDs come in handy as a substitute for a lot of household items. They can serve as mouse pads, drink coasters, soap holders, Frisbees…"

"You must think I'm nuts."

Caitlin placed her hand lightly on Sarah's knee. "You were in the middle of a bad breakup. Those CDs were important to you. It doesn't matter what anyone else thinks."

Sarah was growing more attracted to Caitlin and her sincere compassion by the minute.

"Plus," Caitlin added, "I've taken stranger things."

"Oh really? Tell me."

Caitlin looked enchanting as she stared out over the deep end of the pool. "Once, I took six boxes of vacuum bags without taking the vacuum."

"You did?" Sarah said, fascinated.

"But the strangest…"

When Caitlin paused, Sarah urged her on. "Go ahead, say it. I won't laugh."

"Once I was so pissed, I took a bicycle built for two."

Sarah's eyes grew wide and Caitlin started to laugh.

"Go ahead," Caitlin said. "I laugh every time I think of it!"

And they did as Sarah added, "I don't know what's more amazing, that you took the bicycle built for two or that you actually bought one!"

Caitlin wiped the tears from her eyes as the laughter died down. "Aren't divorces a pain?"

"I could live without them."

In the silence that followed, Sarah could tell that Caitlin was studying her. And it felt remarkably comfortable.

Then Caitlin spoke in a hushed but serious tone. "Those CDs are important to you."

"It was the principle."

"And the hurt."

"That, too." Looking down, Sarah said quietly, "They're great CDs. I'd painstakingly collected and catalogued them. It's good music. Romantic music. I suppose they were my pride and joy. My ex told me to leave the collection as I'd have no use for it without the stereo. And without a girlfriend to play them with."

"Ouch."

"Yeah, that hurt."

Caitlin rocked her knees back and forth, nudging Sarah's. "Don't ever let her or anyone else ever convince you what is or isn't valuable to you. She didn't appreciate you or what mattered to you. But you know what matters."

Suddenly, Sarah wanted to hug her. She was overwhelmed that this beautiful woman understood her, understood what she needed, so quickly and so easily. Caitlin was so close now, Sarah caught wisps of the sweetness from the beer she'd been drinking. The rippling reflections cast by the underwater pool light danced across Caitlin's face.

For a few seconds while they looked into each other's eyes, there seemed no need for words. Sarah smiled at Caitlin, who smiled back.

When Sarah eventually looked away, she scanned the garden and announced, "Geez! Everyone's gone."

"It's Sunday night. There's work to go to tomorrow."

Sarah glanced at her watch. "Or today, actually."

"Wow, it's pretty dark." Caitlin's voice hummed low and sexy. "I can barely see you."

Taking a chance, Sarah hesitated slightly before moving closer to Caitlin. "Is that better?"

"Yes." Caitlin paused a moment. "You know, you may be scared about this whole new life you've started, but it doesn't show."

Sarah looked down, swirling the last of her beer in its can. "Spending time with you has helped a lot. You've helped me to feel less nervous."

Caitlin's voice grew soft and gentle. "Nervous about what?"

"This big bad city they call L.A." Sarah looked back up to the warmth of Caitlin's eyes. Her heart faltered an instant.

"Believe it or not, you help me to feel less nervous, too," Caitlin said.

"How so?"

"It isn't often I meet an attractive and delightful woman. So tonight, I should be pretty nervous sitting here with that incredible combination."

"Not that incredible…"

"Don't underestimate yourself," Caitlin said, covering Sarah's hand in hers.

The touch happened so quickly, Sarah couldn't tell whether the jolt she felt was the excitement of Caitlin reaching out to her or the disappointment that it didn't last.

Unsettled and unsure, Sarah finally said, "I'd better get upstairs."

Caitlin nodded and stood when Sarah did. "Thank you for this evening."

❖

Sarah stomped around her living room, frustrated with herself. She should have stayed and talked to Caitlin more. Unlike her ex, there were people who were actually nice. And more than that. Caitlin had sparked attraction in Sarah that had her buzzing like a downed electrical line in a thunderstorm. Every part of her body tingled as she recalled the evening and every one of Caitlin's words, her smiles, and her laugh. She paced the floor, full of pent-up energy that had nowhere to go.

Why had she ended the evening as she did? She and Caitlin were connecting! Caitlin was so beautiful and nice. She wasn't pushy or intimidating. She was funny and genuinely cared about what Sarah was saying. Caitlin looked so comfortable, as if she could have stayed there talking with Sarah the rest of the night!

But then Sarah would be a wreck the next morning on her first day at her new job.

Her new job. Oh, Lord! A new job, a new apartment, a new life. She looked around the apartment at the few meager things lying around—all the possessions she had in the whole world. What was she doing here in California? Was she so sure that she'd done the right thing? Would Monday prove to be a colossal calamity? Maybe she shouldn't have moved. She could have stayed in Texas and just moved across town. But running into her ex would be a disaster. On the other hand, her friends would have her back. Her friends! Anxious at being so far from everyone she cared about, she picked up the phone but realized it was too late in Texas to call anyone. How would she get through the night and the next few terrifying days?

Cursing her hasty move, she paced the room until a subdued knock at the door penetrated the gloom. Sarah opened it to find Caitlin in the doorway with two small bookshelf speakers, a tuner, and a CD player piled in her arms, cords dangling everywhere.

Caitlin chewed slightly on her lower lip. "I know it's late, but I didn't want the night to end." Then she grinned. "Wanna listen to some CDs?"

Sarah's heart suddenly danced in her chest and tomorrow didn't seem as frightening. Yes, her move had been a good decision. Toluca number nine was exactly where she wanted to be. And holding the door open wide, she realized something else.

"There's nothing else I'd rather be doing right now."

KIM BALDWIN is a former journalist who has published six books with Bold Strokes Books: *Hunter's Pursuit* and *Whitewater Rendezvous*, both finalists for Golden Crown Literary Society Awards, *Force of Nature, Flight Risk, Focus of Desire*, and her latest release: *Lethal Affairs*, the first book in the Elite Operatives Series, co-authored with Xenia Alexiou. The second book in the series, *Thief of Always*, will be released in early 2009. She has also contributed short stories to four previous BSB anthologies: *Erotic Interludes 2: Stolen Moments, Erotic Interludes 3: Lessons in Love, Erotic Interludes 4: Extreme Passions*, and *Erotic Interludes 5: Road Games*. She lives in Michigan.

Contact her at baldwinkim@gmail.com or visit her Web sites at www.kimbaldwin.com and www.myspace.com/authorkimbaldwin for more information.

PARADISE FOUND
KIM BALDWIN

I generally hate traveling for business, though I have to do it at least a couple of times a month. All that living out of a suitcase and tedious waits at airports. But there are far worse destinations than Palm Springs in February when your home base is buried under five feet of snow, so I was in a much more upbeat mood than usual this trip, and Southern California didn't disappoint. Temperatures were in the eighties when I arrived, the sky was a brilliant blue, and the mountains overlooking the city were breathtaking in their awesome purplish brown majesty.

What I wasn't prepared for was the accommodations my assistant had booked for me. Meg usually opts for one of the upscale chain hotels, but she was apparently determined to make sure I had ample opportunities this trip to really relax, so she'd booked me at Casitas Laquita, a lesbian resort with a walled-in, palm tree–bordered courtyard and pool. The minute I passed through the big wooden gate and into the inner sanctum, I knew I was in heaven.

It'd been nearly a year since I'd come to grips with my growing attraction for women and realized I'd been driving on the wrong side of the road the whole of my adult life. But I hadn't yet had the perfect opportunity or irresistible inclination to indulge in any of my fantasies. I was too busy becoming the first woman division head of Flights of Fancy.

If Meg was determined to do whatever she could to change all that, who was I to argue?

Fifteen minutes after my arrival, I was happily ensconced in a plush lawn chair in my emerald green two-piece, bathed in sunscreen and relaxing to Mozart on my MP3 player. Other guests passed by en route to their rooms, but for much of the afternoon, I had the poolside paradise to myself.

I was so relaxed I actually dozed for a while, and when I awoke, I had company. A stunning blonde, in a very brief black bikini, was lounging on a chair directly across the pool. Her expression was serene, her face relaxed, but her sunglasses made it impossible to tell whether her eyes were open. I wanted to think she was watching me, as I was surreptitiously watching her.

The quiet was broken by a feminine voice, hailing the object of my scrutiny. "Ansley! Hey, girlfriend!"

Ansley. The name suited her. Different, unusual. She sat up as a petite redhead in shorts and a tank greeted her with a brief kiss and embrace before sitting on an adjacent chair. They talked in low voices, and something Ansley said made the other woman laugh. After a couple of minutes, they both got up and headed toward one of the rooms.

Just as I was thinking what a shame it was that the ones I liked were always taken, Ansley stopped, turned, took off her sunglasses, and looked right at me, smiling.

I was instantly smitten. Something about her was different from all the other women who had caught my eye. She stirred that sweet inner ache in me, that longing to touch and be touched by gentle hands and soft breasts and ample lips. Her hair was the color of honey, her lips rosy and full.

Unfortunately, as much as I'd have loved to linger there, awaiting her reemergence, I had a business dinner with a client, so I reluctantly returned to my own room to shower and change. An hour later, as I headed toward my rental car, I got the first hint that my resort was hosting some kind of special gathering. Thirty or forty women—I glimpsed Ansley and her friend among them—were about to sit down to a private dinner at a cluster of tables set up at one end of the courtyard.

At the risk of being late for my meeting, I paused to study her. There was a sort of cocky arrogance in the way she stood, like the star athlete in an interview after the big game, not really flaunting that trim, toned body, but standing in a way that showed it off. She was about my height, five-five or five-six, but leaner than I was, and her jeans and yellow tank top were skin tight. She was talking to a trio of women, but as though she could feel my eyes on her, she pivoted to face me and shot me that melt-me smile again before returning to her conversation.

I forced myself on to my appointment, wishing like anything I was part of her group.

The next morning I awoke at the ungodly hour of four a.m., my body steadfastly refusing to budge from Eastern Time. I showered and dressed, made a pot of coffee, and took a mug outside to watch the sun rise over the mountains.

I didn't see her there at first. The only lights were the soft blue spots in the pool, and she was sitting on a bench in the shadow of a palm some distance away. It was only when she spoke that I was aware I had company.

"I don't suppose you have more of that coffee?"

"Sure," I managed, before hurrying back to my room like the devil himself was after me and pouring another mug with shaking hands. I didn't stop to wonder why she was asking me for coffee—she had to have a coffeemaker in her room as well—I just accepted my good fortune. She smiled when I offered the steaming mug to her, and invited me to sit with a nod of her head. I settled onto the bench beside her.

This close to her, my infatuation flared from an ember of interest to a conflagration of heat. The dawn was starting to break, so I could just make out her expressive hazel eyes and see the tiny little indention in her cheek when she smiled. Damn. She was hot as hell. One look at her and I was ready, anxious, and eager to finally become a full-fledged lesbian myself, if I could be one with her. But her next words doused my enthusiasm.

"Thanks. I didn't want to wake my roomie, but I was about to die for a hit of caffeine."

Oh, how I wanted to believe the redhead was only her roomie. A friend she liked to vacation with. "I know the feeling," was the only brilliant remark my befuddled brain could manage, sitting this close to her. She smelled of jasmine, and I wondered whether it was her shampoo or perfume. I forced myself not to sniff her hair, though the temptation was maddening.

"Beautiful here, isn't it? Almost worth being an insomniac."

Her comment turned my attention to the glorious pink and orange hues painting the sky above the mountains.

"Indeed." I'm normally much more profound than this, but the combination of the awesome surroundings and proximity to her just took my breath away.

"How long are you staying?"

I could feel her eyes on me, but I remained pointed toward the sunrise, hoping she might mistake the pink on my cheeks for a reflection off the colored sky.

"Just five days," I answered somberly. "My work consumes far too much of my life."

"Me, too," she said with equal sadness, clearly as distressed as I at the prospect of ever leaving.

The answer gave me strength. More likely then, perhaps, that the woman with her was just a business associate. My mind was desperately searching for that witty or insightful phrase that would make an indelible impression on her, when redheadus interruptus struck again. "Hey, Ansley!" she called from the doorway of their room, fifteen feet away. She was wearing a white terrycloth bathrobe, her legs were bare, and her red hair was tousled. "Please come make the coffee. You know I can never get it right."

"Thanks again." Ansley handed me the mug with an expression I wanted to believe was regret, then disappeared back into her room.

I couldn't stop thinking about her, and wondering whether she was involved. All day, meeting one client after another, the memory of her smile was a constant distraction. I hurried through the last sales pitch, hoping I might find her poolside upon my return.

Instead, I heard laughing as I approached the wooden gate. Inside I found a virtual sea of lesbians. Eighty or so women, of all ages, many of them with books in their hands. A literary club? Ansley stood out, her blond hair shining in the sun. She had on a royal blue tank top and short khaki shorts that showed off her toned thighs. I made it my mission, after I changed, to flirt with her. At least find out her last name.

A lot of people came over to say hello to her while I watched her for the next half hour, but no one stayed too long. The redhead put her arm around her waist at one point, but I just didn't see the spark of two women hot for each other, and managed to convince myself they were just friends.

It wasn't long before most of the women left and only the guests of the resort and a few others remained. I'd never tried to pick up someone before, but I didn't want to miss this opportunity. I'd finally laid eyes on someone who put a zing in my step, and I believe in living a life of no regrets. So I went for it. Ansley was just so damn sexy it made me obscenely brave. I guess I figured since I certainly knew what *I* liked, and I'd had plenty of practice in that department, I couldn't do too badly my first time with a woman.

I made a quick run up the street to Ralph's and back. A few guests were still about, but Ansley was alone, stretched out on one of the lounge chairs. Her eyes were hidden behind sunglasses, but I'd not been gone long enough for her to fall asleep.

I gathered my nerve and approached her. "Espresso. The good stuff. I recognized a fellow coffeeholic this morning."

She took off her sunglasses and looked first at the cup in my hand, then up at me, that smile beginning at the edge of her magnificent mouth. My stomach twisted, and it felt awful and wonderful. "Well, thanks very much," she said, reaching for it. "That's a sweet thing to do."

I shrugged, feeling my cheeks warm as her gaze trailed over my body in a way that excited me beyond belief. Her open appraisal lingered on my breasts—well, okay, they are a rather nice feature of mine, I'll admit—but I'd never felt this way when men had done what she was doing. I loved her eyes on me.

I sucked in a breath and swear I heard a faint moan in response. And boy, that really encouraged me. *What now, idiot?* I asked myself. *How do women do this?* Start simple. I stuck out my hand. "I didn't introduce myself this morning. Maggie Cassidy."

She took my hand in hers, lingering a moment. Her hand was warm, and soft, and her touch was making me a little weak in the knees. "Ansley."

We stood there staring at each other and I saw *it* come to life in her eyes. The same want, the same desire, the same flush of excitement that was pouring through my body.

Of course that was when the redhead swept up beside Ansley and put her arm around Ansley's waist.

Ansley's hand left mine. Its absence was like the loss of a cool breeze on a humid summer day.

"Dinner. You can't refuse," redhead said to Ansley, before turning her attention to me. "Hi. Sorry to pull her away, but we're going to be late if we don't go right this minute."

"Uh, no problem," I stuttered. "Just saying hello." Girlfriend after all, it looked like. I could feel myself getting red again, so I turned away to hide my embarrassment. But I stopped at the sound of Ansley's voice.

"Thanks again so much."

I ventured a glance back to see her hoisting her espresso in my direction. I waved and kept walking.

I spent the rest of the night feeling foolish, and inexperienced, and frustrated more than anything else. Damn, she was fine.

I was up at five, my internal body clock not caring that I didn't have a two-hour commute today and could sleep in if I liked. A half hour later, I headed outdoors with coffee and my laptop to watch the sun rise.

This time, she was sitting in plain view, illuminated by the pool lights on a lounge chair, also with a mug and her laptop. She smiled as though she was every bit as happy to see me there as I was to see her.

But the girlfriend thing had sobered my intoxication with her, jolted me back to reality, at least enough that I was able to maintain my decorum and choose a seat close enough to see her, but not near enough to be intrusive. Or to tempt me to flirt any further with her.

I answered my e-mail as she typed away on her computer, sitting some fifteen feet away. I glanced up to find her looking at me at least as often as she caught me watching her, and I could swear I saw the same smolder of desire in her eyes that I had glimpsed the night before. But what the hell did I know? This was new to me, and so I chalked it up to wishful thinking and tried to let go of the fantasies she'd been inspiring in my waking and sleeping moments since I first laid eyes on her.

I was so intent on the e-mail I was typing I didn't see her get up or hear her approach. But suddenly she was there beside me, and I glanced up to find that damn sexy grin directed my way again. How was I to resist her when she smiled at me like that?

"Will you watch my stuff for a couple of minutes, Maggie?" She gestured toward her laptop and a leather bag beside her chair. I loved the way she said my name. A subtle emphasis, like she'd been looking forward to using it.

"Sure," I replied, as nonchalantly as I could.

"Great. Be right back."

She left through the gate, and I said a prayer of thanks for the warm Palm Springs weather as I appreciated the well-toned legs beneath her snug denim shorts.

She was back in a flash, carrying two grande cups from Ralph's, one of which she set down on the table by my laptop. "You were right," she said. "The good stuff, for sure."

"You didn't have to do that." But I was charmed she did, girlfriend or no girlfriend.

"Oh, I know. I just wanted to return the favor, and say I'm sorry I had to rush off so abruptly last night."

"Hey, uh…uh…no prob," I stuttered. *Smooth talker.* I tried to think of something clever, but everything that sprang to mind with her was much too sexually charged to repeat under the circumstances, and so I kept silent.

"Well, I'll see you around."

I detected disappointment in her voice as she turned to go, and that pleased me no end, but I didn't try to stop her from returning to her laptop. She stayed another forty minutes or so, but with fewer sidelong glances at me, and left without saying good-bye.

Still, I could not let go of the chance to be near her. I had meetings that day until late, so my next chance would be the next morning. I set my alarm for four thirty. Screw sleep. I prayed she would be there.

She was. Back in her chair, head down, working on her laptop. Coffee mug by her side.

Somehow it felt like it was my turn again. So she wouldn't be my first female lover. I still wanted to get to know her better, so I gathered my courage and took a chair six feet away. Not crowding her, but near enough that we could exchange a few words if she wanted to.

She glanced up as I sat down, and her eyes raked over me and that small indentation appeared in her cheek. "I wasn't sure you were coming."

Her words warmed me, and I decided if she was going to flirt, I'd flirt right back, girlfriend be damned.

"Seems we keep the same hours," I said. "My turn to run to Ralph's today when it opens."

Her smile got bigger. "You're on."

Redhead appeared right on cue, poking her head out of the door, begging for coffee. I returned my attention to my laptop, feeling a bit like I'd been caught with my hand in the cookie jar. Ansley, however, looked unruffled.

"Just press the button, Cheryl. It's all set up for you."

She caught me smiling at that, and grinned back.

Now was my chance. "Missed you last night," I said flippantly, as I turned on my laptop.

She chuckled. "I need at least two more cups to be even remotely charming."

"I doubt that."

"Why haven't I seen you at any of the readings?" she asked.

So she'd been looking for me. *Cool.*

"Because I'm not with your group. I'm meeting with clients for my charter flight company."

Her eyes widened. I could tell she was surprised at the news. "You're not here for the Lesbian Book Festival?"

I shook my head.

"So…you're not a reader?"

"Well, I do *read*," I said. "But not lesbian fiction. Nonfiction is more my speed."

She took a couple of seconds to absorb this. "No lesbian fiction at all?"

"Nope. I like true-life stories. Mountain-climbing adventures, shipwrecks, polar exploration…that sort of thing."

"I see." Ansley still had the oddest look on her face, and I couldn't figure out why. "So…so, how do you know about me, then?"

Now I was really confused. "Know about you? What do you mean?"

"You have no idea who I am?" Her eyes narrowed. "None at all?"

I started to get this kind of funny feeling in the pit of my stomach. "Should I? Are you famous or something?"

As if in response to my question, one of the owners of the resort approached, a pen in one hand and a trade paperback in the other. "Sorry to interrupt, but…would you mind, Ansley?"

"Of course," Ansley responded cheerily. "I'd love to. Shall I inscribe it to you both?"

"Yes, please."

"My pleasure."

As Ansley signed the book, I stood and took a couple of steps so I could see the cover. A photo of a woman restrained spread-eagle on a bed, with a lustful look in her eyes. The title read *Handcuff Holiday*, and beneath it were the words *The latest steamy sensation from Ansley, the Queen of Lesbian Erotica.*

All my bravado, all my hormonally charged self-confidence withered in an instant under the weight of her world of experience, and I fled. Yup. Picked up my laptop and ran like the coward I was. Never even said good-bye. *What the hell was I thinking?*

And I didn't even know the half of it then.

I showered and dressed for my day with clients. My first wasn't until ten that day, so I stayed in my room, hiding from her, until it was time to go. When I emerged I saw that chairs had been set up. *Readings*, she'd said. So she was here to read from her novels.

Near the gate three large tables were covered with piles of books. A woman behind them was carefully arranging them to maximize the space. I made sure Ansley was not around before I stopped to look. There were dozens of titles. Romances and mysteries, thrillers and anthologies. There was horror and science fiction, even, and it was a revelation. I had no idea there were so many books out there written by and for lesbians. *Way cool. Time to give fiction another look.*

"Can I help you find a particular title?" the woman offered.

"Well, I'm, uh…I'm looking for… Do you know the author named Ansley?"

"Oh, of course!" She beamed. "Isn't she *great*? No one can *touch* her when it comes to writing the really hot stuff." She laughed at her own double entendre. "We don't have all her titles. Lack of space. But a good representation down on the end here."

She led the way to the last table, which looked eerily like an Ansley shrine. In the middle was a photo of the author dressed only in a leather jacket and torn jeans, and posed in that sure-of-herself-but-not-really-flaunting-it stance. *Sexy. Oh, so sexy. And so far out of my league.* I winced when I thought about how naïve and clichéd my efforts at flirting must have seemed.

Around the photo were her books, with names like *Passion's Pursuit* and *Forces of Femmes* and *Racy Rendezvous*. I read the cover blurbs on several and could feel myself getting redder and redder. Then I leafed through a few, and read a paragraph here and there. *Oh. My. God. I was flirting with the woman who wrote this?*

I bought every book of hers they had, cut short every meeting that day, and stayed up all night to read.

The first book I chose, *Handcuff Holiday*, her latest, I read cover to cover in three and a half hours, including the four breaks I took to imagine myself in a scene with the author. I had never been so sexually charged in my life, but the orgasms were not as satisfying as they should have been. I wanted *her*.

To think that hundreds of women thought this way about Ansley bothered the hell out of me in an odd way, but excited me, too. The next several books I just skimmed, diving into the sexy parts, growing more aroused all the time, knowing *she* had written all of this. But every book also made me feel more foolish that I had dared approach her, and grateful I'd not gone further. Apparently I had a lot to learn about what women do to each other. And for all my false bravado with her in the flirting department, I wasn't sure I could be anywhere near as unrestrained and insatiable and explicit as most of the women she wrote about were. Were they all her ex-lovers?

It doesn't matter, I kept telling myself. *She has a girlfriend, idiot.*

I glanced at the digital clock by the bed. Five o'clock. Would she be there? I fought the urge to go to the window to look, though I knew it might be my last chance to see her. We both would be going home tomorrow.

I lasted until seven, then I went to the window, heart pounding. I couldn't understand my tumult of emotions. I just knew I was far too stirred up to face her in the flesh. Disappointed and relieved to find the courtyard empty, I ventured outside and fired up the laptop.

In less than two minutes, she materialized. "Are you avoiding me?" Her voice was soft, and I looked up into sad eyes.

I shrugged. I couldn't lie to her. "I had no idea who you were. I'm sorry."

She flinched in disappointment. "You're not interested in me because of my writing?"

"No!" I blurted out, and that made her smile. "I mean, for one thing, of course, I didn't know you had a girlfriend at first…"

"Girlfriend?" she repeated, her forehead furrowing. "I don't have a girlfriend."

My heartbeat picked up. "The redhead?"

She draped that great body of hers over the end my chair, so we were within touching distance. That endearing indentation appeared in her cheek. "You mean my editor?"

"Editor?" My body started to tingle in anticipation. She had *that look* in her eyes again.

"Yeah, we had a reader appreciation dinner last night. And a book signing the night before. She keeps me on schedule." She looked me up and down, her eyes lingering on my breasts again, and my body reacted as if she was really touching me. "But I'm free tonight."

I could hardly breathe for the adrenaline racing through me. "Look, it's real obvious that I'm attracted to you, but I'm just not...I mean..." How could I admit to this woman that I was completely clueless?

"You *really* didn't know who I was."

I shook my head.

She reached over and put her hand lightly on my shoulder. I was acutely aware of the soft pressure of her fingertips. "Then why me?"

I looked at her. "I'm not sure," I answered as honestly as I could. "There's just something about you."

"Simple as that?"

Damn, I loved that smile. "Yes."

"Then why did you run?"

She was so close. Kissing distance. And there was no girlfriend between us, after all. I couldn't stop staring at her lips.

"Wouldn't work," I mumbled.

"No?" She leaned in closer to me. "Sure about that?"

"Mmm-hmm." I responded in the affirmative, but found myself shaking my head no, and that made her laugh.

"Why wouldn't it work?" She leaned in farther until I could feel her breath on my cheek.

I'd spent the last several hours being seduced by her words, and like I said, I believe in living a life of no regrets. I suddenly didn't give a damn about my lack of experience. I just felt I should warn her.

"There's nothing I'd like more right now than to invite you to my room, and see how many of the scenes in your books we can re-create in however many hours we have until our planes home," I said. "But..."

"You've read my books?" She looked confused and very pleased.

"I bought eight yesterday morning. Read all of *Handcuff Holiday* and parts of the others," I admitted with a sheepish grin. "I really liked *The Depth of Desire*, and can't wait for *Torrid Affairs*."

"You're serious!"

I nodded, feeling my face flush again.

"Which *parts* of the others did you read?" Before I could answer, she leaned in and pressed her lips to my neck, kissing me so sweetly I shut my eyes and luxuriated in the touch for a moment before I continued with my effort to warn her.

"I love your writing," I said as she continued to nuzzle my neck, "but I have to admit I'm scared to death at the prospect of being with you."

She pulled back to look at me. "Why?"

Now or never. I had to be honest with her, though I knew it might kill the chance I'd have a hell of a memorable evening.

"I've never been with a woman before." I stared at my shoes.

"Never?" Her voice was soft.

"I've known for a long time. Just never met anyone I cared to... you know." I couldn't believe I was talking like this to someone who regularly wrote most explicitly about doing everything imaginable to the female anatomy.

"You sure you want it to be me?" she asked in that breathy half-whisper.

"I'm sure. If you're not put off by my lack of experience." I didn't want to sell myself too short, though, I decided. I looked her in the eyes. "Not that I haven't been paying attention to what I read today, and I certainly am a willing and able student."

Ansley did something then I totally did not expect. She blushed.

Smiling, she cocked her head and looked at me as if considering something. Then she glanced around to make sure we were alone before she leaned in to whisper in my ear. "I'm going to let you in on a little secret, Maggie. My name is Stephanie O'Ansley and I live in a small village in Maine, where I work part-time in a bookstore and then come home alone to my cat. Writing about something convincingly doesn't mean you've necessarily experienced it—it just means you're good at research and have a knack for words."

She kissed me on the neck again, then pulled back to look me in the eyes. "Now, I *have* been with women, yes. But only a few, mostly in college. Nothing to really write home about, and no one in a while." She grinned. "There are lots of things I've written about that I've never experienced, but would like to. I mean, you *did* mention re-creating some scenes, as I recall?"

It was amazing how a little insight into your favorite author can suddenly quell all your fears. "I'm in 33," I said, getting up.

She took my hand and pulled me toward my room, and all the arousal from her words, both written and spoken, came rushing back at me. I stopped at the door and turned to her, and she shot me a questioning look. I could see she was as turned on as I was.

"Remember your hot hotel room scene in *Passion's Pursuit*?" I asked.

That endearing smile turned truly rakish as she nodded with heavy-lidded eyes.

I opened the door. "We can start there."

Julie Cannon is a native sun goddess, born and raised in Phoenix, Arizona. Her day job is in Corporate America and her nights are spent bringing to life the stories that bounce around in her head throughout the day. Julie and her partner Laura have been together for sixteen years and spend their weekends camping, riding ATVs, or lounging around the pool with their two kids.

Julie has selections in *Erotic Interludes 4: Extreme Passions* and *Erotic Interludes 5: Road Games*. She is the author of *Come and Get Me*, *Heart 2 Heart*, *Heartland*, the upcoming *Uncharted Passage* (October 2008) and *Just Business* (2009), all published by Bold Strokes Books.

6,239

JULIE CANNON

Did you ever wake up one morning and have no idea who was lying next to you? That in and of itself didn't bother me. I'd woken up with acquaintances, casual dates, and more than my share of complete strangers, some of whom I couldn't even remember *going* to bed with. The woman on the other pillow was average looking, with eyes set a little too wide apart, lips full and just a bit pouty this early in the morning. Her eyebrows were so pale they were hardly visible even from seven inches away, and her short blond hair didn't even hint it was anything other than the real thing. My memory verified that just below her appendix scar and just above long, muscular legs, she was in fact a natural blonde.

A small tattoo of a woman running peeked out from the rumpled sheet that had fallen down low on her back. Her arms were tanned and the large muscles of her biceps were clearly defined beneath what I knew was very soft skin. Her hands were thin with long fingers that knew just where to go on my body and what to do when they got there. And last night the journey was just as exciting as the destination.

It was as clear in my mind as it had been a few hours ago. We had a quiet dinner talking about this that and whatever. I felt slightly intimidated that she knew more about the presidential candidates than I did. Hell, I didn't even know who some of the people were that she was talking about. And when she started talking about the guest on last Sunday's *Meet the Press,* I'm sure my eyes started to glaze over. Her choice of wine was delicious and she asked the waiter for two spoons with the Tower of Terror Chocolate Sundae.

We didn't say much on the ride back to the house, and we didn't say anything as we walked down the hall and into the bedroom. We weren't holding hands, kissing, or ripping each other's clothes off. It was as if by unspoken agreement, mental telepathy, or some other kinetic connection, words were not necessary. I was aroused but calm, aware of exactly what was going to happen once we hit the cool sheets.

My friends have always laughed at me when I tell them that every time is fundamentally the same regardless of who you are with. There are lips and hands, breasts and vaginas, and every woman has a clitoris even if she hasn't found it yet. You do the same basic things and if you do them correctly, you are rewarded with a climax. Pretty straightforward, wouldn't you agree? I can't help the way I think. I'm a scientist, and I think in analytical terms. I'm not good with the squishy, feely stuff. I had to look up the word *metaphor* in the well-worn dictionary that owns the corner of the coffee table in the front room.

I pulled my wayward thoughts back to the woman sharing the morning beside me. Last night, her hands trembled when she unbuttoned my shirt. Obviously she'd had lots of practice since it didn't take her more than a few seconds to open all ten buttons. Her eyes roamed over my upper torso as she slowly slid the shirt off my shoulders and let it drop. For the first time in a long time I didn't care that there were clothes on the floor.

She licked her lips when her gaze stopped at my breasts. Her breathing quickened and she lifted her hands as if to touch my erect nipples. She must have had second thoughts because she stopped and detoured to my belt buckle instead. The sound of the metal tip sliding through the metal loop echoed in my ears. They'd started to ring in anticipation a few seconds before.

I balanced myself with my hands on her shoulders as she helped me out of my jeans and boots. Her face was even with my crotch and I was glad that I had thought enough ahead to wear my good undies and not the ones with the slight rip in the waistband. Being the practical woman I am, I couldn't throw them away just because they had a little tear in a place that really didn't matter anyway.

I stood there nekked, as my favorite aunt used to say. *Naked* was a technical term whereas *nekked* was nasty. And we were about to do the *big* nasty. She stopped me as I reached for her, and made me stand there perfectly still while she slowly stripped. She was beautiful. I will never forget how she looked bathed in the light that snaked into the bedroom from the bathroom.

I don't remember how we got on the bed, but the next thing I remember is her leaning over me with the most peculiar expression on her face. It was a cross between longing and lust, with just enough hesitation to give me a passing fear that she might not do *it* at all. But she did, God help me, she did everything with a familiarity of my body that took my breath away more than once.

Her kisses were soft and warm as she covered my lips with hers. Minute after minute she made love to my mouth as if she had nowhere else to go and nothing else to do for the rest of the night. She alternately nipped and massaged first my upper lip, then my lower with soft strokes of her tongue. This woman could kiss, and I desperately wanted her tongue inside my mouth. I wanted her to arouse the inside of my mouth as much as she had done my lips. I wanted to suck on her tongue and have her tongue fuck me until I came.

She never gave me the chance to say as much, but I must have done something right because she was soon echoing my thoughts, thrusting in and out and driving me crazy. She was still leaning over me, our bodies not touching. Every time I reached for her, she raised her lips from mine. Like a new puppy eager to please her master, I quickly learned what she wanted me to do, or in this case, not to do. From her position, she dominated me, and I'm not accustomed to being the bottom. But she made me not care. Finally she allowed me to capture her tongue, and I sucked it while my orgasm shot through my body. I should rephrase that: while my *first* orgasm racked my body.

She licked my neck like it was a Popsicle melting in the hot sun. Up and down her magical tongue traveled, from the tip of my collarbone to the edge of my jaw. Long, slow strokes as soft as a rose petal were punctuated with nibbles and extra attention to those sensitive spots that made me shiver. At one point I thought she was giving me a hickey. A hickey, for crying out loud! I haven't had a hickey in thirty years. But again, surprisingly, I didn't care. It was cool enough to get away with wearing a turtleneck if I had to.

She moved farther south, and it felt like she spent an hour exploring my breasts before she captured my nipple in her mouth. She nuzzled and licked and sucked, giving extra attention to the fading scar just below my left nipple. Her teeth were the body part of choice to create the exquisite sensation shooting through my body right to my clit. My nipples have always been ultrasensitive almost to the point of painful, but under her practiced caresses, I was in heaven. When I grasped her hair and pulled her closer she froze, and I quickly remembered my earlier lesson and let my arms drop back to the bed. She sucked greedily on one nipple while she toyed with the other, and the last thing that crossed my mind before my second orgasm was that I wasn't sure who was enjoying it more.

She found the spot on my stomach that is ticklish, and we laughed together as she teased me by returning to that spot often as she explored the flatland between my ribs and pelvis. Okay, so it's more like soft rolling hills, but it used to be flat many years ago. If she didn't mind the extra landscape, neither did I.

Her breasts were tantalizingly close to my crotch, and when she got close enough I could feel her hard nipple sliding in and out between my wet lips. My hips instinctively thrust forward, wanting more contact than I was getting, and I felt her smile against my stomach at my feeble attempt. I wanted her to touch me. I need her to touch me. She knew it and I groaned, realizing that relief was nowhere in sight. But I surprised her when I came a third time just as her nipple grazed my clit.

She traversed across the hard expanse of my hipbones and pubis. Her tongue left a trail of moisture and I shivered when she backtracked, lightly blowing across the wetness. And speaking of wetness, I was so stoked it was starting to slide out of me and onto the freshly washed sheets.

Her hair fell across my stomach and thighs as she moved her mouth lower. *Finally*, my brain screamed. *It's about goddamned time she got down to business.* But I was wrong. Way wrong. She had the nerve to skip the best part. Who did she think she was, anyway? We were here for one reason, and that reason was pounding hard on the door to be released. *How dare she glance over it without even a second fleeting look?*

I forgave her when her fingers began to trace an intricate pattern on the inside of my thigh. I concentrated trying to picture the artwork she was searing into my body. The longer she did it, and the closer her strokes came to the juncture between agony and ecstasy, the less I tried to think and just concentrated on feeling. Thankfully that wasn't difficult because my legs are long and if this sensation was going to continue to my toes, it would be a lengthy ride. But she was driving tonight and I was simply in the passenger seat. And that was more than okay with me.

I didn't think I could feel anything better than my three orgasms so far, but when her hands began long, firm strokes on my feet, I knew I had died and gone to heaven. I never really understood the difference between sensuality and sexuality until my feet were in her hands. She caressed them as gently as she had my breasts. She rubbed and massaged them as she would my tired, sore muscles after a long day at the office. I felt worshiped and relaxed, but considering that my feet were cradled between her full breasts there was no risk I'd fall asleep.

I came again when she slid her tongue between my toes over and over, mimicking what I prayed she would do to other parts of my body. Back and forth she went, slowly at first, then increasing her tempo to match the thrusting of my hips. Or was it the other way around? Who knows? Who cares? Despite my analytical brain, I'm not really one to quibble on the details, especially when it comes to things that make me cry out in the night.

Finished with my legs, her eyes locked with mine and she moved upward. This was it! She was finally going to the one place on my body she had not yet ventured tonight. I was disappointed when her mouth didn't even hesitate in that area, but continued up until her lips were a hairsbreadth from mine. Her breath was warm as it caressed my lips. Time stood still as she searched my eyes, as if she were looking for a sign, or the bottom of my soul. I can't say if she found what she was looking for, because she raised off me and turned me onto my stomach.

I hate being on my stomach when I'm nekked. The sun never shines on my butt, which has gotten bigger as the years have passed, and I have more dimples in that region than I ever had on my face. Thankfully I had shaved all the way up, front and back, so I didn't have that embarrassment to deal with.

She must have turned the map of my body over with me, because she followed my backside with as much tenacity as she had my front. She licked and kissed and caressed the soles of my feet (which tickled), my calves, the backs of my knees (which makes me crazy), up past the back of my thighs and onto the acres of my ass. She was obviously one of those women who thought the more the merrier, because she didn't bypass an inch in her exploration of the dark side of my moon.

She planted a kiss on each vertebra in my spine and lightly traced my ribs with her fingertip, then her tongue. Her hands and mouth drifted close to my breasts more than once and I turned on my side just enough to give her what she needed. Correction, what *I* needed, before returning to my shoulders and neck.

She took the pillow from the other side of the bed and slid it under my stomach. My lily-white, too-big butt was pushed up into the air. A shudder ran through me that was a combination of desire, anticipation, and cold. Seconds later her body covered mine and the cold was immediately forgotten. Her breasts were firm on my back, her hard nipples pushing against my shoulder blades. Her curly hair tickled my butt which, seeming to have a mind of its own, rubbed against her shamelessly. Strong hands caressed my arms, starting at my shoulders and not stopping until they reached the tips of my fingers. All the while her hot breath and wet tongue teased my left ear. Shivers ran down my spine as her body completely covered mine. She was not heavy, but more like a comfortable familiarity settling onto me.

She moved against me in a slow, sensuous dance, teasing me with the full contact of her body and then lifting, leaving me practically bare, my body aching for contact. Each time she returned she would stay just a little bit longer, grinding her pubis into me, obviously enjoying herself as much as I. With her body draped over me, she slid her hand under me and finally, *finally* touched me. It didn't take her long to realize that was all I needed this time. I felt her smile against the back of my neck.

I was still coming down from my orgasm when she rubbed her clitoris against me for her first orgasm of the night. Notice I said her *first* orgasm. More on that later. Her arms straightened, her body arched, and the most wonderful sound of ecstasy came from her. She fell against me, her body enveloping mine.

It took her a long time to recover, but it was well worth the wait. She turned me over again, and this time when she traveled down my body she stopped and settled in exactly where I wanted her. I always wondered if other women could have seven or eight or twelve orgasms in the span of one hour like me. I didn't know, but I thanked my lucky stars I could.

That's pretty much how we spent the rest of the night. Kind of reminded me of the instructions on a bottle of shampoo. Wash, rinse, repeat. Just when I thought I couldn't go again, she didn't seem to agree and off we'd go again. Finally, sometime during the wee hours of the morning, we fell asleep exhausted.

I hate mornings after. What do you say to someone to whom you have done the most intimate things and who has done them to you besides, *How do you like your coffee?* Sometimes I am so embarrassed I want to disappear, and oftentimes I have. I know it's ridiculous, but that's the way I think and I'm not going to try to figure it out.

So here I am again, the morning after. But what is so different *this* morning, so stunning that it hit's me like a brick, is that I've woken up with this woman for the past six thousand two hundred thirty-nine mornings give or take a few for business trips, visits to ailing parents, and an occasional serious fight or two. She is my wife, my partner, girlfriend, lover, or whatever other label you want to apply to the woman I have shared my life with for the past seventeen years. She is my housekeeper, my landscaper, my cook, maid, pet sitter, accountant, doctor, and shrink. She is a teacher, a motivational speaker, a miracle worker, Santa Claus, and the Tooth Fairy. She is the mother of my children, a thoughtful daughter, a caring sister, and a fabulous daughter-in-law. She is the half that makes me whole, and I have no idea who she will be today.

I leaned over her and kissed her gently on the lips, ready to begin another day. Last night was not our anniversary, Valentine's Day, or my birthday. It was just the end of another day in a long cavalcade of days we have shared together. Every day with her is a new discovery of what life will bring us. What new adventure we will encounter and work together to overcome. We will agree, disagree, and take different paths, but in the end we will always come together at the same place, side by side.

Rachel Spangler's first novel, *Learning Curve*, was released in January 2008, and her second, *Trails Merge*, is forthcoming from Bold Strokes Books in December 2008. She and her partner, Susan, are raising their young son in western New York. During the winter they make the most of the lake-effect snow on local ski slopes. In the summer, they love to travel and watch their beloved St. Louis Cardinals. Regardless of the season, she always makes time for a good romance, whether she's reading it, writing it, or living it.

Baby Steps
Rachel Spangler

H oney," my wife, Grace, said, "the baby is asleep."

"Thank God," I replied without looking up from the stack of papers on my desk. "I have really got to get this report done for work tomorrow."

"Kale," she said, placing special emphasis on my name, "the baby is asleep…fast asleep…in her own bed…all the way down the hall."

This time I looked up. Grace was standing in the doorway of my home office wearing one of my old T-shirts, a pair of threadbare sweatpants, and some well-worn blue slippers. Her sandy blond hair was pulled back in a ponytail with several loose strands tucked behind her ear. It wasn't until my eyes met hers that I realized she was giving me *that* look. The one that says all systems are go. The look I hadn't seen since our daughter, Rory, was born over two months ago. The look that used to send me running for the bedroom removing my clothes in the process. I froze.

It's not that I didn't know this was coming, mind you. The doctor had given us the green light two weeks ago, so I knew it was only a matter of time before we reached this point again. Still, I had not expected it to happen like this. Not on a Tuesday night when we were both exhausted. Not when neither of us had had a spare moment to shower in at least forty-eight hours. Not when she had a large spot of dried spit-up on the front of her shirt. Not when I was on a major deadline for work. I had envisioned wine and candlelight, perhaps some soft music, or at least both of us having bathed recently. This wasn't how I pictured it at all, but what was a woman supposed to do? She was giving me *that* look.

I stood shakily and crossed the room, taking Grace in my arms and pulling her close. I wondered briefly if making love was like riding a bike. It wasn't something you could forget how to do, was it? Then again, maybe it was like a foreign language and if you didn't use it regularly you'd lose your ability. I had a brief moment of panic, realizing I barely remembered anything from my high school Spanish class. Then Grace kissed me, one of those deep, searing kisses that had always made my toes curl. Now this I remembered just fine.

I kissed her back, allowing myself to enjoy the feel of her tongue as it wrapped around mine. I placed my hands on her hips and worked my fingers up under her shirt. As I brushed against her skin, I heard her moan softly into my mouth. She leaned into me, her breasts pressing against mine as the kiss deepened. I moved my mouth down along her jawline, then nibbled on her earlobe. Tilting back her head, she gave me access to the soft curve of her neck. I ran my tongue along the delicate skin, licking and biting my way to her shoulder and across her collarbone. Grace's chest rose and fell more rapidly as her breathing quickened. She clutched at my back, holding me tightly to her. It felt so good to feel her responding to my touch again; anything I might have forgotten was certainly coming back to me now.

Eager for more contact between us, I broke the kiss long enough to strip off my shirt. Then I reached up to do the same to hers. We resumed the kiss, this time with more flesh exposed to be touched and stroked. Her breasts were larger now than they had been before, a pleasant side effect of the pregnancy, but I also knew they were tender, so I caressed them softly through the fabric of her nursing bra. At the same time I began walking us backward to our bedroom. I knew that if I didn't get there soon, I would end up taking her on the floor. Halfway down the hall I had my hands in the waistband of her sweatpants, pushing them down over her hips as we went. I wanted her so badly now I could hardly stand it.

By the time we entered our room, Grace had tugged my pants to the ground, and I stepped out of them before we both tumbled onto the bed. I positioned myself above her, supporting my weight on one elbow. I buried my face in her neck and ran my hand up the inside of her leg. She felt so good, so familiar. We had been so preoccupied with the baby in the past two months that I had almost forgotten how much I missed this. Almost. Part of me worried that I was moving too fast, that

I needed to stop and savor the moment, but then Grace arched her hips, urging me to take her. My fingers were inches away from the apex of her thighs, so close I could feel how hot she was for me when a shrill cry came screeching through the baby monitor on the bedside table.

I have to give her credit—even at two months old my daughter has impeccable comedic timing. The kid is already a real show-stopper. Hearing her shriek was like having a bucket of ice water dumped over our naked bodies. This wasn't your run-of-the-mill, slow-to-wake-up fussiness. This was the full-throttle scream of a very unhappy infant. Grace and I both jumped out of bed and headed for the nursery, picking up our clothes as we went. When we entered the room it was immediately apparent what the problem was: we had an overflowing diaper on our hands. The kind that fills the little footie pajamas and requires the mommies to bypass the changing table altogether and head straight for the bathtub. The kind that ensures there will be as much crying during the cleanup as there was while making the mess in the first place. If the baby simply waking up wasn't enough to kill the mood, this certainly managed to do the trick.

By the time it was all said and done, Grace and I were both beat and Rory was wide awake. It was going to be another sleepless night, and not the kind I had been hoping for.

The next morning I awoke, aroused. After finally going to sleep in the wee hours of the morning, Rory was up again three hours later to eat, then up for good at 6:00 a.m. During the few hours of fitful sleep, I had dreams of making love to Grace. I could still feel her skin under my fingertips and taste her lips on mine. Up until this point I had hardly thought about the sex I wasn't having; too many other things had been taking their toll on my mind and body. But now that I had been given an erotic reminder of what I was missing, I could think of little else. I wanted our sex life back.

Since Grace was breastfeeding and up at all hours of the night, I handled things like early morning diaper changes and playtime so she could get a few extra hours of sleep. I greatly enjoyed my one-on-one time with Rory. Despite her horrible sleeping patterns and diaper-exploding abilities, she was a joy to have around. She was a happy baby. Usually, we spent our time together reading books, singing songs, and bouncing around making silly faces in every mirror in the house. That is to say, I did those things while Rory cooed in approval. We spent most mornings bonding and enjoying each other's company. Today, though, we were on a more specific mission—enable romance.

I knew I had been caught off guard the night before. I wasn't prepared when the right time came along, and I knew it. I let my surprise and my libido get the best of me, and I had ended up rushing into things. Grace deserved better than that, and for that matter, so did I. It had been so long since we'd made love. Our welcome-back affair should be memorable, not some quick grope-fest in the middle of the hallway. As frustrating as it was to have been interrupted by Rory, I convinced myself she had done me a favor. Now that I knew Grace was ready, I no longer had to worry about pressuring her. Now I had time to plan something special. Now I was going to take charge and bring back the romance.

I put Rory into her baby carrier, which allowed me to move, hands free, around the house. We started off by making our way to the kitchen, where we got some steaks out to thaw. Then we made a red wine marinade to pour over them. Next, we mixed up a salad and chopped up some potatoes to roast. I would be playing Chef Kale when I got home from work, and I wanted everything to be done to perfection. Having dinner mostly prepared ahead of time would save Grave the trouble of having to do it herself and let me put a nice meal on the table quickly, which was key given the fact that Rory didn't appreciate being put down for too long. I wanted things to go as smoothly as possible, and with a baby in the house that meant a lot of extra planning on my part. Romance would no longer be as effortless as it had been in the past. In fact, nothing was as simple as it had been before having a baby, but that was to be expected. I told myself that just because things took more time and effort didn't mean they couldn't be done.

With dinner almost ready before we'd even had breakfast, Rory and I headed back upstairs for a bath. Normally bathtime occurs right before bed, but I hoped to be occupied in another way right before bed, so I thought I would go ahead and kill two birds with one stone. Rory and I were both in need of a good scrub-down, so I filled the tub to a suitable depth for the both of us, and we got in together. "This is the way we wash our hair, wash our hair, wash our hair," I sang as I soaped up her barely fuzzy head and then my own short dark curls. Rinsing us both was quite a challenge, though, as I had to hold on to Rory while rinsing myself, and few things are more slippery than a wet baby. Thankfully, I didn't have to maneuver us both out of the tub simultaneously. Just as I had begun to contemplate the logistics of such a tricky move, Grace came to the rescue.

"What a nice surprise!" she said, pushing back the shower curtain.

"Good morning, Mommy G," I said, waving Rory's hand while the baby cooed at the sight of her mother.

"Good morning, my clean girls." Grace grabbed Rory's hooded towel off the rack and scooped her up out of my arms.

I stood up and began to towel myself off, but not before I saw Grace smile suggestively at the sight of my body. I don't delude myself with visions of grandeur. I'm not stunning, nor am I as fit as I would like to be, but I take care of my body. Before Rory came along I got enough exercise to stay relatively trim. While I hadn't been to the gym or played racquetball in months, I hadn't lost too much of my muscle tone. Normally I don't give a lot of thought to my own looks, but it did feel good to have my body noticed once again.

Grace took Rory while I got dressed, taking care to put on a shirt Grace had bought me for our sixth anniversary the year before. She had mentioned several times that she liked how the color brought out the blue in my eyes. It wasn't a grand gesture, but today was going to be all about setting the mood, and the small touches mattered. I was rewarded for my attention to detail when Grace kissed me good-bye for work. Instead of her normal quick peck on the lips, she allowed her lips to linger on mine. I opened my mouth to the gentle probing of her tongue, and if it hadn't been for Rory wiggling between us, I might not have had the strength to force myself away. Once again, my daughter served as a reminder that I needed to pace myself.

I got home from work to find my beautiful wife and darling little girl waiting at the door for me. The only problem was that Grace looked exhausted and Rory was fussing. Not exactly what I was hoping for, but I would have to work with it.

"How's my girls?" I asked, fearing that I already knew the answer.

"Exhausted and cranky," Grace replied with a weak smile as she handed Rory to me. "And how was your day, dear?"

"Obviously better than yours." I bounced the baby in the crook of my arm, which quieted her cries to a mild whimper. "Has she been like this all day long?"

Grace flopped onto the couch. "Not if I hold her and keep moving, but God forbid I try to put her down or sit down myself."

"Well, you can sit down now," I said, kissing her on the cheek. "Mommy K is reporting for duty."

"Thank you." Grace leaned back and closed her eyes.

I took Rory into the kitchen, and we set about making dinner. I hadn't planned on playing chef and mom at the same time, but if that's what the situation called for, I would just have to find a way to do it. I was tired after a day at the office, but Grace looked dead on her feet. I knew my options were either to take care of both dinner and the baby or say good-bye to any chance of Grace staying awake long enough for me to make love to her tonight. So the potatoes went into the oven, Rory went into her stroller, and the steaks went onto the grill. I actually came up with a pretty good system. I walked Rory up and down the driveway, stopping at the grill every now and then to flip the steaks. The constant movement took its toll on my feet, but more importantly it wore out Rory, who finally dozed off just as the meat was medium well.

I wheeled the stroller back into the house, balancing a plate of steaks on my arm, waiter style. I set the table in a flash and was just lighting the candles when Grace came into the room.

"Have I told you lately how much I love you?" she asked, placing a kiss on my cheek.

"It never hurts to hear it again," I replied, pulling out her chair.

"I love you," she repeated.

Everything was in place for a romantic dinner that would naturally lead to romance after dinner. It looked like things were going to be okay after all.

"So tell me about your day," I said, just before I took my first bite of steak.

"Well, Rory and I went to the grocery store."

"And how did that go?" I knew that even the most mundane errand could become a wild adventure when my daughter was involved.

"Well, overall it was good, but—" My wife was cut short by Rory's cry. Grace immediately stood up to go get her.

"No, you sit and eat. I'll take her."

"You've had her since you got home."

"And you had her all day before that." I picked up the baby, who quieted only slightly. I tried not to let my disappointment show. My hopes for a romantic dinner were disappearing quickly.

"What were you saying about the store?" I asked over the noise of Rory's fussing.

"Just that some old lady came up to me and asked if I wanted her to hold the baby while I shopped." Grace chuckled and shook her head at the memory.

"A complete stranger?" I bounced from side to side in an attempt to soothe the baby.

"Yeah, never seen her before in my life."

"That's creepy."

"Oh, it was sweet," Grace said, looking up at me and laughing. "Honey, I should take her."

"Why? I've got it under control." Rory had calmed down considerably, and I wanted desperately to salvage our evening. I was determined that we would have a nice dinner even if we didn't actually get to have it together.

"I know you're doing a great job, but you aren't giving her what she needs right now."

"What do you mean? She's settling down," I asserted as if my parenting skills were in question.

Grace gave me a sweet smile. "Sweetheart, she's sucking on your shirt."

I looked down and sure enough, Rory was making a valiant attempt to nurse through the shirt I had taken special care in picking out that morning. There was a large spot of baby drool now coating the area around my right breast.

"Damn," I cursed under my breath and handed the baby over to Grace, who was already unbuttoning her shirt for Rory. It looked like the rest of our meal would be spent feeding the baby. So much for our romantic dinner.

❖

Later that evening I readied myself for one last-ditch attempt at setting the right mood. While Grace was downstairs playing with Rory, I filled the bath with warm water and some lavender soap and then lit some candles around the edge of the tub. Bubble baths were a favorite luxury of Grace's, and she hadn't had one since giving birth, first because they were off-limits while she was healing, then later because she simply hadn't had time. If there was anything that would relax my wife and leave her feeling sensual, this was it.

Grace looked happy enough to cry when I took Rory from her arms and shooed her off to the bath. Then to make sure she had all the time and privacy she needed, Rory and I went to the nursery to get ready for bed. After only a few minutes of rocking, Rory went right to sleep. After the events of the last twenty-four hours, though, I couldn't help but be suspicious. The bedtime routine had gone entirely too easy, so it was with great trepidation that I laid her in her crib. Then I held my breath and said a little prayer that she remained asleep. A gift from heaven, she didn't even bat an eyelid when I slowly moved my hands out from under her. I tiptoed out of the room and shut the nursery door gently behind me.

I moved quickly into our bedroom and lit candles throughout the room. I started the CD player and put in a mix that I had made of romantic love songs. There's nothing like a little mood music to set the right tone. Then I turned down the covers on our queen-sized bed. Surveying the room, I checked each detail to make sure I hadn't overlooked anything. This was my last chance to make something romantic out of the day, and I didn't want to miss an opportunity to make it special. Once everything was set just the way I wanted it, I went back to the bathroom to see Grace.

She was still soaking in the tub, her head resting on the rim, her eyes closed and only the swell of her breasts visible above the soapy bubbles. She was so beautiful she took my breath away. She looked up when she heard me enter the room. "Where's Rory?"

"Fast asleep," I said, feeling a grin spread across my face.

"Well, don't you sound pleased with yourself." Grace returned my smile. "It's almost like you had something planned."

I shrugged, knowing that Grace could see right through me. "Me? Not at all. I've got nothing going on tonight."

"Well, I could think of some things I'd like to do while I've got you all to myself." Grace stood up, and I stared in awe as the suds and water ran down her body. Swallowing hard, I handed her a towel then watched as she slowly dried her body. She was taking her time on purpose, just to tease me, and it was working. She had always had me in the palm of her hand—we both knew it, and I was thrilled that she was exercising her power over me once again.

"God, I've missed you," I finally blurted out.

"I've missed you looking at me like that." She placed a kiss on my lips. "I was beginning to worry that you weren't attracted to me anymore."

I pushed back and looked her in the eye, wondering for a second if she was still teasing me. "How could you ever think that?"

"I just had a baby, my breasts are saggy, I lost my waistline, I still have an episiotomy scar, and speaking of scars, with the things you saw in that delivery room, well, I wouldn't be surprised if you were scarred for life."

"Grace," I said, still gazing into her soft blue eyes, "you gave me a miracle. I am more impressed with your body now than I ever have been. I love every inch of you. Let me take you to bed and I'll prove it."

Without waiting for any more response I took her by the hand and led her to our room. She smiled when she saw the bed turned down in the candlelight. "Nothing planned for tonight, huh?"

"Maybe I was hoping for a little something."

"Come here," she said, pulling me onto the bed with her.

I curled up beside Grace, propping myself up on an elbow and running my other hand along the curves of her body. I trailed my fingers gently down the side of her breast and across her stomach, then through the soft curls and between her thighs. I felt her relax beneath my touch. She opened up to me, and I brushed past her clit, eliciting a soft moan. Pressing my lips to hers, I stroked more firmly, establishing a rhythm in sync with the slow rocking of her hips. I took my time drawing her body closer to mine, and her breathing became erratic.

"I can't wait much longer," Grace said in a raspy whisper.

"Good, I want you to come for me." Two months is a long enough wait. I pushed into her. All she could do was nod frantically before giving in. I felt her entire body shudder as she clutched my back and then went limp. I cradled her in my arms and kissed her cheek softly.

"I love you," she murmured into my neck.

"I love you too."

Grace placed little kisses along my jawline and down across my throat. It felt divine. She rolled me over onto my back and pushed my pants down over my hips. She leaned over me, circling each breast with her tongue while she worked her fingers steadily lower until they were between my legs. I arched up to meet her touch. It wasn't going to take much for me. I was already so close.

I should have known what would happen next. Really, it was becoming the pattern of our lives, so it shouldn't have been surprising, but I was still caught completely off guard when the baby monitor lit up like a traffic light as Rory's cries came blaring through from the nursery.

"Oh, you have got to be kidding me!" I groaned.

Grace sagged against me and we both held still as if willing the crying to cease, but it soon became apparent that Rory's cries held a purpose.

"It's time for her to eat," Grace said, kissing my forehead.

"She just ate," I whined, my nerve endings still humming from the sudden break in stimulation.

"It's been over two hours." Grace grabbed her robe.

"We were so close," I whimpered.

She smiled a sympathetic smile as she headed for the door. "Just hold that thought. We are going to pick right back up where we left off as soon as I'm done."

Somehow I doubted that. In fact, at that moment I doubted that I would ever make love to my wife again. We had tried a quickie and that didn't work. I had tried to be romantic and the baby got in the way. Taking it slow and easy certainly wasn't happening either. I had tried everything I could think of, but any possibility of restarting our sex life seemed to be flickering and fading like the candles that were burning out around the room. The love song CD stopped playing as if signaling an end to my final attempt for the evening, and I lay there sulking in the silence. Apparently the only remaining evidence of my efforts was the dull throbbing at my core. The frustration was almost overwhelming, so I pulled on my pants and headed toward the nursery.

When I entered Rory's room, my eyes took a few seconds to adjust to the dim glow of her night-light, but when they did I saw Grace sitting in the rocking chair in the far corner of the room. She had the baby swaddled in a soft yellow blanket and cradled against her chest. She was humming softly as she rocked, and Rory was watching her peacefully through heavy-lidded eyes.

They were so beautiful together that my heart ached at the sight of them. This picture in front of me was exactly what I had dreamt about for years and imagined every time I placed my hand on Grace's growing belly throughout her pregnancy. The love that filled the room was the reason we'd decided to have Rory in the first place. That perfect little person who stole my heart from the moment she arrived was fulfilling all of the hopes we had shared for so long. It was new, it was exciting, it was satisfying in ways I had never known it could be.

Rory was drifting off to sleep. Soon Grace would return her to her crib and come join me in our bed. Maybe we would make love, maybe we wouldn't, but that didn't seem nearly as important as it had a few minutes earlier. It would happen when the time was right. Standing there watching the love of my life holding the light of my life, I realized that I had been blessed with a beautiful family, and I intended to enjoy every second of the life we were building.

JLee Meyer utilizes her background in psychology and speech pathology in her work as an international communication consultant. Spending hours in airports, planes, and hotel rooms allows her the opportunity to pursue two of her favorite passions: reading and writing lesbian fiction. JLee's hobbies are photography, hiking, tennis, and skiing, but she hasn't had time for them recently. Writing is her passion, and learning this new craft has been a joy. She and her partner CC live in Northern California with their two dogs.

Her novels are *Forever Found*, *First Instinct*, *Rising Storm*, and *Hotel Liaison*. The sequel to *Hotel Liaison* is planned for 2009. JLee also wishes to thank Joelle for her invaluable assistance with French translations and location information.

Visit JLee at www.myspace.com/jleemeyer, or at her Web site, jleemeyer.com, or email her at jlee@jleemeyer.com. You can also find her at www.boldstrokesbooks.com.

PARISIAN FIRE AND ICE
JLEE MEYER

I felt like I'd been scrubbing and mopping for hours. Each time one chore was complete, Pierre raced up to me and pointed to the next. I was sure he was trying to break me, to get me to quit. I just knew that little guy had a grudge against Americans.

But he paid in cash, and I had no work permit and little money left from my meager savings. I'd spent it all in my dash for freedom and didn't want the U.S. embassy to know my exact whereabouts. I never complained.

I'd been working there for six weeks and my speed was improving, as was the variety of jobs Pierre seemed to trust me with. I was now doing a lot of food preparation for the chef, Ormond, Pierre's lover. Ormond was as big and friendly as Pierre was skinny and reserved. It was like a Newfoundland and whippet had found each other. My French was terrible at best, but I was learning because Ormond was a patient teacher.

I'd found a room that didn't cost much in the home of an older woman who was widowed. Since I had no life other than my job, it was perfect. When I had a day off I helped the widow around her house and tended the small garden. I ate whatever wasn't sold out that day at the restaurant, and there was always a baguette and café au lait in the morning. If there was extra, I took it to Anette, my landlady.

All in all, it was better than I could have hoped. Paris in 1988 was proving to be not so impossible after all. That day I was waiting tables, well, kind of. The regular waiter was on holiday and Pierre had been covering for him. It was midafternoon and few were in the bistro, and those usually just wanted a coffee and perhaps a pastry. He must have figured even I could handle that much.

"Help those customers, I must speak to Ormond." Pierre disappeared into the tiny kitchen before I could look up from folding napkins for the evening rush.

Glancing over to an inside table, I was struck by a woman seated against the wall, speaking very animatedly to some fellow. Her hair was long and dark brown, framing a perfectly heart-shaped face and large, fiery brown eyes that matched her lively gestures. I couldn't stop staring.

I must have bored a hole in the woman's concentration because she suddenly looked across the room right at me. Since I didn't seem capable of looking away, I watched in fascination as she threw down her napkin and marched in my direction, that fire I'd seen earlier laser-focused on me. Realizing I was the intended target, I stood and was surprised at how small she was. Small in size, not in stature. She was pointing and gesturing in a way that I knew wasn't good. *"Que êtes-vous? Pourquoi m'espionnez-vous? Je vais appeler la police!"*

The only word that I got loud and clear was "police." *The cops? Jesus!*

"I'm sorry, m'amselle, I didn't mean to stare. You are...*très belle.* That's all."

The woman stopped, gave me a quizzical look, perhaps eventually even a ghost of a smile. Then she snapped, *"Comment vous appelez-vous?"*

"Uh, Jen." I didn't want her to know my last name, I just wanted her to sit down and forget about me.

"Jen? Jen? *C'est un nom, ça?*" Then she huffed and turned on her heel to go back to her tablemate and resume their intense conversation. I didn't think she thought very much of my answer.

As I sighed in relief, behind me a deep baritone mused, "What a woman."

Ormond was smiling, his gaze still on the mysterious customer. I asked, "Do you know her?"

"*Oui.* Her name is Marina Kouros. She is a Greek journalist who works for Reuters. But she is getting more notice from the television people, because of her beauty and her stories. Have you not seen her before?"

"No. I would remember." I didn't watch television because I didn't understand most of it. I knew I would never forget that face and those eyes. Never. *Marina. What a beautiful name.*

"Why was she angry with me?"

"She accused you of spying on her. She has evidently had others try to steal her exclusive stories. I think, when she heard your, um, accent, she knew she was safe."

I could hear amusement in Ormond's voice. My French was really that bad.

There was an upside to my fractured accent and lack of understanding, though, because Marina Kouros started frequenting the café and insisting that I wait on her each time she came in. I was grateful for any reason at all, because the possibility that she might appear added excitement and anticipation to my otherwise fairly mundane day.

When she did appear, I was happy for the whole day and never minded any of the endless tasks Pierre gave me to do. When she didn't put in an appearance, which was most days, I felt a little let down, saddened somehow. It was odd. More than that, it was silly. I didn't even know the woman.

Yet, because of her, I began to study, no, *learn* French. I read my pocket dictionary like it was a Bible and pestered Ormond and Anette and Pierre to translate and help me with my pronunciation. It was still pretty bad, but my comprehension got better every day. I scoured television news programs for a glimpse of her. I had my landlady search for her articles in the newspaper and then I read them with the dictionary beside me, an arduous process.

Marina, as I now thought of her, liked her café au lait with not so much milk, extra espresso, not too hot. No matter what I was doing when Marina walked in, I dropped it to make sure she had her preferred table, the one in the back corner of the restaurant.

I found myself trying to keep that table available, just in case—piling unfolded napkins on it, a few menus, even whatever cookbook I was studying. All of these instantly disappeared as soon as I caught sight of the lovely journalist. I steadfastly refused to consider why I might be doing those things.

Pierre shot suspicious looks at me occasionally but never scolded me in front of Marina. I wasn't sure how that miracle had happened, but decided it was because it couldn't hurt business to have someone with a bit of fame frequent the restaurant.

Marina was coming in more often, too. She acted as though she didn't notice every special consideration, and only occasionally graced me with a smile meant just for me. I thought I was imagining that part. Still, I clung to that smile at night and in my lonely moments, so far from anything familiar to me.

I had made the choice to run, but that didn't mean I didn't miss parts of my former life. In particular, I missed my niece, Constantina, eight years old when I left. Whenever we were together she was my shadow. We were the only two in the family with blue eyes, the same color. And she was going to be even taller than me. I had strawberry-blond hair but hers was a deep auburn color, with curls. I missed that kid.

There was one child, Manon, whose mother brought her by fairly often after picking her up from school. She reminded me of Constantina, about the same age. Without speaking a lot, we had developed a friendship of sorts. She and her mother would sit at an outside table. I would wait on them and make a very big deal out of writing down the child's order. We did much nodding and laughing and she was delighted to correct my accent.

I caught Marina watching our interaction one time, just before she entered the café. Once seated she asked, "You are good with the little girl. Do you have children?" Her English was pretty good, too. She must have seen caution in my expression, because she waited patiently for the answer and I suspected patience wasn't her long suit.

"My niece. She's about the same age. I miss her." I hadn't meant to say the last part, but I caught myself before revealing anything else. That was the last thing I needed. There was something about Marina that made me want to tell her everything. I now understood why she was such a good reporter.

I thought Manon and in particular Marina were probably my distraction from the ache of missing home, and that's where I forced my thoughts to end. To me, there was no going back, so I studied French, worked, and dreamt of Marina Kouros.

My French quickly improved, and that meant I could be more help in the restaurant. I watched the news and found programs where Marina was featured. I was even reading the whole newspaper, slowly but without constant reference to my dictionary. Of course, I never let on to Marina about my progress for fear she would stop coming to the bistro.

On a few occasions I thought she was studying me. I would be helping another customer and glance in her direction and our eyes would meet. She would usually look away, but occasionally her gaze would linger. Once, her tablemate had to say something to get her attention. Those were moments that were burned into my memory to savor. My rational mind was sure she found me strange. My irrational self thought quite the opposite.

One day she came in with a tall, attractive woman who was obviously enamored with her. She answered Marina's interview questions with flirtatious remarks full of double entendres, from what I could tell. It irritated the hell out of me, and before I realized what I was doing, I slammed her pastry and coffee down, not caring if it spilled on her couture suit.

The woman jumped to her feet, yelped, *"Merde!"* as she swiped at her skirt with her napkin, and said a few more unkind things before marching off to the restroom. I felt my cheeks burn and my thoughts were so chaotic they became no more than white noise. I refused to meet Marina's eyes and miserably wiped up the few drops I had spilled on the table. I thought I imagined her hand gently squeeze my own to get my attention.

She smiled sweetly at me and murmured, "You worry too much." I was so overcome by her touch my knees almost gave out. The return of her tablemate was the only thing that allowed me to break the connection. I barely made it back to my station.

Pierre sidled up to me and hissed in my ear, "That woman is a government official! She's very important and you must treat her well. Besides, Mademoiselle Kouros is not interested in her—if you would open your eyes and *see*."

He gave me a meaningful eyebrow raise and slid his gaze to the table. When I turned I caught a look from Marina that instantly made the feeling of her touch return. At that point I was pretty sure I was losing my mind.

Pierre was still beside me and wouldn't let up. "Can you not see? She likes you. I know it!" Chortling to himself, he bustled back to the kitchen, probably to share his observations with Ormond.

I could only stare, knowing my eyes revealed everything because I'd always been told they did. *Ohgodohgodohgod! She knows how I feel, she* knows*!* My misery deepened as I tried not to twist the bar towel to reveal my trembling hands. Marina now knew what I had steadily denied to myself. I cared about her. I *really* cared.

Forcing my feet to move, I practically fled into the kitchen and begged Pierre to finish waiting on her table. Pierre exchanged glances with Ormond and hurried to the dining area while Ormond held my hand and made me sit on a nearby stool.

"Ormond, I made a fool of myself. Marina knows how I feel about her…I saw it in her eyes. I'm so dumb." My French had gone to hell, and my English wasn't much better.

Ormond patted my shoulder sympathetically. "Not to worry, my friend. Pierre insists she likes you, too. He is a very good observer."

"Pities me, you mean. Ormond, I'm a dishwasher in a restaurant, how could she possibly feel anything for me?"

"That isn't true, my friend. You are a responsible, kind, hard-working woman who is learning a new craft. I think you would make an excellent chef one day. Very attractive, too, in my opinion. A little tall, perhaps… I'm sure she sees what a good person you are as well."

I scrubbed my tears away with my sleeve, not wanting to look any more the idiot than I already felt I was.

"I can't go out there until she's gone. Please."

"Not to worry, Pierre will take care of the table. You take a break. We have a delivery for the freezer coming. Will you check it and put things away?"

Two hours later I was setting up the main dining area for dinner when I heard sirens and people yelling outside. The restaurant's close to the Sorbonne, so with students demonstrating about this and that, it wasn't an uncommon occurrence. I wandered outside to check it out as a welcome distraction from my morose thoughts and heavy heart.

Suddenly people were scattering and running in all directions and police whistles were getting closer. I saw Marina racing down the street, looking furtively around. She spied me and zipped into the empty bistro.

Her finger held to her lips as she ran past told me who the police were chasing. I swallowed hard and stayed put, facing up the street as if watching someone flee in that direction. Three policemen thundered past the bistro at full speed.

I folded my arms and toe-tapped to keep from running after Marina until the commotion died down, then used all of my willpower to shrug and stroll back to the dining room. It was empty. Marina must have run out the back door.

Crestfallen, I returned to the wait station to finish my work.

"Psst! Jen!" The sound came from somewhere in the corner of the restaurant.

Jerking my head up like a dog having just heard the call to dinner, I saw nothing. But I knew that voice, even if it was a harsh whisper. I bent to pick up some imaginary trash and saw something move in the shadow of the corner table. This shadow had intense brown eyes that instantly brought back that warm feeling.

Trying not to look elated, I walked to that part of the dining room, keeping an eye on the windows and doorway. I pretended to wipe the table and whispered, "You can't stay there—a customer might come in!"

"The police will be looking for a while. Any suggestions?"

"We have a supply closet. Run into the kitchen and I'll show you." Spying a uniform crossing the street, I hissed, "Hurry and stay low!"

I did my best to amble to the doorway and nod a hello as he prowled by. Normally I would try to not attract any attention, but here I was, throwing myself under the bus for a woman who didn't even know I existed. I couldn't make sense out of it, so I couldn't expect anyone else to understand either. All I knew was that I had to do it.

Sighing, I picked up some dishes on my way to the kitchen and pushed through the swinging doors. Imagine my surprise when I saw Marina and Ormond laughing and chatting like it was all some big joke. I ignored them and tried to keep busy until I felt a tug on my sleeve. Marina was warmly smiling at me.

"*Merci*, Mademoiselle Jen. I owe you a favor for rescuing me. May I ask, why did you do it?" Her eyes held more questions, but the fact that she was actually talking with me silenced the voice that insisted Marina was only being polite to the fool who had helped her escape.

"It was the right thing to do." The odd look on her face made me worry I'd made another silly statement. Maybe my French was so bad that—wait. My French was perfect. I also understood every word that Marina and Ormond had said and responded to her query perfectly, too. *Uh-oh.*

"Your French is excellent! I didn't think you could understand it or speak that well." Her eyes had grown suspicious and she withdrew several feet from me.

Ormond stepped in and said, "*Oui*, and we have you to thank for that, Mademoiselle Kouros." He quickly filled her in on the reason for my intensive study of the language, with me standing helplessly by, feeling the blush to every part of my body.

I'd heard enough and marched out of the kitchen only to see two policemen enter the café. When they saw me I held up one finger, said, "I'll get the proprietor," and made a U-turn. I grabbed Marina's arm, whirling her until we were face-to-face. "Trust me."

I slid my arms around her waist and lifted her, turning to Ormond. "Police."

I walked us to the freezer locker and put us both inside. As the door clicked shut, we were in total darkness. I flipped the light switch with my elbow and there I was, nose to nose, in a walk-in freezer with my fantasy woman in my arms.

Marina didn't move, maybe even tightened her grip around my neck. But her eyes were on my lips and she licked her own, slowly. The thought crossed my mind that the freezer had broken, because it seemed to be heating up in there.

She whispered, "Turn out the light, they might open the door."

Forcing my attention to the new elbow maneuver, when I turned back I was met with the most incredible softness on my lips. I was lost in the sensation, drowning in emotion, and I responded without thinking, matching the intensity with my own.

We might have kissed for a second or ten minutes, but it wasn't long enough. During that time whatever part of my heart and mind might have been in denial was lost completely to the marvelous woman in my arms. We only parted because the door opened.

I immediately dropped Marina to the floor and stood in front of her, sure my larger frame could hide her from the police. Ormond peeked in and then opened the door, staring at me.

"Well. I thought you two might be cold in there, but I can see that I was wrong. Would you like for me to close the door again? The authorities are gone." He grinned at me.

Only then did I register Marina standing at my side, but I wasn't able to force myself to look. Whether frozen in place or resisting breaking the spell, I was rooted to the spot. Ormond seemed to study Marina, and his smile increased.

"You, too? Well, please come out of there, you are turning blue!"

Marina stepped out first and when she turned, her cheeks were blushing a lovely shade of rose against her olive complexion. She pulled me from the freezer and held on to my hand.

Looking deeply into my eyes, she said, "Why are you afraid of the police? And why did you risk being seen for me?"

"How did you…?" I know I had accusation in my eyes when I glared at Ormond but he shook his head and excused himself, scooting a wide-eyed Pierre in front of him.

Marina had stepped closer and demanded, "Why?"

Miserable, I blurted the truth. "Because I had to. Because you… are important to me." I studied my worn and dirty tennis shoes, refusing to say more.

After a few seconds of silence, Marina tapped my chest to get me to look at her. Once I was locked into her incredible gaze and perfectly helpless to look away, she stared hard at me.

"Thank you. And, Jen? This isn't over. I always get what I want. Always." Her smile was enigmatic, and with those words she slammed the door to my heart, locked it, and spirited away the key.

GUN BROOKE, award-winning author of several romance novels and the Supreme Constellations sci-fi series, resides in a Viking-era village in Sweden with her family. The ancient scenery provides the calm and inspiration she needs to be able to write her stories. During the worst of the Swedish winter, Gun escapes to Texas or other warm areas, and during these trips she encounters the many people that sooner or later inhabit her books.

Her latest romance, *Sheridan's Fate*, is a 2007 Lambda Literary Award romance finalist. Look for her newest romance, *September Canvas*, coming in 2009.

Visit her on the Web at www.gbrooke-fiction.com.

TEARS AND CHAMPAGNE
GUN BROOKE

Wearily, Christina dropped her briefcase on the floor and glowered at the pandemonium in the kitchen. The whole sink area looked as if a bomb had detonated. Pots, bowls, and plates were stacked in messy piles together with slicing boards and knives. Open cans fought for space on the kitchen table with paper bags, empty Styrofoam containers, and a sticky page torn out of a magazine. The sight of the mess Amanda had left behind added to Christina's exhaustion and fueled her anger and resentment. Christina jerked the hairpins out of the tight twist that had kept her blond hair in place during the day. Her scalp ached, and she squeezed the pins tightly in her hand, the small pricks of pain from the pins poking her palms working like a diversion from her headache.

She was so damn tired after a week from hell. Not to mention today. First she had struggled to finalize negotiations with the Italian delegation, and then her boss had maneuvered her into joining him and the three enthusiastic gentlemen at a celebratory dinner. She had looked forward to a quiet Friday evening at home with Amanda, but had to smile politely and play nice with flirtatious Italians instead. Frustrated, she had called Amanda to let her know that she would be late. That had not gone very well. After an ominous silence, Amanda had hissed something inaudible and hung up the phone.

Christina rubbed the aching muscles in her neck, making a face at the memory. *What happened to "I understand that your job is demanding" and the promise of support, Amanda?* It was becoming clear that Amanda's support was not what it used to be.

Christina walked through the hallway towards the bedroom. When she passed the large mirror she neatly put the hairpins in the little ivory box on the dresser she used for this purpose. A quick glance at her reflection confirmed how she felt—dark rings under her eyes and a haggard appearance made her look older than her thirty-eight years. Christina didn't particularly like the way her mouth was pressed into a fine line of discontent, or how two deep wrinkles marred her forehead between her eyebrows. The sullen look was not becoming.

Christina stopped on the threshold to the bedroom. Amanda's dark head on one of the pillows indicated that not only had she not waited up for her, she'd ignored the mess in the kitchen and simply gone to bed. Amanda was most likely still in a lousy mood, even in her sleep. Christina knew her partner pretty well after five years together. Amanda had a temper of volcanic proportions. Astonishingly, she worked as a kindergarten teacher, which she loved and where she demonstrated endless patience with her little pupils.

Looking down at her sleeping lover, Christina wanted to wake her. It wasn't the first time she had come home from work and found the apartment a disaster area, but tonight, with all that had been going on lately at work, she was furious. After all, she took care of her part of the household chores meticulously and thought her expectations that Amanda do the same were fair and reasonable. Amanda didn't. She often called Christina a nag when all she wanted was for their condo, their home, to look neat and tidy.

Christina turned and stalked back to the kitchen. She didn't bother trying to be quiet. If she happened to wake Amanda, all the better. She could join Christina in the kitchen and do the dishes.

The coffee Christina had craved after the large meal she'd suffered through with the Italians now burned in the back of her throat. She opened the fridge, looking for mineral water, and noticed bowls and platters covered with plastic wrap. Curious, she peeled back the cover on one. Assorted vegetables, asparagus, peas, shredded carrots, and broccoli—all her favorites—arranged beautifully in even circles made her mouth water despite the heartburn.

Frowning, she put the plate down on the table behind her and took out the next one. Roast beef in large, paper-thin slices covered with spices and roasted onions, surrounded by a bed of potato salad. A more thorough search of the fridge revealed three more of her favorite side dishes. Thinking of the mess on the sink with a sinking feeling in her stomach, Christina put the plates back and checked the wall calendar with their working hours and social commitments. A big red heart circled today's date. Inside the heart, Amanda had drawn a pattern of flowers that created the number five. Five years. Today.

"Oh, damn." Christina leaned her forehead against the calendar and cursed quietly.

A sudden faint memory made her walk out to the living room. Amanda had tidied it up and cleaned it perfectly. Christina had walked right past the living room when she came home, not seeing how the small dining table over by the window was set with a white linen table cloth and their best china. Delicate candles stood unlit in beautiful crystal candleholders next to a large bouquet of red roses and a bottle of champagne in melted ice in a wine cooler. A card was barely visible between the dark red petals, and Christina pulled it out and switched on a table lamp.

Five years of love, Christina, but I'm greedy; I want at least fifty more. I love you with all my heart.

Amanda

All of sudden Christina could hear herself when she had called home four hours ago, how she had rattled off the information that she had to take the Italians out to dinner, not giving Amanda a chance to object. Instead, Amanda had sounded unusually quiet at first, later becoming angry and slamming down the phone.

Christina returned to the bedroom, her feet as heavy as her heart. She switched on her bed light and the soft glow confirmed her fear. The proud face with its high cheekbones and curvy lips was damp and flushed. Amanda had not only been furious, she had hung up on Christina because she'd been crying. Amanda hated to show her tears to anyone, even Christina. Or perhaps, Christina suddenly feared, especially to her?

Cautiously, she pushed a dark tress from Amanda's forehead. From the first time she had laid eyes on Amanda, Christina thought she was the most extraordinary woman she had ever seen. They had met during a local film festival where they had literally collided at the popcorn stand. Christina's box of popcorn had rained over them and Amanda had laughingly apologized and bought her a new one. It had not taken them long to recognize the mutual attraction. Christina thought Amanda was charming and stunningly sexy. Amanda, as usual guided completely by her emotions, had overwhelmed Christina with her passion and capacity for love. Christina had found her utterly irresistible, addictive, even, and had fallen in love with her with every cell in her body.

Amanda stirred in her sleep. Christina leaned over her and kissed her swollen eyelids. "I'm sorry, darling," she murmured huskily. "This was unforgivable of me. I should have remembered."

"You're home?" Amanda, dressed in lace panties and a tank top, slowly opened her eyes and regarded her sleepily. In a few seconds, she clearly went from drowsy to infuriated. "You're home."

Her tone was cold and hot at the same time, and Christina knew she deserved it.

"What time is it?"

"Around ten thirty."

"I suppose you saw the mess."

"I did. And I saw the roses, the wine, the lovely table, how you cleaned the living room and prepared my favorite food." Christina took both of Amanda's hands, holding on when she felt Amanda trying to pull back. "I didn't blow you off. I didn't. I forgot. I don't blame you for being mad at me."

"Your work always comes first." Amanda slowly pulled her hands free. "I can never win, can I?"

"It's not a competition," Christina exclaimed.

"Isn't it?" Amanda said, her voice rising. "If you had a lover, I could at least have a face to go with the reason for your absence. Instead it's this faceless, but oh so damn important company that handles more money than I'll see in a lifetime."

"You criticize what I do because it isn't creative or artistic, and you don't care who overhears. I don't see you complaining about my money when we go on vacation."

Hurt and upset, Christina still wanted to take the words back instantly. Amanda recoiled as if Christina had slapped her.

"Your money? I can't believe you said that." Amanda drew a deep breath, and tears made her voice low and trembling.

"Neither can I. I didn't mean it."

"Didn't you?" Amanda wiped quickly at her eyes. "I think you did."

"For a second." Christina knew that nothing less than the naked truth would suffice. "Once that second passed, I wanted to take them back. I love that we share everything, money too. You're entitled to anything of mine. I really mean that, darling."

"You're sure?"

"Yes."

"That doesn't change the fact that your boss and your clients get the best of you," Amanda said, clearly hurt.

Christina slumped back. It was true. At work she was energetic, full of ideas, and ambitious. Amanda got the leftovers, what little remained of her energy at the end of the day. "I suppose so."

"I thought tonight was going to be different," Amanda muttered. "I had such plans, as you can tell from the kitchen. I…I was so sure that you'd remember and… Who was I kidding?"

"I'm so, so sorry." Christina carefully clasped Amanda's hands again, and this time Amanda didn't pull them back. "I feel so bad about it. I don't know what else to say to make you believe me."

"I don't know either." Amanda squeezed Christina's hands. "We always spend our anniversary together at home, just you and I."

"I know. Of course I know that."

"And still you forgot."

"I did. I can't believe how I could screw this up. I've thought of this day for over a month, I even have a present for you—oh, damn." Christina groaned and tipped her head back. "It's still at the office."

To Christina's surprise, Amanda started to laugh, a contagious giggle that was something in between joy and tears. "Only you, Chrissy. Only you."

"I'm a disaster. Please, darling, forgive me."

"I should also ask for forgiveness."

"What for?" Christina eventually asked.

"I never meant to hurt you by teasing you about your work. I have a big mouth." Amanda gestured helplessly, palms up. "You never said anything."

"I knew you were joking, it's just…some days—"

"—I can be a bitch."

"So, apparently, can I."

"I thought you didn't care about our day," Amanda whispered.

"I do." Christina fought the urge to cry. "I'm hopeless."

"Yes, you are." Amanda hesitated for a few breathless seconds longer and then wrapped a slender arm around Christina's neck and pulled her down into the bed beside her.

"But you're here now," she whispered between kisses. "It's all that matters. You're home."

"Yes, I am," Christina whispered back.

Amanda released Christina and gestured toward the bathroom. "Get out of those clothes and get comfortable."

When Christina returned to the bedroom dressed only in a towel, Amanda was sitting up in bed, offering a glass of wine.

"Here," Amanda said, a small catch in her voice. "Let's drink to us."

Christina took the glass and they raised them quietly. "To us," Christina mouthed silently, and the soft smile on Amanda's lips tore at her heart. After they clinked their glasses and sipped the wine, Christina put her glass down and leaned in for a kiss, wanting to close the distance between them in more ways than one.

Amanda abruptly pulled her close and Christina found herself on her back. Amanda's lips and hands seemed to be everywhere as she parted Christina's lips with her tongue and kissed her deeply. Breathless with arousal and relieved that she seemed to be forgiven, Christina returned the kiss with all her love.

Christina cupped Amanda's face between her hands, registering every beloved feature of Amanda's strong face. How many times had she seen these extraordinary slate gray eyes flash at her in anger, or melt her with just one sultry glance? How many times had Amanda kissed her with those full curvy lips, mapped every inch of Christina's skin? Christina ran her thumbs over the elegant black arches that were Amanda's eyebrows. How many times had she seen them knit together in concentration or frown at her in hurt confusion or anger when they fought?

"Oh, God, darling. Darling!" The realization that she'd come to take this woman—this amazing, one-of-a-kind special, remarkable woman—for granted made Christina so furious with herself, her throat constricted.

"What's the matter, Christina?" Amanda asked, sounding worried.

"Nothing, darling. Not now." Christina smiled with trembling lips. "You're just so beautiful it makes me ache inside." She knew she had to be truthful or this extraordinary moment wouldn't count. "I haven't been fair to you, have I? I haven't been honest. I've buried myself in work instead of telling you the truth."

"The truth?" Amanda asked, her voice tinged with concern.

"The truth is, the only thing—I mean the only one in my life who really means something—is you. Without you, all the rest, career, money, status, reputation, is meaningless."

"You are who you are, Christina," Amanda said quietly. "An intelligent, ambitious woman. You shouldn't apologize for that."

Christina pulled Amanda close. "I'm not apologizing. I'm trying to tell you that my work gives me joy, but part of that is because I can share my success with you. Nothing I do, or experience, feels real, or has any true meaning, if I can't come home and talk with you about it. Do you understand what I mean? Without you, it's just...hollow. Empty."

Christina touched Amanda's chin with a finger and tilted her face up. Slowly kissed Amanda's trembling lips, over and over. "I love you," she murmured against the velvet softness. "You mean everything to me, my heart."

"Love me," Amanda breathed. "Make love to me, Christina."

"Amanda," Christina whispered throatily. "Darling…" She shifted a bit, changed her position so that she could stroke along Amanda's body. "Five years," she murmured against her partner's soft hair. "Five years with you, Amanda, with your love and loyalty. That is truly something to be thankful for, but I'm just as greedy as you. I want at least fifty more too."

"Mmm." Amanda purred. "Deal."

CLIFFORD HENDERSON lives and plays in Santa Cruz, California. She runs The Fun Institute, a school of improv and solo performance, with her partner of sixteen years. In their classes and workshops, people of all genders and sexual orientations learn to access and express the myriad of characters itching to get out. When she's not teaching or performing, she's writing, gardening, and twisting herself into weird yoga poses.

The Middle of Somewhere, her first novel, will be coming out in January 2009, published by Bold Strokes Books.

Contact Clifford at www.cliffordhenderson.net.

DISCOVERED IN LIGHT
CLIFFORD HENDERSON

When it comes right down to it, I'm not even sure I *want* a girlfriend, not at this late date in my life. I don't want to have to go changing. I've already done that once; I quit eating meat for somebody. Boy, was *that* not worth it. My friends think I'm being stubborn. Tell me I should at least get another chair, maybe even a second wineglass—their idea being I'd appear open to the possibility of a girlfriend. But I've tried both these things, too, lots of times, and it never works. My place isn't big enough for two anyway. And I like my routines, or ruts as my more tactless pals like to call them. My routines are all I've got. And *they* don't talk back. Well, mostly they don't. Evenings can be a little tough. Especially on weekends. That's when my imagination kicks in and starts begging for something besides the usual microwave dinner and TV marathon.

That's what brought me here. I thought to myself, *what would keep me busy on weekend evenings?* And the answer that came to mind was, *community theater.*

I was a techie in college. Did all the lighting and set building for the shows. I was good at it, too. Just couldn't make a living once I graduated—not one with benefits and a decent paycheck. Not that the job I have now is all that glamorous, driving a forklift at a paper company. But I'm the only woman in the warehouse and that gives me some satisfaction—when it's not giving me a pain in the ass. Like the time I decided to give those boys a reason to stay off my forklift.

They were treating Bessie like she was community property, which they never did to Jerry's or Don's forklifts. If one of them didn't feel like walking the quarter mile from one side of the warehouse to the other, they'd snag Bessie like she was a go-cart or a taxi—which pissed me off royally. So one morning I got there early and duct-taped a bunch of tampons around the roll bar, let 'em dangle by the strings like little pom-poms in a low rider. Problem solved. Nobody gets within ten feet of Bessie now.

I don't like to take shit. Especially from guys. Women, now, that's a whole other story. I get kinda soft around women… But don't get me started. Suffice it to say I've had my share of heartbreaks and I don't fancy getting my heart trampled again. I'm too old for that shit. Besides, I've got a bad hip—which is giving me a hell of a time tonight as I try to keep myself busy while waiting for the actors to show up.

I'm stage managing for a new comedy that opened last weekend. *Minutes Ticking* it's called, written by some local hotshot. I don't think it's had the reception anybody'd hoped for. The reviews weren't bad, but they didn't exactly call it a "must see," which is what it takes these days to get people off their lazy duffs and into a night of live theater.

It's the story of a couple of empty-nesters, which is part of the problem. Hollywood's got us so jacked up on the young and beautiful that nobody seems to care about the middle aged and frumpy. Once you're over thirty you're not interesting anymore.

The other problem with the play is Mark. He's playing across from this beautiful actress, Camille, and it's like he doesn't see her. All he can think about is the cute, *young* light board op, Lucy, who I'm stuck running the show with for the next month. I tell you, she may be cute but she's dumb as a tack. I'm having to call light cues a couple seconds early because it takes her that long to hear the cue, then send the information down to her pretty little French tips to execute. The girl is dense. But when Mark's onstage he's delivering his lines to *her*, acting for *her*. Or that's how it looks; he faces out instead of facing Camille, and he's always glancing up at the booth as if to say, *check this move out, Lucy*. And the second he's offstage he's badgering her, asking if she liked his performance, if she noticed his new line delivery or the way he tossed his wineglass into the fireplace. I don't know why the director never called him on it. I sure would have. But now the director has moved on to another show and it's just me to keep the damn thing running.

Tonight we have a brush-up rehearsal. My job is to open up the theater, turn on the lights, and hold a prompt book in case either of the actors forgets a line. I'm not here to offer opinions. Just the basic stage manager routine.

Since I got here early, I decided to replace a burned-out lavender gel. That's what's got me up on this ladder. I turned the house lights off so the place is dark except for this one ellipsoidal I'm working on. I like the satisfaction of slipping a new gel in, watching the light go from white to lavender.

Someone enters.

Since I've got the house lights out, I can't make out which of the two actors it is.

She walks into the pool of light and looks up at me, shielding her eyes with her hand. "Hi, Roque."

As usual, my heart does a triple gainer. She's so beautiful under the light—her light. Tonight she's wearing this fringed shawl thingy tossed over a shoulder, giving her a bohemian look that suits her to a T. She's a classy one, Camille is. Tall, with curly salt-and-pepper hair she's pinned up on her head with a pencil. Loose tendrils curl around her long neck. A particularly impish curl falls in front of her eye. She brushes it back as she cranes her head up to see me. "That is you, isn't it?"

"Yeah, I was just…uh…putting a new gel in your special."

"*Thank* you, Roque. Is Mark here yet?"

"Nope."

I hear her settling into her usual front-row aisle seat. She's one of those women who carry a handbag that's more like a fancy shopping bag. She riffles through it.

"I'll turn the house lights on," I say. "So you can see."

"Don't bother. I like the theater like this." She riffles some more. "Besides, I seem to have left my glasses at home."

"You shouldn't need them tonight," I say, coming down off the ladder and folding it up. "Your lines should all be in your head, right?"

She laughs. "One would hope, but my memory went shortly after my eyes."

I laugh. "Know what you mean. Spent half an hour yesterday looking for my keys. Turned out they were still in the door. Put my groceries down and forgot all about 'em!" I wait for her to say something, maybe one-up me on the losing memory thing, but she seems preoccupied. I pick up the ladder and carry it backstage. I'm no good at small talk. Never have been.

It's pitch-black dark behind the flats. I lean the ladder against the upstage wall and feel around for the blue-gelled clip lamp, flicking it on when I find it. It bothers me that I get so nervous around Camille. I wind up coming off like a moron. Part of the problem is we don't know each other too well. During rehearsals it's been all business, and after rehearsals, well, we're past the age where any of us want to go out for drinks.

Camille's an accountant. I know this because she offered to help the theater with the books until they hire a new bookkeeper. I also know she has a couple of grandkids she's crazy about. And she's single. Once, in rehearsal, when they were doing some character work, she let on that she's experimented around with women. I forget her exact words, but she glanced at me when she said it. Guess it's pretty obvious I'm into women, although I've never mentioned it. No reason to.

Another thing about Camille is she likes her chocolate. She brings in bags for everyone to share, but I notice she dips in the most. I always take a handful just to be polite, but I don't much go in for sweets. Salt, that's my vice.

Having done everything I can backstage, I come out from behind the flats. There's still no Mark.

"So…" I say.

"So…" she says.

I'll be damned if I can think of anything to follow this inspired bit of dialogue. I bend down and secure a peeling spike mark in the lavender light. It's Camille's spike, where she places her feet each night so the light will hit her perfectly.

"Shouldn't we call him?" she asks.

I think it's sweet she says "we" because we both know it's *me* who should be doing the calling. "Uh, yeah. Let me get some lights on and find my contact sheet…"

"That's okay. I have him programmed into my phone. I'll call." She takes out her phone and pushes a few buttons. The glow from the phone dimly lights up her face. She smiles at me while waiting for him to pick up.

Now I feel like a total moron. Why haven't I ever taken the time to learn how to program numbers into *my* phone? It's the damn buttons on the thing. They're too small. I pick up my folder of replacement gels and walk it up to the booth, then bring the house lights up to half, a nice golden glow, and a few other muted stage lights. No use us sitting in the dark.

When I return, her eyes are brimming with tears—not the sad kind, but the mad kind.

"You okay?"

"No. I am *not* okay. That *jerk* just told me he's in L.A. auditioning for a commercial."

I feel my chest tighten and remind myself to breathe. The guy's not worth a heart attack. "Did he act like he *knew* there was a rehearsal?"

"Oh, *he* knew." She blows her nose on a giant colorful hanky, then mimics Mark's don't-you-wish-you-could-sleep-with-me voice "'Sorry, babe, but my agent thinks this could be my big break.'"

"Camille, I'm sorry…" Ultimately this kind of screw-up is my responsibility. I'm supposed to keep my actors in line. "I'll give him a call."

"What for? He's *seven* hours away." She takes a deep breath and pinches the bridge of her nose. "Anyway, he says he'll be back in time for tomorrow's performance." She pulls out a plastic bag of what look like chocolate-covered peanuts. "Want some?"

I reach into the bag and pull out a couple.

She takes a handful and pops one in her mouth, then begins to rant while at the same time fiercely chewing. "Here I left my ninety-one-year-old mother—who just flew in from Phoenix—home by herself. Well, not by herself exactly, my neighbor's going to look in on her, but *basically* alone, and this *jerk* doesn't have the decency to even call and tell me he's not going to make it. He is so arrogant!" Another chocolate down the hatch. "I've never worked with an actor like him. He ad-libs half of his lines and mugs through the rest of them. I don't think the guy would know truth if it hit him on the head." Then, seemingly out of nowhere, a smile creeps onto her face. "I just wish I could be there when the advertising people find out he's not as young as his headshot."

This cracks me up. When he came in for auditions, I didn't even recognize him from the twenty-year-old glossy. Mostly, though, I'm relieved she's stopped crying. I'm not too good with women crying. She reaches over and takes one of my hands, sandwiching it between her own. "Roque, you have truly been one of the best parts about working on *Minutes Ticking*. You are a real gem."

I want to say something about how I've liked working with her, too, but all I can think about is the softness of her hands, and how my fingertips are acting like a conduit to my whole body. "Maybe we can fit a brush-up in before Friday's performance" is what I come out with.

She releases my hand. "I can't," she says. "I told Mom I'd take her to dinner before the show. You're just going to have to stand in for him."

My throat tightens. "Me?"

"Why not? You know the play better than anybody."

"Like a line run-through?"

"I'm going to need you to walk though his part, too. The blocking stimulates my memory. So if you could just read his lines, do your best to get his blocking..."

"Uh...sure...why not? I mean, if it would help you..."

"It would *more* than help," she says, standing. "And, who knows?" She places her finger on my chest and gives me a devilish smile. "It might be fun."

An involuntary quiver shoots up my spine.

Ten minutes later, we've got the set pieces and props in place. The play is basically a series of vignettes that happen in a bedroom, a slice of this married couple's life.

"Are the board ops scheduled to be at rehearsal?" she asks, double-checking her hand props on the night stand.

"No. Just you and Mark."

"Anyone else likely to show up? Box office? Maintenance?"

"Nope. All ours."

She cocks her head and looks me right in the eye. "Well, let's get started."

The first few scenes go well enough. They're just your basic humorous scenes about life after kids. Remarkably, I've got most of the lines memorized. I guess this should be no big surprise. I've sat through tons of rehearsals. Still, I'm feeling pretty proud of myself and even start to try out a little acting. You know, *feeling* it and all. I strut around the stage like I *am* Doug—a seemingly self-satisfied sporting goods store manager who, on the inside, longs for meaning in his life.

Living, I discover, is easy when the words and movements are already figured out for you, when all you have to do is recite. And Camille gives so much back. She really listens, for one thing, and even though she knows what I'm going to say she acts like she doesn't. She finds nuances inside of nuances for her character, Anna, a woman searching for ways to invigorate her empty days.

Then we get to *the* scene, the one that turns the play on its side. Anna has bought a book to reignite their sex life.

"Back in a second." I consider bolting for the exit. "I've got to use the restroom. Too much coffee, I guess." Does Camille expect me to play this scene, too?

In the tiny actors' bathroom, I can barely get myself to pee and I spend forever washing my hands. How am I going to do this? The whole scene takes place on the bed.

By the time I return, Camille is already in place—smack in the middle of the king-sized bed. "So," I say, trying to sound as casual as possible. "We discover you in the light. Doug is offstage in the shower, singing."

"Aren't you going to walk though it?" she asks.

I notice she's removed her fringy shawl and is now wearing just her spaghetti-strap cornflower blue sundress. "Uh, sure. You want me to?"

"Well, it would help," she says, removing the pencil from her hair. Locks of salt-and-pepper curls cascade around her shoulders. "This scene is always hard for me."

"Okay. So I'll just go out here and be Doug taking a shower." I retreat backstage and begin singing *All of me...why not take all of me...* just like Mark does. Admittedly, this is one thing he has up on me. I'm a rotten singer, but I give it my best. Anything for Camille.

I can't stop thinking about what I know she's doing onstage—looking at the sex manual and trying out different poses. It's a hot scene, even though she plays it for laughs.

I notice the wrench still in my pocket. Croaking away, I set it on the prop table. I check my fly, too, just in case, and run my fingers through my hair. I've watched Mark's overacting kill this scene night after night—but will I be able to do it justice? The words of the baby dyke sound op, Jan, filter through my mind. "That Camille is damn sexy for an old lady."

Kids, what do they know about growing old?

I finish the song and take a deep breath, willing myself into a Doug that is worthy of Camille/Anna, one who knows how to make a woman feel her beauty.

I peek past the flat to see if she's hit the part where she's on her knees rubbing her breasts—that's when Doug is supposed to enter—but she hasn't. She's still reading the manual. So I pick the song back up. *All of me. Why not take all of me...* She puts the manual down and spreads her legs, pretending to beckon Doug toward her. She pooches out her lips in an attempt to look seductive. The audience always laughs here. She abandons the posture and checks in with the book, turns it upside down, and raises an eyebrow. Our middle-aged audience members always get a big chuckle out of this. I guess they relate to grasping for that one magical thing that's going to make them feel young, alive. I watch Camille flip over and raise her tushy in the air, then study the book one more time before putting it down and rising to her knees...

Blood rushes to my head.

Camille puts her hands on her breasts and begins massaging, like she's polishing a couple of hubcaps.

One chimpanzee, two chimpanzee, three chimpanzee...

Here I go...

"Anna!" I say in a deep voice, a Doug voice. I imagine myself wearing just pajama pants.

"Sweetheart," she says, taking her hands from her breasts.

"No," I say. "Don't stop. I *like* what you're doing."

"Really?" she says, returning her hands to her breasts and caressing them. "I've just been reading from this chapter, Enticing Your Mate."

Big laugh from the audience.

"I'm enticed," I say, walking over to the bed. "What else is in that book of yours?"

"Well, most of the positions take two people," she says, flopping onto her belly and paging through the book.

I'm supposed to join her on the bed, I know, but my legs won't move. "Shouldn't we just run the lines for this part?"

Camille laughs. "Scared?"

"I just don't see how we can do it with the script..."

"Just get up here. We'll figure it out."

I force one foot in front of the next, climb up on the king-sized bed and, finally, straddle the back of her legs, my faded-denim crotch framing her soft, round tush. Trigger, my clit who's been sleeping for at least a decade, wakes right up as if from a brief nap. My breathing quickens. The blast of oxygen gives me a major head rush and I can't remember what Doug is supposed to do next. Stage directions reel through my mind: Doug climbs on bed left and looks over Anna's shoulder at manual. He points to something on the page and leans forward.

My heart is threatening to pound through my chest. I'm not as lean as Mark.

I lean forward, my belly pressing into her spine…

"Ouch! My back!" she wails. This always gets a huge laugh from the audience.

I swing my leg off her, minus the stupid look that Mark usually tosses to the audience. "You okay, honey?"

She rolls to her side and looks at me, and honest to God, I can't tell if it's Camille or Anna. "You said that line much sweeter than Mark," she says, touching my nose—a move that's definitely *not* in the script.

"Well, uh, I thought maybe I really did hurt you."

"You're doing just fine," she murmurs softly. "Shall we continue?"

"Sure…" I'm both excited and terrified by what comes next.

"Maybe we should start with something simple. Something from the first chapter," she says, taking my hand and placing it on her breast. And I know I have a line here, but I can't for the life of me remember what it is. The softness of her breast through the limp fabric of her dress short-circuits all thought. It's been so long…

I try to shift my focus to the script on the bed, but the blue pools of her eyes won't let me go. She gives me a prompt. "Sounds good."

"Sounds good," I repeat, the nerve endings in my hand shooting sparklers through my whole body.

"This is the part where the phone rings," she whispers.

"Oh yeah…" There's this whole funny part where Doug pulls away to answer it, knocking the lamp over.

"Aren't you going to answer it?" she says.

"Do you want me to?"

What she's supposed to say here is, "It might be one of the kids. Mattie usually calls around this time." At which point she reaches for the phone and has a long conversation with our daughter. But she brings her mouth to mine and the next thing I know, our tongues are circling together, velvety chocolate. My elbow gives way and I fall back onto the script. Camille pulls it from beneath me and flings it to the floor.

No script, I think. Now what? But my body knows what. I pull her on top of me, feeling a confidence I haven't felt in years.

A whimper escapes from her lips as our hips begin to rock rhythmically back and forth...back and forth... I take hold of her tush and pull her to me.

"Roque..." she whispers with each thrust. "Roque..."

And then somehow we're rolling over again and she's beneath me. "Am I too heavy?" I whisper.

"No..." she says, running her hands up and down my back. "You feel so good...soooo good..." Then she takes my hand and slides it into her panties.

The plumpness of her lips, the wetness...it's been forever since I've felt anything like this... I drive my fingers inside her and she tenses for a moment, then reaches to meet my hand. "Yes...yes..." she utters, her back arching, her head tossed back. "Go deep. Go deep."

I slide my fingers back and forth inside her, Trigger pulsing, hot.

"Yes..." Camille cries. "I'm...I'm..."

Suddenly, I'm engulfed in white light. I can hear Camille coming too. "Oh...oh...oh..." she's howling. And I think I'm yelling something, but I've no idea what. We end in a giant quiver and both flop onto our backs, breathing heavily.

"Whoa," she says, gasping.

"Yeah," I gasp back.

"It's been a while."

And I know I should say something, but I've temporarily lost the ability to speak. I look above us at the lavender-gelled light glowing softly, then reach my hand over and squeeze hers.

She squeezes back.

And just when I'm thinking I might as well go on and die because life couldn't possibly get any better than this, she runs her fingertip down my nose, stopping just above my lips, and asks, "Shall we run it again?"

GILL McKNIGHT is Irish and lives and works in Ireland, England, and Greece. She loves messing about in boats and has secret fantasies about lavender farming. She has contributed to the award-winning *Best Women's Erotica 2008* (Cleis Press) and the e-Anthology *Read These Lips 1*. Her debut novel *Falling Star* (Bold Stroke Books) was released in July 2008 and will be followed by *Green Eyed Monster* (Bold Stroke Books) in December 2008.

My Lagan Love
Gill McKnight

N o."
"Can't you do just one little thing to help me?"

"No."

"Why are you so bitter?"

"'Cos we're exes. And I wouldn't touch you with a rolled-up newspaper. Not even if it were doused in petrol and set alight…and wrapped round a brick."

"The question was *why* are you so bitter? I wasn't asking for an example!"

"'Cos…we're…exes," Roisin spelled out.

"Some people become friends after they break up."

"Not us."

"But…" Marley almost whined, but remembered at the last minute they were exes and it wouldn't work anymore.

"I won't do it. You can go tell them the truth. I'm not playing any hurtful games for you."

"I can't. It would ruin Sharla and Jen's wedding. I'll tell them after, okay? Happy now?"

"No, I'm not happy now. I haven't been happy for weeks. Or have you forgotten already?"

Marley sighed deeply, took a big breath, and put on her most pleading look. She radiated hope and remorse in equal amounts, a subtle and well-practiced combination. "Please help me here. They're our friends. It's their wedding day. I'm a freakin' witness, for God's sake! I can't just bounce in the day before and tell them we've split up. Talk about throwing a wet blanket all over the happiest day of their lives."

"I know, let's lie to them," Roisin snapped. "Let's pretend we're happy when secretly we're not. That will fool them for a little while—say four years—until the truth comes out. Now, where have I seen that recently? Where did I pick that nasty little trick up? Oh, I know. From you."

Marley winced. Roisin's point of view stuck like a knife in her belly. But their broken relationship wasn't what today's conversation was about. She couldn't get distracted by that old argument. She had to be back in her office in an hour, there wasn't time to talk about this.

They sat almost nose to nose across the table in the Belfast coffee house. Any passerby could have seen through the steam-clouded window and thought them an attractive, passionate couple. And they were, but today for all the wrong reasons.

"Please, Ro," Marley said with a sigh. "They're friends of yours, too. I know you met them through me, but they see you as a good friend in your own right. It would hurt them to know we're through a few days before they jump in at the deep end. Please...please."

"I think you're overestimating how much we mean to them."

"I'm not. I'm really, really not. Look at me...I'm on my belly here, beggin' ya! Please escort me." The hangdog expression was genuine this time.

Roisin stared hard; she knew her ex-partner inside and out, through and through. At least she used to. A few weeks ago she would have sworn to it, until the bombshell. She reined her mind back in. She didn't need to go in that painful direction, she left that for times when she was alone and could cry. "I'll need new shoes."

Marley just looked at her, then, with a resigned sigh, drew their joint credit card from her wallet. Roisin had cut hers in half in a grand gesture a week ago. "Here. Get a whole new outfit."

Roisin snatched it away quickly and secreted it in her voluminous handbag. "I'll get my hair done, too. I'm thinking of going blond."

"Blond?" Marley threw a startled glance at the auburn curls that drifted down past Roisin's shoulders.

"Yes. I was blond before I met you. Remember the photos of Tenerife?"

Marley vaguely recalled some ancient holiday snaps of Roisin by the poolside with Bernie McMillen, a woman Marley had very little time for. Disgruntled, she muttered, "No."

Roisin just snorted in response, gathering her shopping bags, ready to leave.

"So, we're on for Saturday?" Marley looked up for confirmation.

"Yes. Pick me up at ten. I'll be the blonde in new shoes, living in your old home. And you'll be…what? Tell me again?"

Marley sighed. "In a lavender tux. God help me."

Roisin smirked and leant in to drop a good-bye kiss on the top of Marley's head, like she always used to do. Marley's belly contracted. It had been in knots all afternoon, both before and during the meeting. Her face flushed and her chest went tight, and suddenly she wanted to cry.

Roisin left in a happy bubble, her shopping spree extended with the ageless gift of plastic. Oh, how she'd missed her flexible friend. Oh, how she wished she'd never ever cut him in two to make some stupid point about financial independence. Financial independence was all well and good, but spending your selfish ex's money was far, far better; especially as she watched you do it. Lavish, lavish, lavish…that was the order of the day. Oh, and she needed her nails touched up, too.

Marley rubbed a circle in the steamed-up window and watched her ex-girlfriend disappear down the street, her head buried in an umbrella, the wind and rain whipping at her raincoat. She watched the shapely calves and the small feet strapped into the ridiculously high heels whisk along, skirting the puddles. Roisin would undergo any future orthopedic calamity to avoid being the five-foot-one nature had intended. Marley smiled to herself. It was so easy to pick her little lover up to kissable height and set her on a counter top, or table, to simply hug her.

She noticed three teenage construction workers out prowling on their lunch hour nudge each other with some leering unheard comment as her ex flew past. Roisin was an attractive woman and looked much younger than her thirty years.

Jealous rage flared in Marley. Dropping her head onto her hand, she played with her cup and stared fixedly at a print of coffee beans on the wall opposite. She was in trouble here. She'd made a terrible, life-altering mistake, and she didn't know how to fix it. She didn't have time to fix it. Her wristwatch told her she was going to be late for her next meeting if she didn't hoof it quick, and she dashed out into the rain toward her office suite on the Lagan riverside.

❖

Roisin checked the time on the wall clock. Ten past ten. Marley had been on the phone for nearly an hour now, rambling on about next to nothing. They'd had coffee only that afternoon, so what was this call all about? Her first thought had been, *Is she checking up on how much I spent?*

But the conversation never really touched on money. Just silly things like, what colour was her hair now? Highlighted and layered, but no, not blond. And did she know the happy couple were going to Cancun for their honeymoon? Yes, she'd heard that. So...had she ever been there herself? No. Okay...so...had she got a man out to check on the dodgy guttering yet? No. Ah, perhaps Marley should come round and do it herself, she could get a loan of her brothers' ladders? No, she'd rather phone the repairman. Was she sure about that, because Marley could collect the ladd— Yes! She was absolutely sure. Oh... well...okay...so...what kind of shoes did she buy, then?

"Marley, what's going on?" Roisin finally exploded at the unending, ridiculous questions. "You're asking me about my shoes! They're burnished copper leather and they match my new handbag and my new hair. They cost over a hundred and seventy-five pounds...in the sale. I love them and I keep opening the box to look at them. If I ever get pregnant I want to have copper-coloured twins to remind me of these shoes." She blew steam down the phone. "Is that what you really wanted to hear? You've been on for over an hour now...what do you want?"

Silence. A long moment of silence. Then... "I never knew you wanted babies."

"Holy Mother of God!" She hung up.

❖

The next night the phone rang.
"Hello?"

"Guess what?"

Sigh. "What?"

"The tuxedo isn't lavender! Guess what colour it is?"

"Lime."

"No…be serious."

"Silver sequins and you look like an astronaut."

"Wise up. Guess proper."

"Gold sequins and you look like a moonbeam?" A huge huffy puff greeted that. "Okay, I give up. You've outfoxed me, Marley. What colour is it?" Roisin rolled her eyes in exasperation at the stupid, time-wasting, attention-seeking game.

"It's indigo," came the pleased-as-punch answer.

"Good. It will match your bruising if you call me again tonight. I'll see you at ten on the dot tomorrow morning." Roisin hung up and went to run a bath.

At 9:40 the next morning Roisin's doorbell tinkled out "I Will Survive."

"God damn it!" She was running late and halfway through her makeup. In bare feet and dressing gown she ran all the way downstairs and swung open the door.

"You're early," she accused while taking in the handsome indigo figure before her in one scowling sweep.

Marley stood frowning on the doorstep, her gaze locked on the brand-new BMW Z3 Roadster parked in the driveway. Her beloved twelve-year-old Jaguar XJ6 nosed up tight behind it.

"Whose is that?" Marley gestured with her car key, face like thunder.

Roisin smiled and turned away to go back upstairs, leaving her guest to show herself in. She was on the top tread and heard the front door click closed before she deigned to answer. "Mine."

Marley, already scanning the lounge for clues of some other occupant in the house, heard the answer with great relief.

"A red car?" Marley called up the stairs. "Sure it clashes with your hair?"

The Jealous Vixen lipstick froze on its way to Roisin's lips as she stared into the bathroom mirror. *She's right. It clashes with my hair! Well, it's back to the shop with you on Monday. I'll go for the silver. Maybe.* The car was a test model on loan for the weekend to see if she'd buy one. It did no harm to let Marley assume she had. The vivid red lipstick continued its journey to her mouth.

Finally puffed and powdered, dressed and shod, she swanned down the stairs totally confident with her ensemble.

Marley met her in the hall. "Wow. That's a beautiful colour on you. You're like...like a brand-new penny."

Roisin paused on the last few steps so she was eye to eye with her former lover. She gazed at her sternly.

"You're like a wet autumn day. I mean...kinda shiny." Marley groped for appropriate words to describe this goddess of liquid fire before her. Then she caught Roisin's expression.

"Stop it now."

Marley had never been poetical, so she took the advice.

"Whose car will we take?" Roisin asked as she fixed the buttonhole she'd bought onto the tuxedo's lapel. A pure white rosebud with stem and leaves stained the copper of her own dress.

Marley was momentarily stunned. Incredibly touched that Roisin had even thought about the buttonhole she had forgotten about altogether, and astounded that her ex had the audacity to even think they weren't going in the Jag.

"My car. It's got class." Marley held open the front door as Roisin gathered her matching purse and gloves. "And it complements your hair," she murmured into subtle perfumes that lingered long after Roisin brushed past.

"Pity it clashes with indigo," Roisin said as she headed directly for the forest green Jaguar with tan leather upholstery.

The reception hall at Belfast City Hall echoed with joyful laughter and cheerful conversations. The chandeliers tinkled, and gilt-framed portraits twinkled, and even the plush carpets seemed to warm to these events.

"Look at you, sure you're gorgeous. Indigo and copper, what a lovely combination" was the first greeting.

"When will we all be here for your big day?" soon followed a few dozen times.

Roisin smiling warmly, ducked, dived, and deflected with her usual wit and charm. Marley was granted a reprieve by being a witness and having to slide off to wait with an overanxious Sharla. Jen was arriving later, determined to be a traditional bride.

Her best friend raised a forefinger and gently prodded the rosebud on Marley's lapel. "Trust Roisin to get the finishing touches just right. Copper leaves."

Sharla and Jen had decided on rich cream for their outfits. Now Sharla sported an indigo waistcoat. Marley's ears shone pink. Sharla continued, glad to have a diversion, it seemed.

"I'm glad she suggested the indigo. You'd have looked a right poof in lavender. She said it would clash with her outfit and something had to go—either you or the tux! So indigo it is. Good call, heh?" She tugged at the hem of her own silk vest.

Marley's face caught up with her ears. "Roisin told you to change my tux to indigo?"

Before Sharla could answer, the registrar called them from the annex. Jen had arrived, they were about to begin.

On entering the Registry Hall Marley's eyes swept the tiers for Roisin. She found her almost at once, beside an overly attentive Bernie McMillan. Marley turned her back and stood facing the registrar, shoulder to shoulder with Sharla.

Several rows behind, Roisin could see her ex's ear glow pink and knew it was nothing to do with the light through the stained glass window. Smiling, she leaned over and shook hands with Bernie's partner. They'd both come all the way from London for the wedding, happy and excited as they were soon going to tie the knot themselves in England. Then the music began, a traditional Irish air, "My Lagan Love," and Jen floated up the center aisle with her sister, both beautiful in stylish cream organza with indigo sashes. They were allowed to sit and the ceremony began.

After cheers and confetti, and warm kisses and handshakes, the guests convoyed up the Antrim coast to Cairndhu House for the reception. The sun shone, the sea sparkled, and Scotland stood out crisp and clean on the horizon. The Mull of Kintyre and below it the mountains of Arran etched against the crystal blue sky.

Cairndhu, an old ancestral estate now turned over to commercial activity, specialized in boutique weddings. It had splendid halls and reception rooms, beautiful bedrooms and libraries. And magnificent, well-established gardens including a famous maze. The wedding party posed repeatedly for photos in the rose garden with the sundials, by the ornate Italian fountain, on small benches by the two-hundred-year-old yew tree. And in the glasshouse with the tropical palms, and on the carved granite steps with the stately home in the background.

Marley, as witness, was on call for most of them. Roisin, as her partner, appeared beside her in dozens of shots, too. All the while they spat out the beaming smiles of barefaced liars. Roisin's eyes shone with a million *I told you so*'s. It was agony to pretend to be so happy, so bloody perfect.

"Well, when you eventually tell them they can look back over these and say, 'At least they were happy on our big day. The rift must have happened sometime after.'" She flashed another radiant smile, clinging to Marley's arm like life itself. "God, my face hurts!"

Music and drinks followed a splendid quail dinner. The happy couple cut cake. Speeches were enjoyed, toasts were made, and soon it was time for Sharla and Jen to change clothes before heading for the airport.

Jen had one more tradition to perform. Marley escorted her a few steps up the grandiose curved stairway whispering in her ear as they giggled in co-conspiracy. Jen then stood before all assembled as Marley slid back in behind Roisin, the smaller woman only visible in the crowd by the crown of her flaming hair. Marley stood close behind her, and reached round to hold both of Roisin's hands just as Jen launched her bouquet at them as straight and true as a linebacker with a hand grenade. Roisin's eyes widened in dismay at the incoming fragrant missile. It had to be traveling at over a hundred miles an hour! Marley stretched out with both their hands and plucked the posey out of midair, crushing it securely into Roisin's chest amid cheers and laughter and crows of "You're next, you're next!" and "Cheaters!"

"A rose for a rose," Marley whispered into a flushed ear.

"I hope they throw your Oscar at you as hard as that bleedin' bouquet," Roisin managed to whisper back through an outwardly delighted laugh.

The afternoon had lengthened to early evening shadows, but the lowering sun still held its heat. Most guests moved to the outdoor tables to socialise or wander the beautiful grounds. A bottle of grand cru and glass flutes in hand, Marley found Roisin sitting quietly at one of the more secluded tables, partially hidden by topiary. She was concentrating on a flower plucked from the bouquet, carefully denuding it petal by petal.

Trying desperately to act debonair, Marley sat and poured the champagne, quipping roguishly, "She loves me, she loves me not?"

Roisin fixed her with a hard, unwavering stare before fiercely ripping another petal off a creamy blossom.

"No. Burial, cremation, burial, cremation..." She continued with her floral divination.

There was no doubt in Marley's mind whose the body was.

"Roisin, there you are." Bernie McMillen descended upon them, for once at an opportune moment. "I just wanted to say good-bye before we left. Hello there, Marley. How's it going? Great day, wasn't it?" She rested a hand on Roisin's shoulder and gave it a warm squeeze. Roisin turned in her chair and smiled up at her old friend. Marley tried to turn a glower into a sick smile.

"I'm fine, Bernie. Good to see you, too. And yes, it was a grand day for them." *There, answered all in one, hopefully she'll go away now.* But Bernie turned her attention to Roisin, who rose to hug her good-bye.

"Darling, you looked wonderful today. That outfit is amazing on you. You're like a phoenix rising from the ashes," Bernie crooned.

Bleedin' drunk. Marley smouldered at the wordsmith. *Phoenix... fuck. That's what I wanted to say.*

The hugging finally broke and Bernie turned to leave. "Now remember, you have to come and visit us in London, okay?"

"Bernie, the taxi's here," a small Asian woman called and Bernie had to hasten her exit, waving good-byes over her shoulder. Marley glowered at her back all the way out.

"When she said ashes, was she talking about us?" she immediately demanded, watching Bernie disappear into a cab with the woman who had called to her.

"No. I've said nothing. She was just telling me I looked nice."

"Who's she with?"

"Abir. Her partner. They're getting married this October in London. We've been invited."

"Oh." Marley blinked at this. "Bernie lives in London?"

Roisin sighed. "Don't you know anything about anybody except yourself and your own small world?"

Marley wasn't sure how to answer, so she sat quietly, feeling chastised and a little lost. Finally, unsure of what to do, she topped up Roisin's glass.

"Are you plying me with free booze? Isn't that kinda cheap?"

"Hey! I'm plying you with the best they had on offer. I bought this."

"And why am I being plied at all?"

Marley's colour heightened and she nodded over at the tall green avenues and aisles. "So I can get you drunk and chase you round that maze?"

"Darlin', we've been in that maze since the hour we met. We've only just come out, and by different exits. Why do you want to plough straight back in again?" Roisin's eyes were sad and haunted.

Marley felt as if she was pushing molasses through her heart. Her whole body seemed heavy and slow, and her ears hummed in a high frequency. The sound of panic. Her voice, when she found it, was as thick and sluggish as her blood. "Sometimes life gets too busy. Too pressured, and I feel like I'm running in a maze, lost in circles…like a lab rat."

"I can understand that. Well, the rat part."

"Roisin, I forgot you were in there with me."

Roisin watched her struggle silently.

"Please let me try and find you again." Marley hung her head as she gazed unfocussed at the little hope-filled bubbles bursting in her glass. The silence lengthened and she hadn't words to fill it. Just feelings that pulsed out into the space between them.

"I'll give you a clue." Roisin spoke very quietly. Marley strained to catch her words.

"I'm right over here."

JD Glass lives in the city of her choice and birth, New York, with her beloved partner. When she's not writing, she's the lead singer (as well as alternately guitarist and bassist) in Life Underwater, which also keeps her pretty busy. Her novels include *Punk Like Me, Punk and Zen*, *Red Light*, and *American Goth* from Bold Strokes Books.

CLAIMING THE ANGEL
JD GLASS

These are the things that go down hard. In these last few weeks work has been changing, home has been changing. We're working the same shifts, we're working split shifts—it seems like we're never not working. And something else is changing, too: you. In these same last few weeks, I see the way they look at you, our coworkers, our peers, the way everyone responds to your smile, their gazes lingering as you walk by. And I see too what they want.

They want you, and you don't know it. You're mine, but others want you. I hate that the only thing I have for you lately is snappy jokes or sharp retorts—because in these last few weeks of overwork and undersleep, of not enough "us" and too much of everything else, I've forgotten how to speak.

But Shannon hasn't—and she makes you smile. Oh, it's not the same smile, not the one you had for me, but all the same, it's something I can't seem to do lately.

What I can do, what I've been *very* successful at, is eliciting the surprised snap of shock and hurt in your eyes before you shrug it off. I think you're turning off to me, I think I'm pushing the buttons to do it.

The other day at dinner with your family you said something, the sort of thing you're likely to say, and I shot you down, another quick joke, another bitter smile.

Your cousin's dark appraisal under raised eyebrow said more to me than a thousand words ever could—and mute again, I couldn't even apologize. I wanted to.

I think your family hates me.

Even mine has noticed—I ran into my brother Pat today after

that call, outside the ER entrance where so many emergency vehicles parked it seemed like a tailgate party.

"So how you guys doin'?" he asked after the usual catch-up are-you-okay inquiries and the squaring away of details that always follow these sorts of incidents. "Anything, uh, going on?"

We'd been so busy, I'd forgotten about even that, and the combination of concern and awkwardness in his question seemed to me the perfect reason to make yet another one of my dumb jokes, at my expense, at yours, about the whole thing. That's a lie—I didn't even think about it—I just answered.

Pat stared for a moment, as shocked at me as I was. "Baby girl, you're fucking up," he told me quietly.

Anger and remorse made something squirm painfully under my ribs. "I know."

"You're gonna lose her if you keep this up."

"I *know*," I answered again. "I'm handling it."

"You better," he warned, "because"—he nodded, and not twenty feet away where another unit had parked behind mine was patrol, and who else but Shannon was the first to greet you as you stepped out from the ER doors—"you've got serious competition."

"I'm not worried about it," I told him, but inside? Inside I wondered if you noticed her the same way she did you to my eyes. I wondered if you had a clue of what she wanted, and if ultimately she could bring something to you, give something I couldn't—not lately, not anymore. It left me scared and silent, "outside" voice forgotten, or maybe even gone from disuse, along with the words I needed to tell you something other than "I'm tired," or "I'm in a bad mood." Those…have been the nicest things.

I didn't really notice Pat's friendly slap on the shoulder of good-bye, and I barely nodded to Shannon. God, she always managed to piss me off lately, and instead I walked over to you and opened my mouth wide and far enough to kill the spark of welcome in your eyes.

I push you, I wound you, and all I really want to do is throw myself at your feet, swear it will never happen again, then swim in you, under you, through you.

But I don't know how to speak, and all I do know is that when Shannon said something that made you smile again, I really wanted to see her teeth scatter like Tic Tacs from somewhere under my hand.

I seethed instead, steaming on a cool gray day like the fog and mist that rose from the ground, only I was hot, so hot I thought I'd explode.

During the call, it was your hands that covered mine briefly, a split second of the brush of your wrist where it was bare above the gloves on mine as you handled the tools that breathed for our patient.

Our eyes met just as briefly in the jostle and jolt of the rig and nothing else mattered but what we were doing—and we did it together.

This one…it *was* bad, really bad: a member of service went down, and if we did our job right, and if luck was on his side—lots of it, the miracle kind—he might come back up, eventually. We acknowledged it in that glance, the silent pact made: we'd fight like hell and try any way—anything, everything, to save that precious spark. We barely managed it, but we delivered something viable to the ER as opposed to a forensic package—though that still might happen, later, out of our sight, out of our hands.

There was a lot of paperwork afterward thanks to the multi-service response and involvement; Shannon ambushed me with more of it when I finally returned to the station at the end of my shift, perhaps not quite an hour after yours. The sly smirk I wanted to wipe off her face in the worst way widened when my cell rang—and it was you, telling me you're home.

"Home and alone?" the smirk said. "And you've at least another"—she glanced at the forms—"hour. Maybe an hour and a half."

I focused on the paper and the line of print before me. I wondered why the pen didn't melt or snap in two as I shoved it across the white field. I heard a low, steady sound and realized I ground my teeth while spearing through the page. It wasn't loud enough to drown Shannon's words as she placed her hands on my shoulders and spoke.

"Jean…Tori's going to promote soon, and everyone knows it. She'll be transferred, her shift will change. You know how this works—and who determines the 'needs of service.' You need to play ball and work with me, baby girl, so this can all work out all right."

Her touch was more than familiar, it was intimate: the touch of family, friends, and once, for a little while, something…more. She rubbed her thumbs over the knots in my neck. It was gentle, sure, effective, but it wasn't you.

Suddenly, I didn't know and I didn't care that Shannon was my superior officer, or my cousin, or anything, and I stood up and tossed the papers across her desk.

"I'm done," I snarled out as I faced her. "Report me, write me up, suspend me—I don't fuckin' care anymore—I'm not gonna just let you come on to my wife." Teeth like Tic Tacs flew through my mind's eye again and it took real effort not to clench my fists. I couldn't stop the hot that flowed through me.

"Temper, Jean," Shannon said softly. She leaned back against the wall next to the door frame. Eyes lighter than mine calmly, coolly, considered me, and the smirk was gone. "You're sharing that a little too much lately. I'd like to see you both remain in the same battalion—same days on and off. She still thinks she's in love with you—maybe, just maybe, I'm looking out for *both* of you—instead of *just* you—for once."

All the anger flew away, leaving me somehow deflated, except for the little bit left that I focused on myself. Of course. I'd been suspicious of seemingly everyone and their motives lately, which made me moody and raw, and now, I felt guilty on top of it—for accusing my cousin, my first cousin, as related to me as if we were half siblings—of something she wouldn't do. Oh, I wasn't stupid, I knew there was a real attraction to you underneath whatever Shannon said, but she wouldn't poach. Not unless she thought I was really fucking up.

Not fucking up meant doing my job, doing it right. I sat back down and finished the paperwork without another word between us. "Take tomorrow," Shannon said when I finally managed to finish everything without requiring either new forms or writing instruments. "I think you need it," she told me as I walked out the door. "Tell Tori the same."

My hands were numb on the steering wheel as I drove home, as numb as my mind, and when it hit me, I swore to the uncaring radio I hadn't even been listening to. We'd had plans, you and I, we'd had dinner plans—I had the impression you wanted to tell me something, and I have fucked up again.

In addition to forgetting how to speak, I am also guilty of being too late to recover any of whatever it was you had in mind. So now I'm tired again, frustrated, feeling the itching in my fingertips that still want to do grievous bodily harm to my cousin just for looking at you the way she does no matter what she says, and when I finally walk through our door, even Dusty, our dog, doesn't bother to say hello.

I find out why after I chuck my jacket and hang it on the peg as she raises her head from her paws to acknowledge me from her place on the rug: by your feet, where you've fallen asleep on the sofa, waiting—for me.

"Good girl, Dusty," I tell her softly, and pat her head briefly as I close in on the sofa. She's watching you, guarding you. I'm proud of her for doing it—she does it better than I do, and without any snappy comments, either.

I can't help the soft sigh that escapes me as I see your face. The last few years have left some gentle lines, but they're all gone now in your sleep, in your dreams, and as I watch you, I sit lightly on the edge, next to you, and you shift unconsciously, making room for me.

I'm not tired, I'm not angry, I'm just a little sad. I gaze down again and can't help but trace the defining lines of your face, smooth through the hair you've let get a little longer lately, silky and soft as it pours through my fingertips. I'm sad because I can't make you smile anymore, sad because if someone else, someone worthwhile, made you happy I'd step aside, sad because despite all the dumb muteness I can't seem to shake, I know that no one loves you the way I do—not that they don't want to try.

I don't want to be mute anymore—I don't want to be *me* anymore—and I just give in to the way I feel, the overflowing in my chest that hurts because I love you so damned much even as I hug you to me, fit my body to yours, every curve known, precious, familiar, and as necessary to me as breathing.

You call me "angel" all the time, but it's not true, baby, it's not true. You're my heart and my light and I can't help but kiss you, run hands filled with love and desire and possession over you, and you begin to wake even as I feel your skin, warm, soft, your heart beating under my palm before I skate it over your breast, the tip that hardens for me, and your kiss…your kiss is sleepy, achingly sensual, and even while you protest as you try to shift once more to reach me, I hush you with my lips.

"Please, baby. Let me," I beg silently with my tongue on yours, and instead of under your shirt, I'm unbuttoning it, revealing the silky expanse of your skin, my hips pressed solidly against your firm backside. You flash eyes ringed with deep forest green around ale-red center over your shoulder at me even as I lean over you, fill my hand with your curves, pause to feel your heart, the beat strong, steady, real, under my palm before I trace it down the length of you, and I don't know how your jeans disappeared and I don't care either as I claim your mouth once more, and while once more my tongue visits yours, so too do I let a finger slip between lips that welcome me in a hot embrace, a hint of hardness and slickness as I travel, a stroke of promise along this groove, this part of you that you give to me—and it is a gift, I know that. Every downstroke finds the tip of my finger against your wet welcome, every upstroke brings that wetness against the sensitive hardness that pushes insistently, an insistence, a need my body feels and answers, a need I want to fulfill.

"Skin," you half gasp, a welcome hot breath against my throat because we have shifted together and I lie on top of you, your thighs embracing mine, and you lean up to kiss me even as your hands pull my shirt from my waistband. I don't want to stop what I'm doing, don't want to stop touching you, loving you.

"Skin...*now*," you growl against my lips, and it's a demand, another desire I want—no, I *need*—to meet, and for a moment I savor the taste of you before I comply: fire meets fire, your hands with my hands, we do this together.

We are close and hot and tight and I am beautifully lost and wonderfully found, no longer mute. I know the things I've forgotten, remember and relearn you, me, the sacredness of us—it fills my heart as you enter me, then stretches my mind, my body, my soul. I am forgiven, I am absolved, and my heart, so full, now overflows from the beautiful whispered "oh yes" that warms my ear as I enter you, and the knowledge that floods me when I do, because you are so soft and so smooth and the way you feel is like nothing I've ever felt before. I know, I *feel*, the physical proof literally in—on—my hands, a pliant close fit around me, showing me what you wanted to tell me.

"Tori...baby," I choke out, amazed with what I've learned, with the way you make me feel. I kiss your neck, the tender skin just below your chin, catch your mouth with mine as I feel the fine line edge building through you.

"Perfect, angel. That's perfect," you tell me, the words throaty, low, and you're already doing what I love, what I need, showing me in every way you can what you feel, *how* you feel, bringing me with you to that place we're both shooting for—because we do this together, the cascade-chain-reaction of love and lust as you say the words your body proves, and I echo them in the same ways.

There is such perfect trust in your eyes, such open, honest, love for me in your gaze…I have been a jerk, and you love me. I have been surly, and you embrace me. You are my heart, you are my life, you are—the realization chokes me with its fullness, and you reach for and wipe away the first tear before it even falls.

"Angel, what's the matter?" There is nothing but gentle concern in your voice, the same in your touch on my face.

"I've…I've been such a jerk lately," I answer honestly. "I'm so sorry, baby, so sorry." I hold you closer, kiss you between each word.

"Well," you tell me, "I'll pass on the jerk thing again, but"—and you trace a very delicate trail down my nose—"keep the sexy arrogant thing. That I like."

"Just 'like,' huh?"

You're already pulling me even closer to you when you say, "Maybe more. I'm gonna show you."

Sometime later you stir next to me, and under the blanket one of us has pulled from the back of the sofa. "Stay, baby," I tell you and pull you back into me, on top of me, because I'm in love with how it all feels, "we're both off tomorrow."

"Yeah?" you ask, then nuzzle against my neck.

"Yeah," I confirm, then kiss you as nuzzle becomes a taste, "and good thing, too," I add because kiss and taste have become the knowing reach of hands to re-mark and re-map claimed and beloved territory.

"Why's that?"

We are already fitting together; the familiar entwine only adds to the anticipation because each experience with you still feels like a first. I gaze up at your face and my heart lifts, expansive and light at the sight of your smile, "my" smile on your lips as I ease beneath you. "Well," I tell you with a smile of my own, because I love you, because I'm happy, because I don't think you know what your body has told me, and I am eager to touch you, to feel that, to learn and know it all over again. "We've got lots to talk about."

Larkin Rose lives in a "blink and you've missed it" town in the beautiful state of South Carolina with her partner, Rose (hence the pen name), a portion of their seven brats, a chunky grandson, and too many animals to name. Her writing career began two years ago when the voices in her head wouldn't stop their constant chatter. After ruling out multiple personalities and hitting the keyboard, a writer was born.

Larkin's work now appears in *Ultimate Lesbian Erotica 2008* (w/a Sheri Livingston) and *Wetter 2008* (w/a Larkin Rose). Her novel, *I Dare You*, releases from Bold Strokes Books in September 2008.

The voices continue. The clatter of keys continues. The birth of erotic creations carries on.

Come, step inside your fantasies.

THE PROMISE
LARKIN ROSE

Jimmy Choos!" Lindsay draped the dry-cleaner bag across the open suitcase and shot back to the closet. "If you insist on taking me out to some overcrowded place for dinner, those are a must."

Andrea sighed as she watched her partner of ten years wade through at least fifty pair of designer shoes. Lindsay would know the name of each pair, something Andy couldn't care less about. "How about jeans, T-shirts, and a good pair of sneakers? We're only going for the weekend."

Lindsay poked her head around the door frame and rolled her eyes. "I wouldn't be caught dead in jeans, as you well know, and I'm not prancing around anywhere in a damn pair of tennis shoes."

God forbid you look human, or comfy, Andy thought. She pushed away from the wall and rechecked Lindsay's bags. Hell would burst loose if anything was missing when they arrived in San Diego. What happened to the down-to-earth, humorous woman she'd met ten years ago today? The one who squealed with delight every time Andy jerked her up in a bear hug, wearing a smile to melt the moon for everyone? The one who walked barefoot in the grass, low-rider jeans resting dangerously close on her hips, not a care in the world?

Hopefully, tonight, when the sun kissed the ocean, she'd bring back the old Lindsay. Or so she prayed, because if she couldn't...

"Got 'em." Lindsay stomped back to the bed and carefully slid the shoes into the side pocket. She zipped the bag and exited the room without bothering to carry any of the load.

Andy picked up the bags, then followed Lindsay to the car.

"I don't see why you're making me go. I have a deposition to get together, files to read over, a new secretary to find right after I fire the bitch I have now, and, my God, I don't have time for a romp in San Diego even if only for two days," Lindsay complained while Andy packed the backseat. "I've heard the place reeks of crime and prostitution. Couldn't you find another place to take me to, another place I've never been? I won't be missing a thing if I never see San Diego, or California, for that matter."

Without a word, Andy tossed in the last bag and slid into the driver's seat.

"Are you even listening to me? I have work to do, and I sure can't get it done with all this going on. And, God forbid, all those screaming children! What parents in their right mind take brats on a plane?" Her eyes widened. "Did you get my laptop? And the cord? The last time you dragged me off to some romantic getaway, you forgot everything."

Andy reversed out of the driveway, biting back the fact that Lindsay was the one who forgot *everything*. "I got the laptop, and the cord, and the cell phone charger, and your files you left in the bathroom last night."

Lindsay huffed and propped her elbow on the window, nervously chewing the edge of her French-manicured nail. "We're going to miss the flight."

"We're way ahead of schedule. Stop worrying."

"It's my job to worry. You sure as hell don't."

Andy shook her head and wove into the thicker traffic heading for the terminal.

"Do you have the tickets? First-class, right?"

"Of course." Andy tried to keep the sarcasm out of her voice.

"I hope they have better champagne. The stuff they served on my flight to New York tasted like well water. Took me three hours to get that foul taste out of my mouth."

Andy remained quiet. She'd already heard the story a hundred times. After parking in the garage, she found an empty cart and unloaded their bags, then led them across the parking lot.

With any luck, check-in would go without a hitch and they could be on that bird destined for the sky, right on time. As soon as the security tech gave them a quizzical stare, Andy knew she'd have no such luck, and wondered what Lindsay had managed to sneak into her bag.

"Ma'am. I need you to step over here while we go through your luggage."

Lindsay's eyes narrowed into a death stare. "Me?"

"This way, ma'am." He motioned her out of line while Andy pushed her own bags forward.

Once cleared, Andy moved through the scanner. Down the hall, Lindsay waved her arms angrily while the guards unpacked her belongings and placed them on a table. Andy slowly approached, careful to stay far enough behind the red line.

"It's a freaking pair of knitting scissors. Who could I possibly murder with those tiny things?" Lindsay ranted.

"They're not allowed on the plane, ma'am."

"Since when?" She glanced around the terminal. "Where's your superior? I want him out here right this instant. This is ridiculous! I want your badge number!"

The men continued removing and repacking, ignoring her loud complaints. Andy sighed and slid onto the bench.

Lindsay shoved her hands on her hips and glared at Andy. "You're just going to sit there while these assholes manhandle me?"

When the agent finally closed the bag, Lindsay yanked it from his grasp and stormed around him. "You haven't heard the end of me, I promise!"

Andy gave him an apologetic look and followed her fuming girlfriend through the terminal to their gate, then down the ramp to the airplane. Lindsay shoved around people and stomped down the aisle. With a huff, she dropped her carry-on bag in the vacant chair and plopped in the window seat. "Well, this romantic getaway is starting with a freaking bang. I don't know how I let you talk me into this shit."

Andy pushed their bags into the overhead compartment and sat down.

She carefully took Lindsay's hand and pulled it to her lips. "Because you love me?"

❖

Once they were airborne, Andy breathed a sigh of relief. Her plans were in motion, even if Lindsay hadn't settled down from her rage over having her scissors banned. She made a mental note to buy a new pair and smiled as the flight attendant approached.

"Champagne?" She looked between Andy and Lindsay.

Lindsay dragged her gaze away from the window and stared at the woman, then down at the bubbly. "You know, as much as we pay for these tickets, you'd think you could at least serve Dom. I don't expect Cristal but, really, Cordon Negro? Could you be any cheaper?"

The woman's smile faded. "I'm sorry. Is there something else I can get for you? We have Wattwiller bottled water."

"I suppose that'll have to do. I'll buy some real champagne in the VIP lounge when we land in Dallas."

Andy shook her head at the offer and the flight attendant walked away. Plain old Fiji water was just fine with her.

"You don't have to be so nasty. She's not in charge of ordering food and drinks." Andy wanted to retract her words as soon as they slid from her lips.

"Why do you find the need to protect the world against me? Would it kill you to agree with me once in a blue fucking moon?"

Andy only grinned and nodded toward the flashing sign. "The seat belt sign's off. Why don't we make a bathroom trip, then you can nap until we land for our layover."

"Why, so I'll shut my damn mouth?" Lindsay removed her seat belt, stepped over Andy's legs, and started down the aisle.

"Hell, yes," Andy muttered and followed her.

Just as Lindsay started to shut the bathroom door, Andy stuck her foot in and gently pushed it open. "We can share."

Lindsay gave her a hard glare before she stepped back.

Andy shut the door, grabbed her hips, and pulled her against her chest, turning Lindsay to face the mirror. "See that pretty face? When you put a smile on it, it's breathtaking. You should try it more often." She cupped her breasts through her silk shirt. She was sure the blouse had a brand name and was sure Lindsay would scold her for any wrinkle left behind. Right now, she didn't give a shit. She wanted the growling bitch fucked out of this woman before they landed. Lord knew what hell she could unleash there in this foul mood.

"Flattery gets you nowhere, sweetie. You know that."

Andy smiled and circled her thumbs over the hardening nipples. "Of course I do. But it calms your tiger."

Finally, a smile appeared on Lindsay's face. God, how she loved that grin. She'd give anything to be back on the East Coast in

Myrtle Beach, South Carolina, where they'd met, without a care in the world and crazy in love. She'd met Lindsay online in a chat room for lesbians. There was something about her that was wild and sexy. She was drawn to her humor and found herself addicted to the e-mails and chats. Being a starving artist, she didn't have much to offer a city girl, especially one who was accustomed to the finer things in life. Andy had juggled two jobs to pay her way through art school. Lindsay's tuition had been paid in full by her parents. Andy lived in a shack of an apartment where a bungee cord had been her only defense against drug addicts roaming the streets for a score. Lindsay had been given a condominium as her high school graduation present, furnished with everything a daddy's girl could dream of. Yet somehow, Andy had snagged the city slicker's attention. Now she didn't know how to keep it…and wasn't sure Lindsay even wanted her to anymore.

Andy was still the same person, no matter how many paintings she sold, no matter how fat her bank account grew. She still loved with fire. Lindsay loved with stones and daggers, only looking at the career ladder in front of her, never looking over her shoulder to see if Andy was still connected to her.

Lindsay turned in her arms. "The mile-high club. We've never done that."

"There are several things we've never done."

Lindsay's smile softened and she pressed her lips to Andy's. "True. But who has time anymore? We knew it would be like this once I became a lawyer. And now, you're a famous painter. Our lives are chaotic."

"We're supposed to make time."

Lindsay shrugged and pulled herself onto the counter. "What was it about a tiger you wanted to calm? Have you ever considered that maybe I'm a bitch because you tame me so well?"

Andy wished that were true, knowing it was far from fact. Truth known, Lindsay went above and beyond the call of duty to claim her title of queen bitch. Even their sex life had changed, going from whenever the mood struck, to making appointments on a calendar. Hell, even their dates had to be scheduled…and most were rescheduled. She was still waiting on a few rain checks. She unfastened the clasp of Lindsay's soft slacks and yanked them down while Lindsay lifted off the counter.

"Easy with the Elizabeth McQueens, hot stuff. They cost a fortune."

Andy slid her finger along the edge of Lindsay's lacy thong and dipped a finger into her wet pussy.

Lindsay arched against her hand, her head falling back. "Oh, God, yes."

Andy added another digit and pumped against her slick walls. "Can we finish this trip without you complaining, or being rude, or huffing, or cursing?"

"Yes. Oh, man, yeah. I'll shut up." She jerked her hips to the rhythm of Andy's thrusts. "Hurry, baby. I need to come."

Andy knelt and pulled the string of her thong to the side. With a soft lick, she lapped at Lindsay's clit, then nursed it between her lips. Lindsay leaned back and arched toward the suction, her breath coming in rushed gasps.

"That's it, baby. I'm coming!" She arched into a bow and clenched her teeth to muffle her scream.

It was a sound Andy lived to hear. It meant she had Lindsay all to herself…if only for a few minutes. However, this tiny cubicle on an airplane wasn't where she'd be granted that sweet music. But tonight. Oh, tonight. She didn't care who heard her howl with pleasure.

When Lindsay's orgasmic clenches subsided, Andy rose to stand between her legs. "Did I calm your bitch?"

With a weak smile, Lindsay nodded. "Don't you always?"

Andy pressed a kiss against her lips. God, how she wished she could.

❖

The rest of their flight was quiet, with Lindsay staring at anything other than Andy. So Andy focused on the movie instead, hoping by the end of the day, she'd have her lover's attention back…and a new beginning to their life.

What if she didn't? What then? Lord help her, she didn't know where that would leave them. It terrified her to think of her life without Lindsay in it. More than anything, she wanted her angel back. She fucking missed her more than she dared admit.

Once they arrived in San Diego, Andy followed the signs to the baggage claim and waited for their flight number to appear on the monitor. Lindsay waited on the bench, her luscious lips set in a grim line. If Andy didn't love her so much, would she have gone through so much trouble to keep the promise?

She knew without a doubt that she would have. A promise was a promise. As aggravating as Lindsay was sometimes, she was her life, her entire world, and no amount of griping and bitchiness could stop that. Andy's friends called her pussy-whipped. She called it love. And no matter what they said, no matter what her head told her, her heart knew the love of her life was hidden beneath that hard shell somewhere. It was up to her to find her and bring her back.

She was now out of options. She'd used up all of her resources to cling to the love of her life. Today, she would make good on her word and pray her angel found her way back. The alternative didn't bear contemplation.

Andy found their bags, spotted a shuttle, and motioned the driver over. Lindsay ambled their way, and with a humph, climbed onto the front seat, her gaze fixed straight ahead. Andy tossed the bags onto the back and directed the driver to the car rental.

When they arrived at their destination, Andy realized with a jolt that the sun was starting to sink from the sky. While Lindsay waited, she hurried to fill out the necessary paperwork, took the keys from the clerk, and headed back outside.

"The rental's parked right there." She pointed toward the Jeep, hoping to catch a glint of remembrance in Lindsay's eyes. She knew it was foolish but couldn't help herself. Add chipped paint and bald tires and the vehicle was identical to the very one she drove to meet Lindsay for the first time. Lindsay'd been so fucking gorgeous with her long hair flowing and twisting in the breeze. They hadn't had a care in the world as they explored the coast, and each other.

Lindsay crinkled her nose. "A Jeep? You've got to be kidding. Don't they have a freaking car with a goddamn cover?"

"Don't forget your designer luggage." Andy pulled her own bags from the car-rental office and started across the parking lot.

Lindsay grumbled and cursed as she lugged the suitcases into the backseat. She huffed a loose strand of hair from her face and hurled herself into the passenger seat, immediately folding her arms across her chest. "Are you just trying to fuck with my nerves?"

"Don't I always?" Andy slid her sunglasses into place, cranked the car, and pulled out of the parking lot.

Lindsay was quiet for several miles. Though it wasn't Andy's first visit to the stunning ocean city, she couldn't wait to live that first experience through Lindsay. But the look on Lyndsay's face said she wasn't impressed with the palm trees and blue skies.

"What's the funky odor?"

"The ocean."

"Jesus. How can anyone stand that raunchy smell all day, every day? Give me Atlanta any day of the week. I can't handle this gross odor. Tell me again why we had to come here?"

"First off, it's not raunchy, it's sea water. Second, people get used to it the same way I got used to that potent stench you use every morning."

Lindsay's mouth flew open. "Stench! I'll have you know that's Dolce and Gabbana."

"I don't give a shit what it is. It stinks."

"What the hell is your problem?"

"I'm tired of your complaints. All day, every day, twenty-four fucking hours a day. You can't give it a rest even for what was supposed to be my romantic getaway." Andy clamped her mouth shut. Lord help her, if she didn't stop now, her plans, her promise, would be forever ruined. Only silence and the rush of wind through the windows greeted her as Lindsay turned away.

Andy took several deep breaths, wishing she could conjure up an apology, but knowing even that would be a lie right now. She wasn't sorry for anything she'd said. She was sorry her love had lost her soul, and prayed she could help her find it again.

God help her if she didn't.

❖

"Is the traffic always this horrible?" Though it was another complaint, it was asked with softness. Maybe she'd heard the roar in Andy's voice and finally realized she'd gone too far.

"Yes." Andy wanted to remind her that Atlanta traffic was just as brutal, but found the point moot. She wove through the traffic, watching in horror as the sun sank lower in the sky. Only minutes left to keep her promise. "Do you remember the day you met me?"

"Of course. At the beach. We went camping with the sand fleas. I had welts on my legs for weeks."

Andy smiled, remembering the red marks beneath Lindsay's sunburn, Lindsay's attempts to scratch them...Andy kissing her, making her forget.

"I followed them like a dot-to-dot path for my dining pleasure." She glanced over at Lindsay, saw a smile creep across her lips. She resisted the urge to slam on the brakes and kiss her before the smile faded.

"I had a paper due and I couldn't drag myself away from you... drove all night to get back to Florida, stayed up all morning to get it done, then fell asleep at the keyboard. When I woke up, class was over and I never turned it in."

"You aced the next one, and the one after that." Andy drove onto the exit ramp, searching the sky again for the closure of her promise, regretting she hadn't at least reached out for Lindsay's hand before the complaints restarted.

"But I flunked that one."

"Well, you lived. And look where you are today. You're an awesome lawyer. That one grade didn't hurt your career."

"But it could have."

"It didn't." Andy pulled to the red light, impatiently tapping her fingers against the steering wheel while idling behind a line of cars. "What else do you remember?"

"Um, getting sick at the seafood restaurant you picked, you holding my hair back while I puked." She glanced over at Andy. "What a way to meet and greet, huh? I was hugging the porcelain god two hours after we met and didn't even have the pleasure of getting drunk to get there." She actually laughed.

Andy closed her eyes and let the sound filter through her mind. She'd never forget that laughter. For years, she'd gotten to hear that sweet music. Then Lindsay graduated with honors, was grabbed up quickly by a prestigious firm, and was caught up in the whirlwind. Fuck, where had that sweetheart gone?

Andy reached for the good. Always the good. "We spent our first Friday night together curled up in the tent."

"With the sand fleas. Don't forget those little critters shared our sleeping bag."

Andy would have slept in a pit of snakes to be with Lindsay. She checked the sky again. Was it just her, or was the sun setting faster by the second? Was it a sign to give up her attempt?

"And Saturday?" She gunned the engine as the cars moved forward, then took a sharp right, heading straight to the beaches.

"We went to the amusement park and waited in those long-ass lines, strolled all those little shops on the boulevard spending way too much money, bought matching T-shirts with our names spray painted, and walked the beach until it was too dark to see. Almost got lost trying to find the campground."

Andy couldn't help looking over at her, wondering if they'd been at the same beach at the same time. They'd gotten to know each other in those lines, hadn't cared about the money they spent on each other, and if she remembered correctly, they'd been kissing too much when they missed their entrance to the campground.

"I still have that damn shirt."

"You still have that old thing? I have no idea what happened to mine. Oh well. No telling."

"It's in a box in the garage." Andy sensed Lindsay look at her, but kept her eyes glued on the side streets leading to a parking area. Deep orange and purple hues streaked across the sky, threatening to rip the promise from her grasp.

Lindsay shifted on the seat and crossed her legs, her expensive high-heel pump dangling from her toes. "We made love for the first time that night. It was incredible."

Andy smiled, remembering that night. Lindsay was the one. Lindsay was still the one. She'd known from the second Lindsay had rushed across the sand to hug her. The feel of her tiny body crushed against her own, the way her smile lit up her face, her eyes sparkling with joy.

"Yes, we did. All night."

"And Sunday, I cried. I couldn't stand the thought of leaving you. I was ready to U-haul right then and there."

"You had school to finish, a career to make." Andy found the street she wanted and darted down it.

"And you lived in that rat-infested hole," Lindsay said. "I wanted to throw it all away to be near you."

"I wouldn't have let you. You'd worked too hard."

"And then you sold your first painting six months later and moved to Florida."

"It was too hard being without you. My little Jeep couldn't take much more traveling."

As if a beacon had been turned on, Lindsay surveyed the vehicle. "It was like this one, only with less paint and a lot less upholstery."

Andy pulled Lindsay's hand to her lips and placed a delicate kiss against her skin. "Great memories, huh?"

A sweet smile lifted Lindsay's lips. "Yes, it was. Being reckless and out of control was great. Too bad we all have to grow up, huh?"

Andy parked in the public access lot to the beach, killed the engine, and hopped out of the Jeep. Her heart hammered against her chest. Growing up was one thing, but growing into the person Lindsay had become was quite another. Would she hear everything Andy had to say? Or would she stomp off in anger? Would their relationship end on the promise?

She waited impatiently for Lindsay. She wanted to grab her hand and run for the ocean, to scream out how her love was still alive…that she needed her Lindsay back. The sun was inches away from dropping onto the ocean. She casually took Lindsay's hand and pulled her toward the wooden bridge leading to the beach.

"Do you remember you leaving Sunday night?" They crossed the bridge and Andy stalled to kick off her shoes.

"Um, sweetie, I'm not walking barefoot in that nasty sand. No telling what kind of germs are loitering in there."

"Take off your fucking shoes, Lindsay." Andy glared, too damn close to let anything stop her now.

Lindsay's mouth dropped open, but thankfully, she bent and pulled off her high heels. She slowly rolled up her pants legs. "There. Happy?"

"Not yet." Andy pulled her toward the shore. "Answer the question."

"I didn't want to leave, was squalling like the world was ending."

"I've only seen you cry once since then."

"After your week in Florida, when you were going back to Tennessee. God, I hated watching you leave."

Andy nodded and walked faster, her gaze glued to the sunset. "No more than I hated leaving with those tears falling down your cheeks. It broke my heart." She gently touched Lindsay's cheek. "You never cry anymore."

"I don't have a reason to cry."

Andy dropped her hand and approached the edge of the water. She stopped at the shoreline, letting the water slosh around her feet. "Heartless people don't cry."

Lindsay gasped. "What the fuck does that mean?"

Andy faced her. "I love you, Lindsay. I have from the second you stepped out of your cute little convertible. I'd never wanted another person like I wanted you. The fire, the love, the clenching need...it's still here, damn it. Where the fuck did you go? I fucking need you, can't you see that?"

Lindsay blinked hard. Her expression went from cold to soft then to something in between. "Oh, honey, I'm here! What's wrong, baby?"

Andy stepped closer. "Remember, Lindsay. I need you to remember."

Lindsay's eyes searched Andy's, then she looked toward the blazing sun just as it met the horizon. Tears welling, she hung her head.

Andy crooked her finger under Lindsay's chin and forced her gaze up. "We've discovered everything together. Your career, my art, our lives, our home, our fears, our dreams...we've conquered them all side by side. Now I feel like I'm the string holding this relationship together." She held Lindsay at arm's length, her heart catapulting against her chest. "And for the life of me, I don't know how to rediscover that passion we found on a damn beach completely across the map."

Lindsay sobbed, tears streaming down her beautiful face. Andy tugged her down to the sand and cradled her between her legs, facing the flaming orange rippling across the ocean. She held on tight. "No matter how much our lives have turned, and twisted, I had to keep my promise. Do you remember it?"

Lindsay nodded. "You said, 'Ten years from today, you're going to be in my arms while I show you a sunset on the Pacific Ocean...and I'm still going to be just as much in love with you then as I was this morning while I watched the sun rise on the Atlantic with you in my arms.'" Lindsay tightened her grip on Andy's arms. "It was the sweetest thing anyone had ever said to me."

Andy kissed her temple. She'd never fallen in love so fast, or so furiously out of control.

Lindsay twisted around, placed her hands on both sides of Andy's face, and kissed her. There was no argument in her eyes. "It's still in here. I want that back, too, Andy." She bit her bottom lip before more tears fell. "I love you so much. Thank you for giving me this. It's the most beautiful thing in the world."

"I know something far more beautiful." Andy hugged Lindsay to her chest as the sun slid beneath the surface, shutting out the day, sealing her fate on a ten-year promise. "I want *us* back, Lindsay."

"I'm so sorry." Lindsay snuggled closer into Andy's arms. "You were the one, Andy. I knew it from the second I saw you standing there, all tan, and tall, and smiling that Elvis smile. I loved you right then and there. I'm still in love."

Andy felt the love strings reattach, binding her to the love of her life again. The true Lindsay was back. For the next two days, they strolled hand in hand, barefoot through the sand, shopping the stores along the boulevard, laughing and loving like they'd just met for the first time. They bought matching T-shirts bearing both their names in rings of hearts. She knew without a doubt, Lindsay's heart would never be in a box again.

Better yet, not a single complaint escaped Lindsay's mouth. Not even when the waiter accidentally spilled Coke all over her new hip-hugger jeans. Not even when the skateboarding punk ran over her toe in her new flip-flops. Not even when the hotel double-billed them at checkout. Not even when the flight attendant offered them champagne on their return flight home.

As a matter of fact, she had three glasses…one after their first trip to the bathroom, another after their second, and another after the third.

Neither one of them knew what happened to the laptop. Nor did they care.

Since 1994, JENNIFER HARRIS's poetry has appeared in numerous national literary magazines including multiple publications in the *New York Quarterly* and *Fish Stories*. She has also been published in *HLLQ*, *Art Times*, and the anthology *Power Lines* (Tia Chucha Press). *PINK*, published in April 2008 with Bold Strokes Books, is her first novel. She is currently working on a new novel, *The Stars at Her Feet*.

Jennifer received her MFA from The School of The Art Institute of Chicago and her BA from The University of Arizona. She spent a decade as an active literary organizer in Chicago, both as the director of a poetry series at The Art Institute of Chicago and as the founder of a small literary magazine. She also founded and directed a nonprofit that hosted writing workshops for at-risk teens in hospitals and shelters throughout Chicago. For the past nine years, she has also spent most of her spare time raising money for food and medical supplies for the Drepung Gomang Monastery, located in south India. She is a member of the board of trustees of the Chicago Poetry Center.

MERCURY
JENNIFER HARRIS

Mercury is the god of commerce and thievery, the Roman counterpart of the Greek god Hermes: messenger of the gods.

My first kiss was a dare. I was twelve and can't remember his name. He had blond hair and wasn't cute. I remember wanting to kiss him just to prove I wasn't queer because I hadn't yet kissed a boy, and because I sat in the front of our class.

Let me qualify. My dad moved us from Aurora, Ohio, to Laguna Beach, California. I'm talking major culture shock. It was the '80s and I was all preppy this and that, a gay goody-two-shoes, and SoCal was just Dolfin shorts, Vans, and potheads. Also, I had just had my first fight the week before. Jennifer Cohen started yelling at me at lunch and shoving me around. She was all, let's fight. Let's go, let's go. I said, "We're fighting now." I asked, "What do you mean, 'go fight'? Where?" And the girls on my side were coaching me on how to make a fist. I never did understand what it was about, but she broke my nose.

So the next week when what's-his-name's tongue slid inside my mouth, I just thought of eels in the zoo. The way they glide along the bottom of the tanks, swirling up dirt and muck. He tasted like corn chips. I kept my eyes open. Behind us, my best friend Suzie was making faces. He kissed me in the park behind school; there were eucalyptus trees everywhere and the air stank of it.

Suzie dared him to do it. I remember him saying sure, sure, no big deal. "It could be worse," he said. I thought it wouldn't be so bad.

But of course, it was Suzie I loved in that pre-teen sort of way. I knew I was queer but wasn't interested in anyone knowing just yet.

It made me feel aloof, like it didn't matter what those dumb wipes thought.

It was power, you see?

Suzie died a few years later. I was sixteen and didn't go to her funeral. She was shot in L.A.—at a monster truck derby. Some guy stole her purse outside the gates of the Coliseum. It was imitation leather, white, with two bucks and a lipstick inside. Some guy just walked up and grabbed it. Suzie waved down a security guard and they chased him two blocks to an alley. When the guy found himself cornered, he turned around, pulled out a gun, and shot Suzie in the center of her head.

She used to sleep over a lot because her mom was a nurse and worked the night shift. My mom said it wasn't right for her to be alone so much, but Suzie was always sneaking out. It sounds strange, but I always knew she wouldn't make it. It was her eyes. They had this sad thing in them. But back then, we slept together all the time. We would sleep with just our underwear on, arms wrapped around each other.

Sometimes she would touch me but I knew she didn't mean it. She was already having sex with boys. I knew with me, she was just bored and wanted to see if I'd object. But I never did. A month after the dare, Suzie's mom got a job in Huntington Beach, about twenty minutes north, so after a while we lost touch.

The day I learned Suzie was dead I was with my first girlfriend, Anna, and we were driving to go body surfing at the Wedge, in Newport, near Thirty-first Street and Pacific Coast. We were cruising around, blaring the radio and singing along. Anna pulled into a 7-Eleven off Pacific Coast and right there on the front page of the Metro section of the *L.A. Times*, was Suzie's picture. I didn't notice the photo. I read the whole article not realizing that Suzie was my Suzie; was the Suzie who plotted my first and only boy-kiss.

Anna grabbed the paper from me, said, "This is Suzie, isn't it? You and her used to be best friends, didn't you?"

I grabbed the paper and stared at her photo. She looked strange. Somehow removed from the memories I had of her. I couldn't put it together that this dead girl was Suzie Coleman.

Later at the beach I laid out my towel, put on some Coppertone #4, and walked down to the water. The waves were breaking pretty good that day. A slow curl. Anna and I waded out and floated over the swells.

The quote from the security guard had read, "There was blood everywhere, she just sort of collapsed. I didn't know what to do."

In that park with all that eucalyptus in the air, I remember the boy turning away from me laughing. Suzie dared me because she'd been fucking around and I guess she thought I should at least kiss someone. I remember her fragile blue eyes. I remember her telling me that I had to open my mouth more; that guys like it when you open your mouth real wide.

CATE CULPEPPER is the author of the Tristaine series, four novels about a passionate clan of renegade Amazons. She is a 2005 Golden Crown Literary Society award winner in the Sci-Fi/Fantasy category, and was named one of the recipients of the 2008 Alice B. Readers' Choice Awards. Cate's new book, *Fireside*, set in modern day, will be released in January 2009. Her Tristaine series includes *Tristaine: The Clinic*, *Battle for Tristaine*, *Tristaine Rises*, and *Queens of Tristaine*. Thanks to Fecky McFeck for the idea.

Silent Vows
Cate Culpepper

*D*ang, Jesstin!" Dana thumped the door to the sweat lodge with the heel of her boot. "You're getting pruney in there. Brenna's not going to marry a raisin."

When she got no answer, Dana scowled and rested her head against the lodge's pinewood frame. The rising moon was already visible through the thick branches of maple and oak that encircled Tristaine. The handfasting began at midnight. As Jess's second, it was her job to deliver Jess to the village square in time for the ceremony. Bodily, if need be. She heard another hissing rise of steam within the small lodge and rolled her eyes.

"Come on, how many impurities do you need to cook out, for God's sake?" Dana yelled. Then her jaw snapped shut as she spotted a slender figure trotting through the high grass, and she felt a silly smile rise on her lips.

"Well, I've lost her," Kyla announced, waving her arms in agitation. "Two things Shann asks me to do tonight—sing and guard Brenna—and I've already blown one of them." Kyla stopped short and stared at Dana in consternation. "She's not here, is she?"

"Who, Brenna?" Dana pulled her gaze from Kyla's rapidly rising and falling breasts. "No, of course she's not here. Jess is here, so Brenna can't be here." She looked around sharply to be sure. "Shann will scalp us both if we let those two see each other."

"Shann's not really a scalping kind of queen, honey." Kyla grinned as she rested an elbow against the lodge and caught her breath. "Is Jesstin still gazing at her navel in there?"

"Still gazing." Dana thought Kyla looked adorable, but then all Kyla ever had to do to look adorable to Dana was breathe.

"Jess?" Kyla pressed her ear to the sweating wood, then knocked politely. "It's me. You need to come out of there, adanin, your hair's going to go all lank!"

"Right," Dana snorted. "You know how to persuade an Amazon warrior. She'll barrel out of there screaming now."

"Well, you're not doing any better bossing your Amazon around than I am bossing mine." Kyla puffed an auburn lock of hair out of her eyes and stared into the darkening forest. "Where could she be?"

Dana shrugged. "Exactly what sort of torments were you all inflicting on Brenna when she slipped your leash?"

"Just our usual preparations for a handfasting." Kyla ticked them off on her fingers. "The ritual bath, the gauntlet of caresses, the naked knife-dancing—"

"Jeeze, Ky, Brenna's probably run off to marry some *guy* to escape all that."

"No, Dana, it was really beautiful." Kyla's eyes sparkled as she clasped Dana's hand. "I just love the way our clan's spirits rise toward the moment when two of our sisters join for life."

"Okay, but why all this hoopla about keeping Jess and Brenna apart?" Dana couldn't stop staring at Kyla's fingers entwined in hers. "They've been adonai for years, it's not like either of them are vir—"

"Well, Tristaine's Amazons only marry after they've been together for years. That's where the whole custom of celibacy before the handfasting comes from." Kyla's elfin features took on a dreamy cast. "Aphrodite rewards the lovers for their long seasons of waiting for Her blessing. All that hands-off time makes for some very memorable first-joining nights."

"I'm sure." In spite of her lascivious tone, Dana felt color rising in her cheeks. She jerked her chin toward the sweat lodge. "It's just tough to picture old brawny-butt in there celibate for two days, much less a month. Sorry, a moon. Jess figures in the sex fantasies of every dang Amazon under ninety in this clan."

"Ooh, that she does." Kyla bounced on her toes, smiling, and Dana allowed herself a brief flare of jealousy.

She knew Jess and Kyla loved each other dearly, but platonically— their relationship was the essence of fierce devotion that the Amazons called adanin. That close sisterhood described the warm bond between Dana and Brenna as well.

But let's face it, Dana thought. *Jesstin is Tristaine's lead warrior and Shann's second, she's built like some female ideal of Adonis, she's got all that clenched-jaw, broad-shouldered butch thing going—basically, Jess was what some of the younger women called her when Brenna wasn't around—a walking, vulva-clenching climax.*

Dana shook her head. "And she hasn't touched Brenna for *weeks*?"

"I know." Kyla snickered. "Those two keeping their hands off each other that long is a miracle of stamina worthy of…"

Kyla's voice trailed off and she and Dana looked at each other in dawning horror.

"Jesstin," Dana shrieked, and they attacked the door of the sweat lodge in a scrambling fury.

Billows of steam gushed out at them as the door crashed inward, and there was much sputtering and flailing of arms until it cleared. The dark sweat lodge contained buckets of water and a pit of baking stones, filled with glowing coals and smoking cedar chips. The lodge no longer featured two boards in its back wall. And it no longer contained any Amazon warriors, clench-jawed, broad-shouldered or otherwise.

"Shann's gonna *scalp* me," Dana moaned.

❖

Brenna ran faster.

Jess had taught her the cleansing and calming benefits of speed, and it was beginning to help. She leapt nimbly over a dark bank of bushes and kept going, her stride light and effortless, tracing the inner rim of the vast mesa that housed Tristaine.

Brenna was fitter than she had ever been, healthy in body and spirit. She could run all night, and was considering doing so. A light wind gusted through the trees, cool and fresh on her heated face, and the rustling leaves spurred her on.

The laughter and singing of the Amazons had long since faded behind her. Brenna didn't fear pursuit. She doubted her sisters would even miss her in their boisterous revelry.

Ordinarily she loved it—the intricate rituals and ceremonies that were the heart of life in Tristaine. Their customs came from a dozen different continents and theologies, weaving a lush cultural tapestry that Brenna revered and usually enjoyed. But she had been unprepared for the emotional intensity of this night.

She veered around a gnarled maple and headed toward the mesa's east plain. She craved the solace of her private refuge, a small glen graced by a waterfall that had preserved her sanity on more than one turbulent night. Sweeter comfort could be found only in Jess's arms, and that friendly warmth had been unavailable far too long. Brenna's parched heart thirsted for it.

"Adonai," she whispered as she ran. It was the Amazons' word for life-mate, wife, a bond held so sacred in Tristaine that the word itself was a prayer. It described what Jess was to Brenna, what they had been to each other for years. But tonight, they would speak the vows that would join their lives forever in the eyes of their sisters, and the Goddesses who guided their clan. As the sun began to set, the enormity of it had sneaked up on Brenna and smacked her powerfully in the chest. But she was calmin now—she'd find her composure before midnight's full moon.

Twigs snapped beneath her feet and she eased from all-out flight into a more relaxed pace. She would cry during the handfasting, she knew this. She minded it only because her throat would tighten, and she had vows to speak. Now she was afraid the words wouldn't come at all. How could she give voice to the depth of her love for Jess? It was always there, it flowed beneath her every waking moment, but describing that devotion in words was like trying to capture the night wind.

A sudden, enraged churning shook the tree limbs directly over her head, and Brenna's heart jagged in her breast. As she flew past the oak, a black shape skulking in its highest branches leapt from its perch and landed in the tree ahead.

Brenna guessed at once that whatever was chasing her was not Amazon. An Amazon hunted her prey silently, and this eerie stalker made no attempt at stealth. Her pulse rocketed and so did her pace, and the dark demon pursued her, leaping catlike from branch to branch in the closely-packed forest.

The wind lashed through the trees and her legs pistoned against the soft earth. A deep-throated snarl sounded through the quivering leaves behind her, and Brenna put a hand to the dagger in her belt. She tried to turn west, back toward the village, but the shadowed form jumped onto a low limb almost directly in her path, and she was forced to turn back.

Then Brenna knew who it was, even before she raced into the glen and reached the waterfall, and whirled to confront the creature who hunted her. The pounding fear in her heart was real, but so was the tingling of her senses, the sure recognition of her soul reflected in another—Brenna's very blood sang her name. Trembling and pulling for breath, she waited.

Jess dropped soundlessly from the trees, her knees dipping slightly to catch her weight on the mossy ground. She was dressed in a simple tunic and leggings; her thick hair was a wildness around her shoulders, scattered with twigs and leaves, giving her the aspect of a vengeful woodland goddess. Her step toward Brenna was slow and deliberate, her muscled arms relaxed at her sides, but the piercing, predatory cobalt of her eyes held Brenna motionless.

Brenna stood silhouetted by the rising moon, her diaphanous white robes waving softly around her still body, and Jess saw the high color in her cheeks as clearly as if the sun rode the sky. Her young lover's hands were clenched, and her full breasts rose and fell in hypnotic rhythm. Jess drank in the sight, filled the hollows of her bones with it. Her low brogue emerged as a guttural growl.

"No power will keep us apart."

Fear glinted again in Brenna's eyes. She looked up to hold Jess's searing gaze as she reached her. "Don't tempt the fates, Jesstin."

Jess lifted her hand, and her long, cold fingers closed gently around Brenna's slender throat. "No power," she murmured again, "will keep us apart."

Brenna swallowed and closed her eyes, Jess's animal heat spilling over her skin.

"I pledge all my days to your protection and happiness, Brenna." Jess felt Brenna's dove-swift pulse flutter against her rough palm. She slid her hand downward and brushed two knuckles across her wife's stiffening nipples. "I'll cry your name in the night, all my nights."

Ravenous beyond bearing, Jess tripped Brenna and caught her in a single motion, and lowered her slowly into the thick grass. Her shaking hands made short work of the slight robes, and when Brenna lay naked before her, her full curves pale in the moonlight, Jess lifted her face to the star-filled heavens and hissed thanks to her Goddess. She twined her hands in Brenna's lush hair, but then felt slender fingers wrap firmly around her own throat. She looked down at Brenna, dazed. The emerald green of Brenna's eyes was clear and shining, and held nothing of submission.

Brenna waited until the fire in Jess's austere features banked enough to allow her to hear her words.

"You've given me a family of sisters I never dreamed of, and a love I never dared hope for." These were not the vows Brenna had written, she didn't need them, she was just talking to Jess and telling her the truth. "You've saved my life a dozen times, in a dozen ways. I cherish you with every breath." A healer to her core, Brenna shuddered with the knowledge. "Jesstin, I would kill or die for you."

The carnal greed in Jess's expression changed, tempered into a saner, wondering look. In that moment, she was still Brenna's lover, but she became again all else she was to Brenna—her closest friend and fierce protector. Her playmate, her hero. The arms that held Brenna now had lifted her high in celebration and had cradled her as they both wept for Tristaine's lost sisters.

Jess studied the beautiful woman beneath her with something like awe, seeing at first the tormented young medic Brenna had been when they first met. Then her delicate features shifted, changing swiftly through the years into the face of the strong and loving Amazon Jess held tonight. The part of Jess's mind that was still capable of rational thought wondered what she could have done to merit such precious reward.

"What in the world did I do to deserve you?" Brenna whispered.

Jess smiled. Her lips feathered across Brenna's fuller ones, the lightest of tastes after too many nights' fasting.

After that it was pretty much about the sex.

❖

The low, musical chanting of five hundred Amazon voices was about to rattle Dana's teeth out of her head. Not that the song was loud, it was just so *expectant*. They were nearing the time in the ceremony when Jess and Brenna must appear. Dana could hear the creaking of her ankle tendons even over the singing as she bounced up and down on her toes, that's how tense she was.

Even she had to admit the handfasting had been pitch-perfect so far, though. Beautiful summer night, starry skies, huge turnout, roaring bonfire, teary-eyed testimonials. The queen was, with all respect, a knockout in those silky robes, and Dana hadn't seen such sheer happiness in Shann's eyes for entire seasons.

"Will you stop with the jumping jack thing?" Kyla gripped Dana's sleeve until her heels settled into the grass. She was smiling dreamily into the crackling flames of the bonfire. "Relax. They'll be here."

"So you keep telling me." Dana craned her neck to try to see over the heads of the taller warriors. "What did she say?"

"Who?"

"*Who*," Dana snorted. "Shann, Queen of Tristaine, she who we all dang well better obey, *Shann,* what did she say when you told her we lost Jess and Brenna?"

"She told Aria to put on another pot of posole, we'd be starting a little late." Kyla rocked slightly to the harmonious chanting from the women encircling the fire.

"How can we eat posole when Jess and Brenna are going to hell?"

"Dana, darlin'." Kyla lifted Dana's hand and patted it. "I promise you, our adanin are not going to hell." She nodded toward the assembled Amazons. "These are just our clan's customs, honey, they're not natural law. Tristaine's Goddesses are far too sensible to get miffed by a little premature ravishing, and so is Shann."

"Well, where are they, then?" Dana tried again to see through the throng of bodies around them. "Man, even if they blew off the chastity thing, you'd think they'd show up for this. Everybody here loves those guys. You'd think they'd care—"

"They care," Kyla assured her.

Dana heard it then, the ripple of excitement that enlivened the crowd's chanting to a trill of welcome. A dark head appeared above the other warriors, and then Jess stepped into the cleared space in the grass before Shann. At the opposite end of the inner circle, Brenna was nudged forward by another group of grinning sisters.

Jess sauntered into the clearing, smiling slightly, her shoulders relaxed. She never took her gaze from Brenna, who returned it with the light blush of fulfillment still coloring her cheeks. Dana had never seen a more vivid walking proclamation of post-climax content in her life, and apparently others saw it too. An appreciative whistle broke out from the cluster of warriors across the fire.

Jess turned, and Dana felt the trajectory of her frown pass over her head like an arrow in flight, targeting the offending warrior. A quick, respectful silence fell over that curve of the circle. One of their archers lifted her hand in apology, and Jess's nod acknowledged it.

Shann cleared her throat quietly. The queen stood gracefully on a low bench, studying the heavens, the essence of regal patience. Her two errant Amazons finally reached her and faced each other.

"I'm up," Kyla whispered. She rose on her toes and brushed a swift kiss across Dana's cheek, stunning her into paralysis, and then weaved through the circles of women to a position behind Shann.

Brenna smiled at Kyla nervously, hoping against hope that her vision wouldn't blur with tears—she was already immensely moved by the palpable joy of the Amazons around them. The clan's pleasure in their union was heartfelt and universal, and she basked in the warmth of her sisters' excitement. As she watched, an entire silent conversation passed between Shann and Jess while the chanting faded.

From her elevated stance, the queen looked down pointedly at a small leaf still caught in Jess's tumbling hair, and lifted an eyebrow in mild reproof. Jess lowered her head in brief, respectful admission, but then she grinned up at Shann with such bandit satisfaction that Brenna couldn't repress her own smile, and neither could Shann.

The queen glanced over her shoulder and nodded at Kyla. Kyla filled her lungs slowly, and an ethereal melody emerged from her lips, sweet and lilting in the fresh night air. Brenna's throat tightened as she recognized the aria from one of Tristaine's most honored legends. The song told the story of a timeless bond between two Amazons who transcended death itself to claim their love. Kyla had chosen these verses wisely, out of her sure understanding of the almost mystical ties that forged Jess and Brenna into adonai.

"Brenna." Shann's voice was low and a little amused.

Brenna came to with a start. Jess was extending open hands to her, and she stepped closer and took them readily. Her warrior's palms were dry and warm, calming the trembling in her own fingers.

Kyla's rich song continued, the only sound in the hushed night beyond the crackling of the fire. The clan watched silently as Shann lifted the simple ribbon from around her neck and kissed it. The delicate lace of the handfasting braid was threaded with thin strips of leather, butter-soft but strong. Shann draped the ribbon around Jess's and Brenna's wrists, and then straightened.

The first words of the blessing the queen had chosen nearly brought on the tears Brenna had successfully held back thus far. It was one of Tristaine's oldest prayers, and the one spoken when Shann had joined her life with her adonai, Dyan, long years lost now.

"Now you will feel no rain," Shann said, *"for each of you will be shelter for the other.*

"Now you will feel no cold, for each of you will be warmth to the other.

"Now you are two Amazons, but there is only one life before you. May beauty surround you both in the journey ahead and through all the years.

"May happiness be your adanin, and your days together be good and long upon the earth."

A sigh moved through the women, and Brenna closed her eyes as the queen's hand rested briefly on her head. She wanted very much to look at Jess at that moment, but the time had come to speak their vows, and she was afraid her throat might lock entirely if she saw her face. Brenna swallowed hard. Then she felt a small warmth on her wrist and opened her eyes to see a single teardrop darkening the lace of the handfasting ribbon. She lifted her head.

Another tear brimmed in Jess's eyes and slid over her high cheek. Her tears were not many and they fell silently, but easily and without shame. They smiled at each other as Brenna's eyes filled at last, a warm energy thrilling through their clasped hands.

Kyla's lovely voice grew softer, and the watching women stilled to listen to the adonai exchange vows. The warrior and the healer stood close to each other, their locked gaze holding no need for words. All had been said, all promises given and love professed, at the glen, and echoed in every day of their lives since they met.

Several moments passed, and some of the watching Amazons looked at the queen, puzzled at this pleasantly intense but continuing silence. Shann studied the faces of the two women before her. Then she looked out over her clan and nodded, content.

A murmur of understanding rustled through the crowd, then they quieted once more to hear their sisters' silent vows.

No one moved until Jess took Brenna in her arms at last and kissed her, and then a mighty roar shook the village square.

The Amazons danced until dawn.

Author's Note: Shann's blessing was adapted from the oral tradition of an Apache wedding prayer. The words are not my own.

Gabrielle Goldsby is the author of *The Caretaker's Daughter*, *Never Wake*, *Such a Pretty Face*, *Remember Tomorrow*, and the 2007 Lambda Literary Award–winning mystery, *Wall of Silence* 2nd edition. When not writing, reading, or in the gym, Gabrielle enjoys exploring the trails near her home in Portland Oregon, camping—the kind that requires a tent—and watching movies in her home theater with her partner of nine years. Gabrielle's works in progress are *Paybacks* (Bold Strokes Books, 2009) and *The Burning Cypress*.

For information about these and other works, please visit www.boldstrokesbooks.com.

THE PLAYER
GABRIELLE GOLDSBY

H ello, Gianna. It's been a long time."
"Elle, it hasn't been near long enough." With those words,
Gianna Abatoli turned and walked away. There was a time in Gianna's
life when she'd felt honored to have attracted Elle Butler's attention.
But that was a long time ago. Today, the quick flash of anger that
accompanied any mention of Elle's name was magnified by ten—the
number of years since they had last spoken to each other.

Gianna had always imagined that she would be cool and uncaring if
they should ever run into each other again. Maybe even say something
biting, like, "I'm sorry, do I know you...bitch?" Instead, she had
blurted out the thing that came first to her mind: the truth. The hurt and
humiliation were still too fresh for her to pretend that Elle was simply
a college buddy. Gianna had given her virginity to Elle Butler, but they
had never been friends.

Gianna moved through the throng of party guests, outright
ignoring the fact that Cori Hoffman, the hostess of the pool party/
housewarming, was calling her name.

"Gianna, would you wait, please? Damn it! Stop walking so fast,
I can't catch up."

"That's the plan," Gianna muttered, but she slowed just outside
Cori's front door. Still, she was halfway down the driveway before Cori
caught up to her.

"Thanks for slowing down," Cori huffed.

"I didn't slow down to talk to you. I slowed down because I want
my shoes back."

"What?"

"I said, give me back my Jimmy Choos."

"But why?" Cori looked down at the cute little sling-backed sandals that complemented her summer dress, then back at Gianna as if she had just been asked for one of her kidneys.

"You *knew* she would be here, didn't you?"

Cori nodded and looked so forlorn that Gianna would have felt bad if she wasn't certain that Cori was more upset at the loss of the shoes than the fact that Gianna was leaving her party early.

"You said I could wear them. They go with my outfit."

"I changed my mind." Gianna felt tiny and spiteful. Cori had been her college roommate. She knew all of the sordid details of why Gianna hated Elle's guts. Why wouldn't she have warned her?

"Look, she's the one that called me, okay? She said she had taken a coaching job at the junior college and heard about my party through the grapevine. I tried to tell her that you would be here and you wouldn't like it. But she said it was time for you two to work this out like adults. I thought you were over that stuff. It happened ten years ago."

"If you thought I was over it, why didn't you tell me she was coming? Take the shoes off, Cori."

"But there's gravel all over the driveway."

"Good. Take 'em off."

"I thought you guys could talk. Maybe she remembers the situation differently than you do." Cori removed one shoe and held it out cautiously, as if attempting to feed raw sirloin to a hungry lioness.

Gianna snatched the shoe from Cori's hand. "I'll need the left one too. They're a pair." She watched as Cori stooped to remove the other shoe. "And what do you mean, maybe she remembers it differently? How could she? What happened is what happened. The videotape is probably still floating around. Hell, I wouldn't be surprised if it's made it to DVD by now."

"I just meant that maybe you should talk to her. You might be surprised by what she has to say."

"The time for talking was ten years ago."

"She tried, Gianna, you wouldn't see her. You went out of your way to avoid her. You even stopped tutoring the basketball team just so you wouldn't have to hear anything about her."

"You know that's not the only reason."

"I know, but the point is, you wouldn't *let* her talk to you. She tried calling you before she left to play overseas."

"Like I said, we had nothing to discuss. I got involved with a player and I got played. Lesson learned. I don't care what she has to say."

But the problem was, she did care. No matter how many women she dated, how many years went by, and how many times she told herself she should forget, Gianna still caught her breath whenever she saw a tall, athletic-looking brunette. She'd thought she caught glimpses of Elle in crowded grocery stores, above clothing racks, and in SUVs inching down packed highways. But until today, she had always been left disappointed and feeling ashamed that she still looked for the woman who had left her not only devastated, but jaded toward future relationships.

Gianna looked up just as Cori's front door swung open. Her eyes settled on Elle with a hunger that shocked her. She had spent the past decade telling herself that Elle had probably grown lazy and out of shape like many former athletes. She had spitefully named one of the characters in her sixth novel after her. Fictional Elle had married a portly older man for money and had borne him four large-headed babies in rapid succession that served to stretch her once young and perfect breasts into sagging teardrops of flesh. Gianna had taken great pleasure in making that character into such a pathetic creature that even she could see her editor's point that she had given the fictional Elle no redeeming qualities for the reader to get behind. In the end the character, like the real thing, had been abruptly removed from the plot and she had been forced to tie up the loose ends as best she could.

The real Elle was striding toward them, looking as fit as she had in her early twenties. The few strands of silver Gianna had spotted in her hair during their brief conversation brought her no pleasure. If anything, the sign of maturity added to her attraction.

"Damn, she's still sexy, huh?" Cori said.

"Shut up and put the shoes back on," Gianna said through tight lips. Cori snagged the shoes and went so far as to use Gianna's shoulder for support as she slipped them back on with a pleased sigh.

"May I speak with you before you leave?" Elle sounded hesitant, as if she expected to be shot down again.

"I'll just head back to my party and give you two some privacy,"

Cori said. Without looking at Gianna, she scurried back up the driveway and through her front door.

"I'm in a hurry," Gianna said. "Why don't you give me your phone number and I'll call you sometime."

"I'd like the chance to explain my side of things."

"I don't know what you're talking about." Gianna flushed. It was a stupid thing to say. They both knew she remembered. How could she ever hope to forget having her virginity taken by her dream lover and her heart broken within a few days by that same lover? How could she ever forget the humiliation of attending classes daily for three more years with the fear that the jock sitting behind her had seen her nude body, had heard her beg for release? It would never happen. She could never forget that. No matter how hard she tried.

"Gianna, please," Elle said in that soft way of hers.

Gianna felt caught like the numerous lightning bugs she'd imprisoned in glass jars as a child. Like most of her friends, she had thought nothing of using the crushed bodies of those living things to write her most secret of secrets across her chest. *I love Kate Strawberry.* Gianna caught herself staring at two nicely rounded and perky breasts. She tried to look away, but was caught by Elle's intense dark eyes.

"Can we go somewhere and talk?" Elle asked.

"No, we can't. I have nothing to talk to you about."

"Okay, then can we go somewhere and not talk?"

The quirky half-smile on Elle's lips had always made Gianna's tummy flip with pleasure, but the fact that it still did, all these years later, infuriated her.

"It was a long time ago. Whatever it is you feel we need to talk about, I'm sure I've already forgotten." The hurt on Elle's face withered any further words on Gianna's lips. What the fuck? She was still using that lost, innocent look? Of course she was. Why not? That look was all she had needed to land Gianna's naïve eighteen-year-old-virgin ass, spread-eagle and screaming how much she loved her. Gianna flinched at the memory. "If you're still feeling guilty, don't bother. What's done is done. It's time you moved on. I already have." Her words were as cool as the feeling in the pit of her stomach.

"That's just it. I've tried." The lost-girl look passed across Elle's face again. She dug something out of her coat pocket and held it tightly in her hands. "I've kept this in the hopes that I would have the opportunity to give it back to you. But after I left the country and you graduated, I was afraid too much time had passed." Elle held out a thick white envelope. Softly she added, "There's a card inside with an address on it. That's where I'll be tomorrow at two o'clock. If you don't show up, I'll understand. But I hope you do."

Gianna almost refused to take the envelope, but curiosity and the pleading in Elle's eyes made it impossible. She took the envelope and dropped her hand to her side as if she couldn't care less about the contents.

"Thank you. I hope I see you tomorrow," Elle said.

Gianna expected Elle to turn away and head back to the party but she didn't. Gianna was forced to walk away first, unsure of how and what she should be feeling. This had been simpler before. She'd had years of thinking of Elle as a calloused playgirl who had used her star-basketball-player status and charm to take advantage of Gianna, but now she couldn't help remembering the gentle way Elle had made love to her. The look in her eyes as she had relished what Gianna was giving to her had not been cocky or superior, but grateful. It was the same look she had on her face now. Gianna didn't remember if she had said good-bye or not, but Elle was still standing in the driveway when she tossed the thick envelope on the passenger seat of her car and drove off.

Gianna pictured herself tossing the envelope out the window and freeing herself of the burden of Elle for good. But she could no sooner toss that envelope from her life than she could have walked out of that college dorm when Elle had forced her to come clean about the looks they had shared during their tutoring sessions. If only she *had* walked away ten years ago. What would her life be like without Elle Butler to despise?

❖

Ten Years Earlier

Gianna stood in front of Elle Butler's on-campus apartment for several seconds listening to raised female voices. She was loath to interrupt the argument, but reluctant to squander the precious time she had to spend with Elle each session. She knocked twice before trying the knob. Unsurprised at finding it unlocked, she let herself in while calling out a hello. Gianna stepped into the hall just as a girl she vaguely recognized as being either on the cheerleading squad or in her chemistry lab stormed out of Elle's room, straightening her clothes. The girl stopped long enough to look at Gianna's khakis, polo shirt, and flats in disgust. She made a big show of stepping around Gianna and gestured toward Elle's bedroom.

"She's all yours, have at it."

Gianna watched the girl stomp out the door without bothering to close it behind her. Shallon Thompson, star freshman point guard and Elle's new roommate, walked out of the bedroom reading a magazine. Gianna was so relieved Elle wasn't in the room that she forgot her natural propensity for shyness and spoke first.

"Hi, Shallon."

Shallon looked up from her magazine long enough to scowl at Gianna. "Who are you?" she asked, and continued into the living room where she dropped on to the couch insolently.

"Um, I'm Gianna?" Since the look on Shallon's face clearly said "so?" Gianna explained, "Elle's tutor?"

"You're her tutor? Oh yeah, I remember now. Your name came up in a conversation the other day."

Gianna flushed at the thought that Elle might have mentioned her, but she couldn't bring herself to ask what they had been talking about.

"Have a seat. I heard Elle get in the shower. She should be out in a few. You want something to drink? I have some coolers in the fridge."

"No, thank you." Gianna thought about pointing out that it wasn't quite noon yet, but based on the stories she had heard about Shallon, the time of day probably didn't matter.

Shallon unwrapped a grape sucker and put it into her mouth in an oddly sexual gesture that left Gianna queasy. Shallon shifted her feet and slouched lower on the couch, her legs open and one hand stuck halfway into her waistband. Gianna reluctantly sat down across from her and tried to avoid looking up the leg of her shorts.

"So, how old are you?" Shallon asked around her sucker.

"Eighteen, why?"

Shallon smiled, shrugged, and switched the sucker to the other side of her mouth. "Just asking." Her Southern drawl sounded more pronounced for some reason. Her gaze settled on Gianna's breasts and stayed there until Gianna was forced to look down to see if she had food stains on her chest.

Gianna was relieved when the bathroom door opened and Elle walked out. Like Shallon, Elle wore shorts that went to her knees, but Gianna was having a hard time ignoring the still-glistening skin, the damp hair, and the perfect fit of Elle's tank top. Gianna looked away, but not before the image of Elle's dark areolas, confined beneath the sheer fabric, burned into her mind.

"Oh hey, is it eleven already?" Elle said.

Gianna noticed the bags under Elle's eyes as she walked into the living room. "You look like you've been up all night."

Shallon snickered and took a loud slurp of her sucker.

"If you want me to come back tomorrow, I can." Gianna hoped so desperately that Elle would turn her down that the few seconds it took Elle to say "no" felt like a lifetime.

"Let's study in my room. I'm sure Shallon won't mind." The last sentence was spoken louder than seemed necessary, but Shallon just chuckled and picked up her magazine.

Gianna followed Elle toward her bedroom but was brought up short when Elle stopped in the doorway. Gianna had to peer around her to get a look at the chaos inside. Clothing was strewn across both beds, almost every square inch of the floor, both desks and their chairs.

"You out of laundry detergent?" Gianna cursed herself for finding the nerve to crack a joke with Elle when she was so obviously annoyed. "Sorry, I'm guessing Shallon is a little on the messy side."

"You're guessing right." Elle jerked one of the closet doors open so violently that clothing fell off its top shelf, revealing a couple of shoe boxes, three large canisters of protein shakes, a video camera, and a case of noodle soup. "I'm trying real hard not to act like her mother. I understand what it's like to be on your own for the first time and wanting to have fun and stuff, but this messiness and this senseless need of hers to party constantly is starting to get on my nerves."

Elle kicked a pile of clothes into the closet and shoved others on top of Shallon's flat of dehydrated noodles with no apparent regard for whether the clothes were dirty. "It's a good thing I fell asleep on the couch last night. If I had come in here to this I would have been pissed."

"You slept on the couch after that game you had last night?" Gianna said, horrified. "I bet your body is screaming at you."

Elle stopped shoving clothes into a laundry bag and gave Gianna her quirky little half-smile.

"You watched the game?"

"Didn't everybody? You were brilliant."

"I didn't think you were a basketball fan."

Gianna shrugged rather than admit she had only started watching after she had started tutoring Elle.

"I don't know how I got stuck with a freshman, anyway." Standing there with dirty clothing gripped in one fist, her hair still damp from her shower, Elle had never looked more beautiful. Gianna could think of no place she would rather be or person she would rather be with. *Stop it, Gianna, look at her. Why would she want to be with you?*

Elle must have misinterpreted something she saw in Gianna's face because she dropped the clothes she was holding and walked toward her, hand out, but stopping short of touching her. "Oh hey, listen, I didn't mean anything by that."

"No, it's cool. I get what you're saying. Maybe they put you two together in the hopes that you would help her to grow up a little."

"That's what Coach said. But I think all she worries about is sex."

This was a new side of their relationship. Gianna had been tutoring Elle all quarter and they hadn't entered into any kind of personal conversations. Unlike most of the other players on the team, Elle seemed to like to keep to herself. The newspapers had called her driven and wise beyond her years. Gianna thought it was a very accurate description of Elle despite the fact that she had hardly known her at the time.

"Can't you just talk to her? Maybe she doesn't know how much it bugs you."

"I've tried. She thinks I'm trying to be her mother. Do you know she had a girl in here partying last night?" Elle tossed the remaining laundry into the closet and sat down in the now-cleared chair.

"Can't blame her for wanting to celebrate after the game you guys had last night." Gianna opened a book and pretended to look for the right section.

"Huh, I guess. She treats them like shit the next day, and most of them look at me like I should have warned them or something."

"I'm guessing you are going to have one more entry into the former fans of Shallon club."

"What makes you say that?" Elle picked up a rubberband and yanked her hair back into a ponytail.

Gianna stifled her sigh of regret before it became audible.

"Oh, I heard arguing when I came in. The girl she was in here with nearly knocked me over when she ran out of your room. I thought you were busy. I almost left, but Shallon told me you were in the shower."

"You thought that girl was in here with me?"

"Well, she *was* running out of your room." Gianna laughed in the hopes of dispelling the serious look on Elle's face.

"Yeah, but not from my bed."

"I know that now, but even if she had been here for you, it's none of my business." Elle looked confused and slightly embarrassed. Something told Gianna not to probe deeply. "We should probably get started."

Elle agreed and Gianna pretended to look at her notes from their last session. She was finding it hard to concentrate because she kept feeling Elle's eyes on her.

"Hey?" Elle's expression was still too serious. "I hope you don't think I'm like that. Maybe a few years ago, but I'm too old for that now. Shallon is a kid."

"Shallon and I are the same age," Gianna pointed out.

"You know what I mean. I would never sleep with anyone just for the sake of having sex."

"Why are you telling me this?" *Oh my God, she knows! How could she possibly know?*

"I guess…I guess I kind of hoped you'd care."

The answer stunned Gianna into silence.

"Did I make a mistake?"

"No." Gianna felt as if her vocal cords and tongue had turned to stone.

"I'm so sorry, I thought…I hope I didn't offend you."

Elle looked so mortified that Gianna hurried to explain. "I meant you didn't make a mistake. I like you a lot, but…"

"But what?"

"I just figured, I'm a freshman same as Shallon, so you wouldn't be interested."

"Shallon has never been away from home and she's compensating by acting like a kid given free rein of the playground. Look, can we stop talking about Shallon?"

"Sure, sorry. Do you want to open your book to…"

"I want to talk about a different story."

"A different story?" Gianna asked, taken aback by the intense look on Elle's face. "It's not in the syllabus?"

"This one isn't in the syllabus."

"What's it called?"

"The author hasn't titled it and it's not finished," Elle said in a voice so low that Gianna found herself leaning forward to hear it. Elle still regarded her intently, but she had taken the book from her and turned her chair to face her.

"What kind of story is it?" Gianna asked.

"A romance."

"From what era?"

"Present day."

"And this is something you've been assigned in class?"

Elle slowly shook her head. "It's something I came across in the library by chance."

"You picked up a romance at *our* school library?" Gianna felt confused. Elle didn't seem like the type to seek out a romance to read for pleasure. "What drew you to the book?"

"I liked the way the main character professed her love for the other character. No game playing, just a lot of honesty and passion."

"Passion? Was it…were the two characters gay?"

"Yeah, lesbians. At least one of them was for sure. They were a lot like us. One was a basketball player and one was a…"

Gianna went cold. "Elle, I…"

Elle opened her desk drawer, pulled out a sheaf of papers, and laid them on the desk in front of Gianna. "Did you write this? Is this story about us?"

Gianna couldn't answer either question because her teeth were locked together in a fight against tears and rage at her own stupidity. She'd been so angry with herself for misplacing the story when she realized it was gone, but had soon forgotten about it. Never once had it occurred to her that the manuscript would make its way into Elle's hands. Never once did she even consider that Elle would recognize herself as the love interest or Gianna as the author. "Yes, it's mine, but it's just fiction. How did you get it?"

"I found it on the floor in the library after one of our sessions. You had already rushed off for a class. I intended on asking you about it when I saw you again, but it slipped my mind. I brought it back here and put it in my desk and forgot about it. I didn't intend to read it."

"But you obviously did."

"Shallon was going through my desk looking for something. She read it and thought it was a love letter from a fan. I thought it might be from you, but I wasn't sure."

"You told her, didn't you?" Gianna started packing her things, her eyes blurry with the effort of holding back her tears. She grew even more embarrassed as she remembered Shallon's knowing smirk when she had introduced herself as Elle's tutor.

"I mentioned that we were studying in the library when I found it, but that was before I had read it. I wouldn't have told her anything if I had read it first."

Gianna grabbed her bag and headed for the door, unable to bear the humiliation one more moment. She hadn't expected to be caught at the door and pulled back against those breasts she had only ever fantasized about feeling.

She had written about kissing Elle, but she had never really imagined it would ever come true. Her fantasy had nothing on the reality of Elle's lips pressing into hers. Elle cupped the back of Gianna's neck as she urged her mouth open and her head back to accommodate her much taller height. Elle steered them both toward the bed. Gianna didn't protest when her back hit the mattress, but she did groan when Elle's weight settled atop her for the first time. She opened her legs thinking Elle would settle into the V between them, but Elle had other ideas and Gianna was lifted a full inch up the bed as Elle thrust against her. Gianna cried out with equal parts surprise and pleasure. Gianna's hands roamed Elle's back, encouraging her despite her nervousness. She had never felt anything so delightful, so wickedly good.

"We're going too fast. Maybe we should study in the library today," Elle said between kisses.

"Not yet." Gianna rode Elle's thigh, boldly slipping her hand under Elle's tank top to explore the nipples that had been tantalizing her since Elle had come out of the bathroom.

This time Elle let out a raspy moan. "Gianna, let's go get something to eat. Let's go for a walk, we need to get out of this room." Elle's eyes were closed and there was no force to her words. She had caught on to Gianna's rhythm. Her breathing, although still uneven, had taken on a more determined quality. She rested her head on Gianna's moist brow. "Open your eyes. Look at me."

Gianna obeyed. Elle's lips were parted and swollen from the kissing, her eyes were a storm cloud waiting to burst, and yet she was telling Gianna without words that what happened next was up to her. Gianna slipped her hands beneath Elle's shorts, cupping her buttocks, pulling her closer.

"Are you sure?" Elle asked.

"Yes, I'm sure."

Elle sat up quickly and whipped her shirt off.

Gianna's eyes had no sooner rested on Elle's breasts than they traveled to an area of Elle's muscled body she had never dreamed of seeing. By the time Elle lay naked on top of her, Gianna had grown light-headed.

Elle fanned the flames with searing kisses. Soon Gianna was moving without restraint and Elle was panting with a struggle greater than the act of just keeping up with her. With a low growl, Elle lifted up and pulled Gianna's shirt from her pants. In quick secession, Gianna's shirt and bra were gone, followed by her shoes and pants. Then warm, silken-smooth skin glided over hers, a thigh pressed between her legs, and she was riding it toward a pleasure that was kept just out of reach. She could no longer keep her voice down. The sound of their skin gliding together, her own soft gasp, and the harsh sound of Elle's breathing rent the air. A cataclysmic explosion nearly choked Gianna as the first orgasm she had ever experienced from other than her own hand destroyed any resolve she had of being quiet. She screamed Elle's name, begging her for something that Elle seemed to understand, because while she was still shuddering, Elle slipped to the side of her. Watching the whole time, Elle slipped a finger through lips drenched with silky passion. She whispered something in Gianna's ear before parting her and claiming her with one small thrust.

Gianna cried out, pulling Elle closer despite the slight pain that seared through her. She opened her eyes to see the wondrous look on Elle's face, but Elle started a rhythm that forced all rational thought from her head. The pain long forgotten, she arched her hips, urging Elle on, and when a second finger stretched her endurance, she opened her eyes to see Elle's mouth moving. She couldn't hear past her own rasping breath and pleading voice, but she could make out the concern mixed with the arousal. She didn't have to hear to know what Elle was saying and it brought tears to her eyes. Why had it taken them so long to find each other? When her body tightened for her next orgasm she saw Elle close her parted lips, and in the seconds of silence that followed she heard Elle's soft breathless whisper, "oh my sweet love," before Gianna was lost to her own pleasure.

❖

Gianna took a deep, shuddering breath and blinked away the vision of their hours of lovemaking before all hell had broken loose. Elle had pleaded with her to go out, but she had been the one too blinded by passion, too caught up in the pleasure to realize they were moving too fast. Funny how that little fact had faded over the years.

She reread Elle's handwritten note, shaking her head but knowing with a certainty that Elle was telling the truth. She'd had no idea that Shallon had been filming herself having sex and had inadvertently caught Elle and Gianna's moment of passion. Elle also wrote that she had been as shocked as Gianna when the rumor mill had informed her that Shallon was bragging about a tape of the two of them making love.

Elle had forced Shallon to give her the tape, but Gianna had already heard about it and refused to see Elle. Elle had finished her last year and a half at State, then had played basketball overseas until she'd been injured. She claimed to have never forgotten Gianna, a fact that was easier for Gianna to believe when Elle confessed she'd held on to Gianna's first amateur attempt at a romance.

Gianna spent much of the drive to the address printed on the card telling herself that it was a mistake to allow Elle back into her life. That regardless of whether she believed Elle, the past was the past. As she'd pulled into a parking spot half a block from the address, two things intrigued her. First was the fact that Elle was already there, waiting outside the building. Elle glanced at her watch and then up the street in the direction Gianna normally would have come. And second was the fact that Elle had asked her to meet her at a pub theater, which according to the marquee didn't open for three more hours. It was already five minutes past two, and Elle looked agitated. Gianna decided to get out of the car. Elle spotted her almost instantly and jogged across the street.

"Hey, you came."

Gianna studied her seriously. "Did you think I wouldn't?"

"I was afraid you might not. You read my letter?"

"I did. I'm not sure if I would have ten years ago, but I don't see any benefit in you lying now."

"I never set out to seduce you. I didn't know that thing was on, but as soon as I found out I made her give me the tape and I destroyed it. Coach threatened to take Shallon's scholarship if there were copies. People may have heard about it, but they didn't see it. Do you believe me?"

Gianna hesitated. She wouldn't just be saying she believed Elle. She would have to let go of all the anger she'd held on to over the years.

"I believe you."

Elle's body seemed to sag with relief. "Really?"

"Yeah, really. I'm sorry I didn't allow you to tell me sooner."

"That's okay. I was angry at you for believing me capable of that anyway. If we had known each other better before we had sex, things might have been different."

"Maybe," Gianna said.

"I got over being mad at you a long time ago. I've read all your books," Elle said shyly.

Gianna flushed. "What did you think of them?"

"They were all great. I love a good mystery. I kept expecting a romance out of you, though."

"I never could write those."

"I liked the one I read."

Gianna laughed. "I haven't had the courage to read it again. Nothing like reading your first attempts at writing to dampen your spirits. I got rid of most of my first attempts a long time ago."

"You won't…"

"No, of course not." It surprised Gianna that Elle would think she would throw away that particular story. She might not read it, but she would never throw that story away. Even ten years later, she still remembered her longing for Elle. The story had been the only way she knew to deal with those emotions.

"Good. Okay then, so do you want to go in with me?"

"It doesn't open until five."

"Not for the public, but it's open to us." Elle held up a key. "My parents own it."

"They own it?"

"Yeah, I worked here all through high school. I always thought it would be a romantic first date. A theater all to ourselves... I don't know, what do you think?"

"Our first date?" Gianna grinned. "I think we're doing this backward."

Elle looked very serious when she said, "Whatever it takes. I had hoped you would finally put an ending on that romance you started in college. It's kind of tough reading it for ten years and always wondering how it would have ended if things had gone differently."

"Maybe we should collaborate?" Gianna said as Elle put the key in the door and turned the lock.

"I'll let you deal with the fiction. I'm going to focus on the real thing."

Jove Belle grew up in southern Idaho and now lives in Portland, Oregon, with her partner of thirteen years. When she's not writing, Jove dedicates her time to chasing her four-year-old around the house, making silly faces at the baby, and being generally grateful for the crazy carnival ride of life. She is the author of two novels with Bold Strokes Books: *Edge of Darkness* and *Split the Aces*.

THREE MINUTES
JOVE BELLE

There are moments, I'm told, that define who you are. Life draws a line and waits for you to step over it. And when you do, you come out on the other side forever changed for having crossed it. Complete rubbish, or so I thought, preferring to believe that change happens slowly over time. And I maintained that healthy bit of cynicism right up until the moment Katie plucked the timer off the bathroom counter and twisted the dial, setting it to go off in three minutes.

I knew, without reservation, this was one of those moments. I swallowed hard, the physical manifestation of the "Oh my God, what have we done?" screaming through my head and out the tips of my super-spiky hair. Katie pulled her boxers up over her hips and gave me that half-smile that melted my insides. The same one that sent my heart tumbling along after her in a headlong rush that hadn't eased in the six years since I'd fallen in love with her.

She placed her hands on either side of me and stepped in close. "I need to wash up."

Our bathroom was tiny, too small for both of us, but it hadn't stopped me from following her through the door when she'd held up that slim white stick a few minutes ago and announced it was time. I shuffled to the right, a not-so-subtle attempt to clear her path to the sink.

She pressed closer, her mouth brushing against my ear. "No, don't move."

This is how we ended up in this position in the first place, that damn smile and her body so close to mine that I couldn't think beyond the need to hold on to the moment, to not let her slip through my fingers.

I heard the splash of water in the sink behind me as I surrendered to the feel of her. Even through the layers of our clothes, I could feel the heat of her skin inviting me in. I wrapped my arms around her waist and nuzzled her neck. God, the smell of her, that light, lingering scent of lavender. Not the manufactured kind that gave me a headache, but the fresh, unmistakable reminder of the garden she loved so much.

That's where I'd found her the first time, only it wasn't her garden, it was my grandmother's. Summer vacation—the three-month reprieve between my junior and senior years at the University of Washington—had just started, and I'd promised to spend it in Boise with my grandmother. The thumpa-thumpa of bass pulsing out of my speakers died abruptly when I killed the engine, and I was instantly surrounded by the Saturday afternoon peace of suburbia—the dull roar of a lawn mower, distant laughter of children, and the unmistakable smell of meat on a grill. I hefted my duffel over my shoulder and started around the house.

"Grams?" I called, more to let her know I'd arrived than anything else. After all, I knew where she would be.

A light breeze rippled across my skin on its way through the neighborhood, carrying the promise of hot summer days and cool, lazy nights. I found her, as expected, knee deep in the field of lavender that made up her backyard. Ambitious wisteria and clematis tangled their way through the chain link that separated Gram's property from the community park on the other side, completely blocking out the dull sheen of metal fencing.

"Lana?" Grams raised her hand to block the sun, an unnecessary effort since her face was already well shaded by a wide-brimmed, floppy hat. "Come give me a hug." For as long as I could remember, that's how Grams greeted every one of us grandkids, with enthusiasm and love. It didn't matter how long it'd been since she'd last seen you.

I dropped my bag and jogged over to her, threw my arms around her waist, and hugged hard enough to pick her up. "I've missed you."

"Put me down." The protest was offered with a smile. "You need to be careful with these old bones."

I knew she didn't mean it, but I placed her back on the ground as requested.

"Yes, Grams." I laughed along with her. Not because anything was particularly funny, but because it was just so good to be in her presence again. Nine months was a long time, and I had the next three to make up for it.

She squeezed my hand, a firm reminder of her love, and stepped to my right until we were both facing the same direction. "There's someone I want you to meet."

Grams said more, I'm sure. She's a well-mannered woman. She never would have left the introductions incomplete like that. Still, I didn't hear another word. My eyes tracked to where she pointed and the world faded away until all that was left was an enchanting woman rising out of the lavender. Her wild tangle of hair tumbled down her shoulders in an untamed wave and all I wanted was to lace my fingers into the reddish gold mane, feel it flow over my skin.

A light spray of freckles fanned out across her nose and cheeks. I wondered if a similar pattern could be found anywhere else on her body and if she'd let me play connect the dots with my tongue. She pulled off her gloves, tucked her hair behind her ears—something I immediately wanted to help her with—and stuck out her hand. She stood there, head tilted to the side, mouth slightly open and curved up on one side, waiting for my brain to stop short-circuiting.

Six years later, she looked at me the same way as we stood together in the too-small bathroom waiting for the timer to wind down. Unlike the day we first met, I didn't repress the need to kiss her. I pulled her in close, dipped my head slightly, and pressed my lips to hers. I tried to impress everything I felt for her, every sweet thought, every dream of happily ever after, into that extended moment of contact.

"Two more minutes," she whispered, her forehead against mine, her eyes, the color of summer sky, full of love, desire, and just a hint of fear.

"Scared?" I traced the line of her jaw with the back of my hand, a promise that everything would be all right.

She took a shaky breath and squeezed me even tighter. "Terrified."

I followed her gaze to the plastic white stick on the bathroom counter. One blue line—the control line, according to the instructions on the box—solidified before my eyes.

"Did you ever think we'd be here?" Her voice was low, husky, with a little tremble tied into it. Her words tore at my heart.

I slid my hands down her arms and laced our fingers together.

"See this?" I lifted her left hand, the diamond and platinum promise prominent on her ring finger. "This is the only place I ever could have been." I brushed my lips over her knuckles. "Here, with you, is the only place I ever want to be, regardless of what that test tells us."

She nodded slowly and closed her eyes. When she opened them again, they were shiny with unshed tears. "Me, too."

I smiled then. Big and real, the kind of smile you can't hide because it starts in your gut and bursts through before you can stop it and once it's out there's no taking it back. "Me, too." It was a faint benediction from my heart, our special way of saying *I love you with everything that I am.*

We'd dated for almost a year before either of us made that declaration. I was too afraid, knowing that my heart would break beyond repair if she didn't share my feelings. But once we said it, we never stopped, until the day of our wedding. When we were supposed to publicly announce our love and devotion, the words that came so easily to us just didn't seem enough.

She walked down the aisle, all flowing white and glowing smile, and my heart was gone. Unfortunately, it took my brain and the ability to articulate along with it. Katie stopped in front of me, those perfect blue eyes mirroring every overwhelming "hold on tight," "run and hide" emotion ripping apart my insides.

The church—stiflingly hot and overflowing with boughs of lavender fresh from Grams's garden—faded into a blur of white noise and static as the minister carried the ceremony forward. I was vaguely aware of a carefully constructed speech about commitment and family extending beyond the bounds of ordinary love, and the words etched themselves into my subconscious to be inspected later. The minister, chosen mainly for her charisma and ability to hold an audience, jolted me back to the moment with the words before "I do."

"Kathryn Mary Taylor"—her voice was laden with serious intent—"do you promise to love, honor, and cherish Lana Corinth Anders, to keep her heart safe for as long as you both shall live?"

Katie looked through her lashes at me, shy with a blatant layer of lust just beneath surface. "I do."

Before the minister, a small-framed, overly serious woman, could ask me the same question, I blurted, "Me, too."

A nervous ripple of laughter washed over the crowd and I touched

Katie's cheek. I was almost there, our lips scant inches apart, when the minister cleared her throat, reminding me that it wasn't time for that yet. I had to earn the privilege of kissing my soon-to-be wife. I pulled back, embarrassed and frustrated. I wanted that day to be perfect. Katie deserved that. More than that, though, I wanted to kiss her.

"Soon." She'd said it quietly, just for me, then tightened her grip on my hand.

Since that day, four years ago, we've relied on that ineloquent, if enthusiastic, declaration when our love feels too big to be expressed by simple words: *Me, too.*

The timer crawled slowly, relentlessly forward. "Who knew three minutes could take so long?" I tried to lighten the mood, ease some of the tension from Katie's body.

"Lana, are you sure you want to do this?" There was that doubt again, like she was waiting for me to disappoint her.

I cupped the back of her neck, willing away her apprehension. "Absolutely. And in a minute we'll know if it worked or if we get to try again next month. Either way, I want this." The sink was hard against my back and I was grateful for the support. No way my legs would have held me up on their own. I wondered if her wavering sense of certainty was about me or her. Did she have doubts that she was trying to project onto me? The walls pressed in and I wanted to lead her out of the bathroom, lay her down, and cover her with my body until she felt safe, protected again, but the timer held me captive.

I pictured us, nine months in the future, a beautiful, tiny version of her curled between us on our bed. I could see the baby, the result of one simple act involving a syringe and some bodily fluid I never wanted anywhere near me in the past. More than that, it was the culmination of our love, the perfect, undeniable, irrevocable expression of our commitment to one another. The magnitude of it humbled me and tears stung my eyes. My throat tightened and I choked on my next sentence.

"I love you." My voice cracked. I swallowed and tried again. "I love that we're doing this, that you want…" I couldn't finish, the emotion building in me too much to hold back. How could I ever express my gratitude, show her the truth in my heart? It was a gift, this precious life I hoped for. How could I quiet the voice of doubt whispering in the back of her mind?

Ding! Katie's mouth hung partially open, her response cut off in the sound of the timer. Her eyes, full of hope and longing, locked on mine. After several moments, we turned and read the results together.

Two lines. Relief and gratitude flooded my body as I wrapped Katie up in my arms. She swayed against me, her breath a hot rush on my skin. I stumbled out of the bathroom not yielding my grip on her and swung her around, too excited to remember her newly defined delicate state.

I set her down, the enormity of those two little lines sobering me, and brushed away her tears with my thumbs, my caress smooth and sure. I pressed my lips to her forehead. "We did it."

Three minutes and two little pink lines and my life was dumped upside down. Forget noble arguments about change being gradual, the culmination of micro-events. Everything good and right in my life—Katie rising like a goddess out of a sea of lavender; saying "I do"; knowing, rather than suspecting, that Katie was pregnant—happened in the blink of time between inhaling and exhaling. I gripped Katie's hand as she marked off days on the calendar, setting the timer for our next life-changing moment nine months in the future.

NELL STARK is currently working on a PhD in medieval English literature in Madison, Wisconsin, where she lives with her partner and their two cats. When she is not teaching, writing, or teaching in the Writing Center, she enjoys reading, cooking, and most sports. She has published two novels with Bold Strokes Books, *Running With the Wind* (March 2007) and *Homecoming* (August 2008). She is also a contributor to several erotica anthologies, including Erotic Interludes *4* and *5* (Bold Strokes), *Wild Nights* and *Fantasy: Untrue Stories of Lesbian Passion* (Bella), and *After Midnight* (Cleis). Nell can be reached at nell.stark@gmail.com, or by visiting www.nellstark.com.

SIGNIFIER, SIGNIFIED
NELL STARK

I hadn't thought seriously about getting a tattoo before I fell in love with Melanie. The idea had always intrigued me, but as I told her—back in one of those early conversations over the phone when we were just getting to know each other—I hadn't found any design or symbol that I was absolutely certain I wanted on my body for the rest of my life. And I needed to be certain.

"Maybe someday," I had said. "If the spirit moves me."

Someday had come and gone. By now, four days after walking into the local tattoo parlor with sweaty palms, the healing itch had faded from maddening to bearable. The tatt was beautiful where it lay nestled in the juncture of my abdomen and left leg, its lines dark and crisp against the vivid whiteness of my thigh.

Mel was going to love it.

For the third time in as many minutes, I glanced up at the clock above the mantle. Just past ten at night. I sighed and shifted in my chair, unable to get comfortable despite the fact that it was my favorite in the house. On my lap, a stack of unread student papers sat neglected. I couldn't concentrate, couldn't focus, couldn't seem to do anything except wait in anticipation for the sound of the front door being opened.

Five days. In the grand scheme of things, five days was inconsequential. But this was the longest business trip Mel had ever taken, and I missed her with an unnerving ferocity. The past several days had felt like the first few years of our relationship, back when we were living a thousand miles apart, unable to see each other for months at a time. Back when all the unchanneled love and need and want pressed in on me so hard that I had trouble taking a deep breath. Back when—

But those times were behind us. Things were different now. Half an hour ago, I had opened a bottle of Silver Oak '95 and poured two glasses, letting it breathe just like Mel taught me. And an hour before that, I had tucked our two children into bed after reading them a story. Now I was lying in wait for her, desperate to cup her face in my palms and kiss her with all the pent-up hunger that had been gathering under my skin since our farewell embrace at the airport. My body was humming and my breaths were shallow, and under the cotton of my sweats, my tattoo ached slightly.

I smiled, thinking about how surprised she would be, and how pleased, when she finally saw it. I already wore her ring and her necklace, but this was a different kind of sign—a reminder that I belonged to her. A vow, inscribed and imprinted. A shared memory etched into my skin for her eyes alone.

"So...last night, while I was taking my shower, I had a thought," she said.

I grinned at the image of her in the shower, water sluicing along the dips and curves of her, and pressed the phone closer to my right ear. "Oh? Was it a sexy thought?"

"I was thinking about us. And these two Chinese characters just popped into my head all of a sudden. I felt compelled to trace them on the wall with my finger."

I sat up straight in my chair, intrigued. "Oh? What ones?"

"The symbol for fire and the symbol for wood."

I bit my lower lip in thought. "Fire and wood. Who...who do you think is which?"

Mel paused then, and I listened to the gentle sounds of her breathing, exhilarated to know that I'd been in her thoughts.

"I think I'm fire," she said finally. "And you're wood. You...you ignite my passion. And enflame it."

Goose bumps broke out on my arms at the strength of the emotion behind her words. "And you make me burn," I whispered.

Mel had given me a lot of grief when I insisted that she'd handed me a tattoo on a silver platter.

"Wood?" she had said, laughing. "You do realize that every single person who can read Chinese is going to see your tattoo and laugh their ass off, right? They'll think you're a dumb white chick who just picked a pretty character without knowing what it meant."

I had shrugged and tried to look mysterious. "Maybe I'll put it in a place where no one but you can see."

Years had passed since that conversation, as I waited for the perfect moment. And now all I had to do was wait a few minutes more. I looked up at the clock and sighed again before finally lifting the papers off my lap and depositing them onto the coffee table. It was useless to even pretend to do work. Where was she, anyway? It usually didn't take this long for a cab to get to our house from the airport. Was there bad traffic? What if there had been an accident? What if *she* had been in an—

The front door clicked open. I sprang from my chair and hurried into the foyer. Mel looked up from kicking off her shoes when she heard my footsteps, dark hair swirling around the collar of her long winter coat. She barely had time to smile before I was pressing her against the door and kissing her deeply. My anxiety disappeared as her lips moved against mine, gentle and yielding.

"Hey, baby," she said softly when I finally pulled back.

"I missed you," I breathed, rememorizing the sight of her face. So familiar, so beloved.

"I missed you back." She tightened her arms around my waist. "Every second."

"Really?"

"Yeah. Really."

She nuzzled briefly at my neck before nipping at my earlobe. I shuddered, but forced myself to take a step back. I watched her smile disappear, to be replaced by confusion.

"Why don't you take off your coat?" I suggested. "Check on the kids. And then come cuddle with me in the den, okay?"

"Okayyy." She looked suspicious. And no wonder—usually I ended up taking her hard against the front door when she'd been away.

"I'll be right there."

I hustled off to the kitchen, threw together a plate of cheese and crackers, and set the plate and our wineglasses on a tray. I found her lounging on the love seat, her stockinged feet propped up on the coffee table. She looked tired. She looked beautiful.

She was mine.

"Wow," she said as I approached. "This is so…romantic."

I rolled my eyes and put the tray down on the table before her, pretending to be hurt. "Why so shocked? Do I not romance you enough?"

She watched me hungrily as I unloaded the tray. "You're an excellent romancer. It's just that usually you fuck me first."

My body tightened at her words. She grinned, loving the effect she had on me. "Well, tonight," I said as I settled in next to her, "we're going to do things backward." I passed her one of the wineglasses, then gently clinked them together. "Welcome home, love."

"Oh," she said after taking a sip, her eyes closing in pleasure. "That's the Silver Oak, isn't it?"

I laughed and draped one arm around her shoulders, relishing the feel of her body pressed against mine. "You're good."

"Mmm," she said, stroking one hand along my thigh. Unbeknownst to her, her fingers skated over the tattoo. I suppressed a shiver. "And you *feel* good."

We told each other stories then, deliberately catching each other up on what had happened while we'd been apart. She made me laugh when she reenacted the performance of a particularly boring speaker. She made me smile proudly when she told me how well her presentation had been received. I fed her bits of cheese and crackers between stories, and she took great pains to curl her tongue around my fingers with every bite. By the time it was my turn to regale her with tales of the kids' antics and my students' rhetorical faux pas, I was reclining on the couch and she was lying on top of me, peppering my neck and chin with kisses.

I was in the middle of a sentence when she finally couldn't stand it anymore and stopped my mouth with her wine-flavored lips. The kiss was hard and demanding, and it ignited the desire in me like droplets of water on hot oil. I cupped the back of her head, pressing her impossibly closer, while I slipped my other hand under her shirt to massage her lower back.

"You feel incredible," I rasped when she broke the kiss. "God, Mel. I need to make love to you. So bad."

She lurched to her feet and silently extended one hand, tugging me up and toward our bedroom. I closed and locked the door while she worked the dimmer switch until a soft twilight bathed the room. I joined her at the foot of the bed, trembling with the force of my need for her.

"I missed you," I said again, unable to suppress the forlorn note in my voice.

"I know, baby. I know." She gathered me into her arms, and I buried my face in the dip between her neck and shoulder, letting her scent wash over me. "It's hard to be apart from you."

I never wanted her to be in pain, but the admission that she needed me—the same way I needed her—was intoxicating. "I have to feel you."

"Then undress me," she whispered, her warm breath cascading over the sensitive shell of my ear.

I stepped back, just far enough so that I could reach between us to unbutton her shirt and slide it off her shoulders. Before it had pooled on the floor, my arms were around her again, fingers fumbling at the clasp of her red satin bra. I kissed her neck as I clumsily unfastened the hooks, and was rewarded by a soft moan.

I let my knuckles brush her breasts as I drew the fabric away from her body, and then I went to one knee to unzip her slacks. I pulled them off slowly, kissing every inch of skin that I revealed. When she stepped out of them, I ran my hands back up her legs before slipping my fingers beneath the sliver of satin between her thighs. And then I looked up to meet her dilated eyes.

"I love you, Mel. I love you so much. I'm starving for you."

She touched my cheek with gentle fingertips. "I'm right here. I'm yours. Take me."

Suddenly, I couldn't do slow anymore. In another moment, she was nude and I was kissing her fiercely even as I walked her toward the bed. But before I could urge her to lie down, she rested one hand over my heart and pushed.

"I need you naked, too."

This was the moment I'd been waiting for. I shucked off my shirt and tossed it into the corner, but then reached out for her hands and guided them to the hem of my sweats. "Take them off."

Her eyes went wide at the command—she loved when I played the top. And then she dropped to both knees, far more gracefully than I had. My pulse surged in anticipation as she worked the pants down over the slight curve of my hips, then down a few inches farther…

"Oh my God." Mel sat back on her heels and looked from the tattoo to me in pure, wide-eyed astonishment. At once pleased and oddly self-conscious, I quirked a smile and shrugged.

"Surprise," I said softly. "What, uh…what do you think?"

She reached out but didn't quite touch it, her fingers hovering just above the crisp black lines. "Can I…?"

"Yes."

She traced it gently with one fingertip, her touch as light as the brush of a rose petal. My skin there was still sensitive, and my eyes closed involuntarily at the rush of sensation. "Oh, Mel."

"Did it hurt?" she asked hoarsely, never ceasing her gentle exploration. Somehow, I forced my eyes open, needing to see her expression.

"It wasn't too bad," I said. "Itched like crazy for the first few days, though."

"It's beautiful," Mel breathed. "I wish I had been there to hold your hand."

I reached down to stroke her hair. "I was thinking about you the whole time," I said. "I needed to do this so…so you'd know."

Gently, she rubbed her thumb along the single vertical line of the character. "So I'd know what?"

I took a deep, shuddering breath. "That I'm yours. All yours. Only yours." I frowned because the words were coming out wrong, as usual. I couldn't tell her how I felt. I could only show her. And that's why being apart from her—even for only five days—was so hard. I looked down at her and shook my head, silently begging her to understand.

"Yes, love," she said. "You're mine." She rested her hands on my hips and leaned forward to retrace the path of her fingers with her tongue. When my knees buckled at the onslaught of sensation, she guided me onto the bed. And when, much later, I begged her to grant me release, she took me with her mouth and her fingers and made me whole again.

We didn't sleep that night. In the early morning hours, we lay spooned together, bodies entwined as the sun broke free of the horizon. I wasn't tired in the slightest—I was at peace. We had half an hour at most before the kids woke up, and I wanted to spend it right here, savoring the advent of a new day with my beloved.

"I love you," I murmured for the thousandth time, pressing a kiss to the base of Mel's neck.

"Mmm," she said, wriggling even closer to me. "Love you back."

"So. When are you going to get *your* tattoo?" I asked, grinning against her so-soft skin.

She turned in my embrace, threaded her arms around my neck, and did her best to look mysterious. Mostly, it was adorable.

"When the spirit moves me."

MERRY SHANNON lives in the sunny mountains of Colorado with her girlfriend and their five pets, and when she's not writing, she works for social services. Her first novel, *Sword of the Guardian*, won two 2006 Golden Crown Literary Society awards, and her most recent work, *Branded Ann*, was released by Bold Strokes Books in January 2008. Keep an eye out for her next project, the second book in the Legends of Ithyria series!

Rebellious Heart
Merry Shannon

Yuri stood outside the apartment door and lifted a hand tremulously, then dropped it again. Had she lost her mind entirely? What had possessed her to visit a *sempai*'s apartment in the middle of the night? It was late, and Jack was probably asleep. But she couldn't get Jack's face out of her mind—the way she'd flinched, the shock that had spread across those beautiful, androgynous features earlier in the afternoon when Yuri had announced her intention to retire.

In all her years dancing for the Takarazuka Revue, Japan's famous all-female theater, Yuri had made only one friend—Jack. She deserved a real explanation, though Yuri still had no idea what she was going to say. How did one express such forbidden, uncontrollable feelings? Her rebellious heart was her curse, and left unchecked, it would destroy them both.

But surely it would be more appropriate to call on Jack in the morning, rather than awakening her at this time of night merely to soothe her own conscience. Sheepishly Yuri turned from the door, but a shuffling sound within caused her to pause uncertainly. Was Jack still awake? She heard another low noise, like sniffling, and before she could change her mind she knocked softly.

"*Dare*?" Jack's voice was even deeper than usual, and Yuri wondered if she had disturbed her friend's sleep after all.

"Kazehiro-san? It's Nagira. I am very sorry to disturb you."

"Yuri-chan?" The door opened. Jack's eyes were red-rimmed and ringed with dark circles. She stared as if she could not believe Yuri was truly there.

"Jack-san, have you been crying?" The words escaped before Yuri could stop them, and she quickly lowered her gaze and bowed in embarrassment. Jack was her *sempai*, her senior, not just in age but also in experience. In the Revue, junior-senior relationships were considered very important. "Forgive me, I have been impertinent. I will leave at once."

"No, please." Jack laid a hand lightly on Yuri's wrist, and Yuri's skin tingled. "Please, come in. I am glad to see you."

Yuri hesitated, wondering if the invitation was made merely out of politeness. She had obviously intruded on a private moment. Sae Kazehiro, playfully dubbed "Jack" by their fellow actresses, had always appeared as strong and self-assured as the men she played on stage. She was the top star of Rain Troupe and received the leading man role in all of their shows. Her natural, friendly confidence made her an excellent leader, and Yuri was not used to seeing her appear so off balance. Her first instinct was to take her despondent friend into her arms, and she quashed that impulse with some horror. It was dangerous to even consider such a thing. She should not have come in the first place, and tried to think of a dignified way to excuse herself. But before she could speak, Jack ducked slightly to catch her eye.

"I am very glad you are here," she repeated. "Those are my true feelings." That was a common saying in Japan—"those are my true feelings"—because the Japanese believed that *tatemae*, the face a person shows to the world, was separate from *honne*, their real thoughts. Yuri knew that people often used the phrase when they did not mean it, but she could not doubt the sincerity in Jack's eyes.

"Thank you," Yuri finally said, allowing herself to be led into the apartment.

"Please sit." Jack indicated the living area. "May I get you some tea?"

Yuri passed through the kitchen and sank with pleasure into the cream-colored leather of the couch. "I do not wish to cause you trouble."

"It's no trouble at all. It's my pleasure."

Yuri watched as Jack filled the silver teakettle with water and placed it on the stove, admiring the graceful, slender fingers that retrieved two teacups from the cabinet and filled strainers from a tin on the counter. Even her smallest movements looked like dancing.

Jack's finely chiseled features, sharp enough to give the illusion of masculinity onstage, were drawn more tightly than usual, as though she was battling some inner grief. Had the announcement of Yuri's retirement truly caused Jack so much distress? Yuri could not believe that. Takarasiennes left the Revue all the time, and some young, fresh face was always right behind, ready to fill the gap.

Jack looked up and caught Yuri's eyes on her. She smiled a little, a charming, melancholic smile that was probably not meant to be flirtatious but made Yuri's heart leap all the same. Yuri blushed, quickly averting her gaze to her hands in her lap. "I must apologize for coming here tonight. I did not mean to disturb you."

Jack made a dismissive noise. "You are always welcome in my home, Yuri-chan. I hope you will remember that even when we are no longer…" Her voice caught strangely and she cleared her throat.

Yuri winced. "Actually, that is why I am here. I didn't mean for you to find out like that. I wanted to explain."

"It's not necessary." Jack brought a tray of small cookies to the low table before the couch and set it down.

Yuri caught the elegant troupe star's sleeve. "Yes, it is." Jack's reddened eyelids, slightly puffy with crying, sent a surge of guilt through her. "But perhaps now is not the time."

"It's me, isn't it?" The question was barely above a whisper, and Yuri stared at her *sempai* in shock.

"No, of course not," she stammered out. "It's my ankle, you know how I've injured it this season. I just can't endure it."

"It's not your ankle. You would dance barefoot on broken glass if it meant you could remain onstage." Jack sat down next to her, though she seemed to be careful not to let their legs or shoulders touch. "I never meant to hurt you. I don't know what came over me." She leaned forward, elbows on her knees, a masculine posture that came naturally after years of practice. "You're the best dancer in the Revue, and I've admired your seriousness and concentration from the beginning. You were so withdrawn when we started in Rain Troupe together. It was like you were afraid of everyone around you and could think of nothing but work. Your loneliness called to me. Even though you were an underclassman, I wanted to be your friend."

"You are!" Yuri interjected, and Jack shook her head sadly.

"A friend would not be so cruel to you as I have been. I had heard the rumors. I knew what you had at stake, how hard you'd fought to save your reputation, and still I—"

Yuri was astonished when Jack covered her face with her hands, her shoulders shaking. She didn't know what to say. She had not imagined that Jack would blame herself for their encounter.

❖

The week before, Jack had asked Yuri for extra rehearsal time after everyone else had left the practice room, as the two of them had been assigned a particularly difficult duet routine for the upcoming show. In typical Takarazuka fashion, the dance told an abstract, melodramatic story about a young boy enticed away from his family home by the seductive Spirit of War. Jack would play the Spirit, in a magnificently garish red-sequined bodysuit and feathered headdress, while Yuri danced the part of the boy.

The complex choreography required precise coordination between the two dancers, and Yuri's role was especially athletic as she repeatedly dropped to her knees or to the floor only to be swept onto her feet again. But even with her bad ankle, Yuri could handle the intricate steps and the heavy physical demands of the routine without much difficulty. The real problem was something far more challenging.

One of the aspects of the Takarazuka Revue that made it so appealing to its fans was the rampant gender bending; the dashing, handsome women sang in deep alto voices, marching around the stage in sharply tailored suits while wooing the smaller, daintier, emphatically feminine actresses. Occasionally a director tried to thrill the audience by taking this gender play a step further, and the dance Jack and Yuri were to perform was one such example. Many of the moves were tantalizingly erotic—torrid embraces in which Jack slid a hand passionately from Yuri's thigh up to her breast, sensual lifts as Yuri wrapped a leg around Jack's waist and was carried through the air. They rehearsed each step over and over again, their heartbeats and respiration increasing, sweat breaking out on their faces and shoulders. And despite her best efforts, Yuri could not help getting caught up in the fire and exhilaration of the music, and the raw sexuality of Jack's body writhing against hers.

As they neared the end of the routine, the young boy lay dying of battle wounds in the Spirit's arms. The Spirit was to bend tenderly over the boy and kiss him at last, drawing him out of his mortal body. Stage kisses were simulated with a well-positioned hand hiding the actresses' lips from view of the audience, and so Jack had taken Yuri's face in her palm and leaned forward, bringing her mouth a few centimeters from Yuri's.

What had happened next had been Yuri's fault. She was supposed to tilt her head back, close her eyes, and pause just long enough to titillate the audience with the suggestion of a kiss—a kiss even more sensational than usual, since both characters were ostensibly male. But as Yuri lay panting in Jack's arms, her blood pounding in her ears, all she could see was Jack moving toward her. Perspiration glistened across her *sempai*'s forehead, unruly strands of hair sticking to her neck, her expression one of rapturous desire as she remained perfectly in character. And instead of closing her eyes, instead of surrendering, Yuri sat up just enough to actually meet Jack's lips with her own.

If that had been all, if it had stopped there, perhaps she could have brushed it off with an embarrassed apology and the excuse that it had been an accident. But the instant their lips touched, Yuri lost all capacity for rational thought. The taste of Jack's mouth, the velvety warmth of her tongue, the soft, deep wetness suddenly open to her… Yuri felt as though something inside her had shattered. She could not stop. When Jack finally pulled back with a gasp, Yuri could barely breathe.

And then, horrified by what she'd done, she'd scrambled to her feet—and ran.

❖

Now Jack's guilt made Yuri feel even worse. What had happened was entirely her fault; she was the one with a history of deviant desires. Now her demons had managed to poison her beloved friend as well. Yuri dug her fingernails into her palms until she could feel the skin part beneath them.

The teakettle whistled sharply and Jack straightened, wiping her eyes and going to the kitchen. She removed the kettle from the heat and the whistle quieted.

"I'm going to make it right, Yuri, I promise. You shouldn't feel that you must leave because of me. Tomorrow I will go to the board and announce my retirement."

"No!" Yuri exclaimed. "You mustn't, the troupe needs you. You're our top star!"

"It doesn't matter." Jack's hand trembled slightly as she poured the boiling water into the teacups, releasing clouds of steam. "My behavior was inexcusable. You love Takarazuka more than any of us, I think. You told me once that you would die if you could not dance. You have worked so hard to be here, and you do not deserve to be forced out by your foolish, clumsy *sempai*." Her smile was probably meant to lighten the mood, but it only increased Yuri's suffering.

"No, Kazehiro-san, I won't let you do that." She went to the kitchen counter opposite Jack. Sliding the teacups out of the way, she took Jack's hands and stared her directly in the face. The anguish she saw there turned her stomach. Yuri closed her eyes. "They weren't just rumors."

"What?"

"The things you've heard. They weren't just rumors. They're true. Well, most of them, anyway."

"Yuri, you don't have to tell me…"

Yuri opened her eyes again and her voice shook. "You need to know. It wasn't your fault. None of this is your fault." Their faces were too close together, and her gaze drifted uncontrollably to Jack's lips, that soft, sensual mouth just centimeters from her own. Her breath hitched for a second before her brain took over. Backing away quickly, Yuri released Jack's hands. "I don't know what's wrong with me. I've always been this way, wanting things I shouldn't. It's already cost one friend her career. I won't let it take yours as well." She began to pace as the words spilled out.

"My second year in TMS I was assigned to supervise the three first-years who cleaned the north cafeteria. One of them, Ayako, began to follow me everywhere when we weren't in classes. She would tease that one day we would be partnered as top stars together. She was a cute girl. I liked her, so I did what I could to help her. Some of her classmates were jealous, I think, because she got so much of my attention. One day they dared her to kiss me."

Yuri could not look at Jack, and her cheeks burned. "So she did.

Not a stage kiss like we'd learned, but a real kiss. I liked it far more than I should have." The admission was embarrassing. "Ayako would have done anything I asked, and I couldn't stop thinking about her after that. I was far too bold then, far too sure of myself. And she didn't know any better. We…" Yuri struggled with the words. "We became…"

"You became lovers."

Yuri's head shot up, but she detected none of the condemnation she would have expected in Jack's tone. Jack was watching her intently, her dark eyes full of unexpected sympathy. Yuri nodded. Jack picked up the teacups and returned to the couch. She settled in the far corner, placing one of the cups down on the table. "What happened?" It was a gentle question, without accusation or judgment. Her relaxed tone calmed Yuri's nerves slightly.

"Well, you can't share a dormitory with two hundred other girls and keep a secret like that forever." Yuri gave a short, mirthless laugh. "We were caught. The school committee wanted to expel us both, but…"

"But you were at the top of your class. Too valuable to lose."

"It wasn't just that." Yuri sighed heavily and joined Jack on the couch. "My father has powerful influence with the Takarazuka board. He makes large donations to the Revue every year. They did not want to risk angering or shaming him by expelling his daughter for…indecent behavior. But Ayako was not so fortunate. She came from a poor fishing village on the southern coast, and the committee decided that expelling her would be punishment for us both. I didn't even get to say good-bye. She was just… *gone*."

The memory was still unbearably painful. Ayako had told Yuri all about the years she had spent training before the entrance exams, learning ballet from self-instruction videos and books since her parents could not afford formal lessons. She failed the auditions two years in a row before she was finally accepted, thanks in large part to her sweet singing voice and likeable, engaging manner. Takarazuka was, she often said, the greatest thing that had ever happened to her. And Yuri had robbed her of that dream before she'd even been able to set foot on the stage.

"I won't let it happen again," she declared abruptly. "What happened between us"—a light tremor ran unbidden through her body as she remembered the kiss—"wasn't your fault. I don't know why I do this to people. I can't help it." She couldn't bear to meet Jack's eyes. "I can't even be in the same room with you without wanting to touch you. It's all I can think about, how beautiful and strong and clever and kind you are." She heard Jack's sharp intake of breath and rose to her feet quickly, humiliation scorching her face.

"I'm sorry, Kazehiro-san. I have no right to say any of this to you. But this is why I have to leave Takarazuka now, before I hurt anyone else. Please don't blame yourself." She stumbled around the low table and gave a brief, polite bow. "It is late. I will bother you no longer."

"Yuri-chan." Jack rose to her feet and placed her hands on Yuri's shoulders.

Yuri squeezed her eyes shut and wriggled away. "Don't touch me, *sempai*, please don't."

"Yuri," Jack said again, her deep tones suddenly authoritative, "you are not leaving until you listen to me. Sit down."

Yuri sat instinctively. Jack used that commanding voice in rehearsals and she was accustomed to obeying it. Jack knelt by her feet, looking up at her, and Yuri turned her face to avoid eye contact. "First of all, you didn't make me do anything I didn't want to do. I kissed you because I wanted to."

Yuri shook her head. Jack lifted Yuri's chin with one hand. Her eyes were bright with tears. "You captured me with your sadness from the first day I saw you. The way you danced, as though your heart would fail to beat if you stopped." She brushed Yuri's cheek softly with her thumb. "You shrank from everyone like a shadow, but onstage you suddenly burst into a thousand stars. I longed to see you carry that smile with you offstage as well."

"Jack…"

"I wanted to be near to you, to get to know you. And once you came to trust me, Yuri-chan, I found so much passion and life behind your shyness. When we danced together I felt like I was a part of that passion. I was honored that you would open yourself to me…and I kissed you because it was the only way to express my feelings."

Yuri could not believe what she was hearing, and she shook her head vehemently. "No, it's not true. It can't be."

"Why not? If you can have these feelings, Yuri-chan, why can't I?" Jack's rebuke was quiet.

"Because you weren't meant to have them," Yuri cried, backing away. "It was me, I…"

Jack caught Yuri's face between her hands and laid a finger to her lips. "Shh. Listen to me. Do you really believe that out of six hundred Takarasiennes, you are the only one attracted to women?"

Yuri's lips parted in astonishment. Wasn't she? Jack's hand traced the side of her face, tucking hair behind her ears. "Are you surprised? The board is anxious to preserve the image of Takarazuka. It's something no one speaks of, but we all know it is there. You have nothing to be ashamed of, Yuri. And you are not alone."

Unexpectedly Jack leaned forward and brushed Yuri's lips with her own. Yuri whimpered and closed her eyes, fighting back the wave of desire and longing that flooded her body, but it was too much. Jack's kiss was tender and impossibly soft, and Yuri felt like she was melting inside. Jack pulled away slowly and Yuri opened her eyes to see the beautiful troupe star gazing at her earnestly.

"*Aishiteru*, Yuri. I love you."

"Jack…" But she did not have the chance to say anything more, because Jack suddenly took Yuri into her arms and kissed her again, more insistently this time, pressing Yuri back into the couch. Yuri could not help herself. She entwined her fingers in her *sempai*'s choppy, bleached hair as Jack trailed a line of searing kisses across her jaw.

"Please don't leave Takarazuka, Yuri-chan," Jack mumbled into her ear, nuzzling sweetly against Yuri's neck. "Please don't go."

As Yuri ran her hands along Jack's solid, muscled back, pulling her even closer, she found herself thinking that perhaps her rebellious heart was not such a curse after all.

LEE LYNCH has been proudly writing lesbian stories since the 1960s when she was a frequent contributor to *The Ladder*, the only lesbian publication at the time. Since then she has published a baker's dozen books, her stories have appeared in a number of anthologies and magazines, and she has written reviews and feature articles for *The Lambda Book Report* and many other publications. Her syndicated column, The Amazon Trail, has been running since 1986.

Her novels include: *Beggar of Love* (2009), *Sweet Creek* (2006), *Toothpick House*, *Old Dyke Tales*, *The Swashbuckler*, *Home in Your Hands*, *The Amazon Trail*, *Sue Slate, Private Eye*, *That Old Studebaker*, *Dusty's Queen of Hearts Diner*, *Morton River Valley*, *Rafferty Street*, *Cactus Love*, and *Off the Rag*.

GIFTS
LEE LYNCH

Their first Christmas Angela made a gift of herself. While Tam showered, she'd put on a white lace bra and silky white panties under a red sateen robe and tied a red ribbon around one wrist. She'd arranged the wrapped gifts around her body as she slid partly under the Christmas tree.

She'd been twenty-two, Tam eighteen. She'd bought Tam a fringed leather vest, a heavy peace symbol necklace, and an olive fatigue jacket from the Army-Navy store. Her own new underwear was for Tam too. She wasn't sure Tam would like the other gifts—they were so new as a couple she didn't know enough about her, but Tam wore bell bottoms and sometimes, a paisley bandana rolled into a headband. With all the long-haired men around, Tam, short-haired, could have been one of them. And to see her among the gay guys when they went down to the city—the men themselves said Tam would have made a beautiful gayboy.

The shower stopped. She gave Tam time to dry herself, then called to her. This gift she knew Tam would like.

"I'm not dressed yet!" Tam answered, moving toward the bedroom.

"Tam?"

It took Tam a minute to locate her. Tam was wrapped in one of their too-small, faded bath towels and Angela promised herself that she'd style some hair off the books to buy them luxurious towels soon.

"What're you doing under the tree, Angie, peeking at presents?" asked Tam, laughing.

Angela held up her left wrist and displayed the red bow. "It looks like Santa left you a great big present."

By then Tam was on her knees, looking at her in her bra and panties. "Oh my gosh," said Tam, who came from the hill on the other side of town where they were too good, or too rich, to let their kids curse.

She'd thought Tam would help her move the gifts aside and they'd go to bed, but Tam, smelling of her Halo shampoo, radiating the shower's damp heat, had jumped her already, was kissing her and running her hands along her arms and sides and up into her hair. The girl was all heat, sucking her nipples though the lacy bra until the fabric was soaked. Angela swung her arms and legs as if to make a snow angel in order to push the packages away, in the process feeling an amazing amount of wetness soak her panties.

Tam was reaching down her stomach. It wasn't often that Tam groaned, but this morning, under the Christmas tree, when her fingers found Angela's heat, she groaned, shaking right along with Angela.

"Take my panties off, Tam. Please, take them off me now."

Tam got cute and pulled them down, first the left side, then the right, with her teeth. Angela found herself lifting up, her mons seeking Tam's mouth. Tam was still trying to roll Angela's panties down her thighs. Her towel was long gone. While Tam was off balance, Angela turned her onto her back, away from the tree, took off her panties, but not the bra, spread herself open, and mounted Tam's thigh, all hard muscle from biking up and down that hill on the good side of town. She snaked her hand between Tam's legs and moved the flat of her fingertips against Tam's prominent clit to the rhythm of her own movement.

"Angie," Tam said with the quiet, urgent voice that signaled she was ready to come, but Angela was too close herself to reply, to worry about the tree, the presents, the neighbors hearing them. They were pleasure stripped of self: no Angela, no Tam, just a melding of two crazy hot bodies that left her limp with adoration. Tam turned her on by doing nothing but being herself.

Five years later, Angela was spending her first Christmas alone; Tam was, as usual, with her parents and grandparents, while Angela had put her foot down. She wanted Tam home with her, like their first Christmas, and she was staying home to prove her point. The night before, she'd gone over to her parents' apartment behind their candy store on Cannon Street and dropped off their gifts. She'd also called them this morning, before they went to the big shindig at Aunt Rosa's. She thought her mother would cry—their first holiday without Angela! Tam, clearly tense and avoiding her eyes, exchanged gifts with her, then left to spend the rest of the holiday with her family on the hill. The Thorpes would keep her as long as possible, bribing their innocent lamb to stay away from her life on the other side of the tracks with that penniless young hair person who knew a good thing when she saw it. Though she owned the shop, Angela didn't make much money yet and she felt as low as they made her out to be when Tam left her for holidays. Someday they would swallow Tam alive and she just plain would not come home.

Idly, she went to the television, but the programs were all about the holiday and the Soviet Union shipping rockets to North Vietnam. Thinking about the guys she knew who were fighting over there wasn't going to help. She made herself imagine the hours stretched ahead of her as a special treat, not a bleak and lonesome holiday. It was only noon. She changed into tall boots and a car coat and went outside.

The sky was a cold blue, with perhaps a dozen small, high, benign clouds, but with no wind off the Hudson to speak of, she was comfortable. Small mounds of snow were left over from two weeks ago. The down-at-the-heels first-floor flat she and Tam rented—in the only section of Roosevelt they could afford with all the commuters moving up from the city—was two blocks from the marina. In summer, the boat slips were filled and boaters' cars were parked well up past their place. While Tam studied on Sundays, Angela watched first the fishermen, then the sailing crowd, and later in the mornings, the yacht owners, lug their gear. The weekly newspaper, printed at the shop where Tam worked, had been full of some developer's plan to level these old houses and pave a parking lot for the boaters. Meanwhile, the area had been home for five years and Angela loved its ramshackle quality: the porches used as storage, kids' new Christmas toys left in the yards, scruffy dogs and children who greeted her like a long-lost friend. And she loved the memories, like that first Christmas under the tree.

It was 1:35, she saw on the tiny gold watch Tam had given her that morning. From most of the houses came the scent of turkey and herbed stuffings. Like her family, the Tabors, they would sit down to dinner at 2:00 p.m.

Maybe next year, or the next, Tam would see that saying no to their families did not end the world. Angela felt saddest about losing the big, warm, noisy holiday meal. Someday her mother and Aunt Rosa would be old and she could offer to cook the turkey. Maybe Aunt Rosa would come over then to fill her home with her big laugh, and her mother would bring her worried nagging. Maybe by then they wouldn't mind so much about Angela being with Tam. If she only knew some gay people, she would invite them all, stuff the house, lure Tam away from the cold, conniving Thorpes with the hot smell of holiday turkey. At least her own family, no less pigheaded about her and Tam being lovers, had it out, yelling back and forth about who was wrong.

It was colder at the marina, where the river sloshed gently against the wooden piles as it ran toward the Atlantic, but it simply was not Christmas without a walk by the water. She didn't want to walk later when she might run into the Tabor clan. That would be too sad. From a marsh to the east of Maple Beach rose a heron, long-legged and bottom-heavy. A few were year-round residents, *like the rest of us working stiffs*, Daddy would intone during every Christmas walk. He tried so hard to use American slang, his accent still as awkward as the lumbering heron's take-off. A smattering of mallards swam under and around the floating docks. Angela tossed them the handfuls of table scraps she'd been saving. Christmas dinner, she thought, as she watched them grab and squabble, quacking at one another.

She didn't want to dwell on the fight she'd had with Tam last night about Christmas. It had been too ugly. Tam had never seemed cold like the rest of the Thorpes before. Her good looks had been deformed by fury and conflict. Her compact, confident body had been slouched in on itself. Tam had turned out to be, so far, as unforgiving as the Thorpes were.

Angela had only asked Tam if they could talk about the holidays. Without anger, she'd added. At the shop when a knotty problem came up, she and the other hairdressers would hash it out, often over a few hours, as they worked. Like the day she'd learned that the guy who supplied her with everything from shampoo to capes was closing up and retiring to Florida. They'd all chewed on that until one came up with a place she'd heard was good, another spent time with the yellow pages, another called a relative who owned three beauty parlors, all about the same size as her own. Each suggestion had its merits and when she'd objected to all the new paperwork if she used more than one supplier, Maxine had volunteered to do some ordering and Karen, as it eventually turned out, had taken over the books altogether.

"Why shouldn't talking about our problem at home work as well?" she'd asked Tam.

Tam's voice was barely louder than a mumble, a certain sign of anger. "You just want to bring me around to your way of thinking."

"That's not true! If we put our heads together we may come up with a new solution."

"There is no solution," said Tam into her textbook, "new or old."

Angela was standing at the windows, about to close the drapes against the darkening sky. "Tam, we don't know that."

"Angie," Tam commanded, holding up her book and the blank page of a notebook. "I'm trying to study."

"And I'm trying to get you to give a little time to solving a miserable mess that gets in our way at least four times a year, honey." She knew she had stooped to pleading. "Ignoring it won't make it any better."

Tam closed her book slowly, marking her place and squaring corners with her notebook. She turned toward Angela, eyes still hard and voice all too low. "All right. So talk about it."

Angela felt silenced, as if Tam had thrown up a wall and simultaneously drained her of will and strength. She sat on the wooden arm of their plaid couch and folded her hands on her knees. "Tam," she said with great sadness, remembering the tomboy freshman with the pixie haircut she'd first seen in high school, "we won't get anywhere if you're angry."

Tam stood and threw her arms in the air. "First you want to wheedle me into something I think is dumb. Now you tell me how I'm supposed to feel while I'm doing it. Anything else you want, baby?"

"What is wrong with you? I'm not asking for the moon. We're two grown-up people, Tam. Lovers. We ought to be able to have a discussion."

"Lovers? Lovers?" Tam cried. "You call this being lovers? Every time I've come near you for the past six months you've shrunk away like I'm some kind of monster."

"Which is one reason I think we have to talk this thing out."

Tam stared at her. "Are you saying this holiday mess has been freezing you up?"

"Don't you think our families are coming between us?"

Tam wouldn't look at her. She stood, mute, twisting her fingers like someone being called on the carpet. She looked up once, then slumped into her chair.

"Maybe it's a fact of your life, Tam, but things are about to change for me." Tam looked up quickly, a frown drawing her eyebrows together. Without planning to, Angela said, "I'm not going to spend Christmas Day at Aunt Rosa's. I'll spend it alone if I have to."

"See?" Tam said, her voice sharp. "Wasn't it easier for you to just announce this, this ultimatum and not pretend we decided it together?"

Angela wanted to push Tam into the Christmas tree, into that deep piney scent, so the lights and bulbs would smash into tiny pieces, like their lives together. "You want to know when I decided that, Tam?" she challenged. "I decided it as I said it. I don't know why you think I'm plotting against you"—oh, no, the tears were coming—"but I'm not. I'm only loving you."

Tam glowered at her. Angela did cry, hiding her face in her hands. She heard Tam leave the room. Drawers opened and closed. *Good*, she remembered thinking, *she's going to bed*. They often made up in bed, cuddling.

There was something about the pure intimacy of cuddling, its undemanding safety, that made sex feel like it was more about loving than at any other time. Tam was such a complicated person, with all the hang-ups her family had instilled in her and her ambitions and beliefs— and her choice to stay in Roosevelt with Angela and support herself through college rather than take her parents' money. It was heavenly when she stopped working, studying, and balancing all her worlds long enough to simply lie with Angela in her arms. They'd talk and laugh, kiss now and then, just be close. As the feeling of closeness deepened, Angela could feel them merging. Sometimes they would fall asleep like that, but other times, at a certain point, a spark would leap between them and they'd find themselves on fire for each other.

"Tam," she would say. "My darling."

The word "darling" never failed to ignite Tam. Her body would seem to gain heft and broaden. She'd feel like Tam could carry her across the river in her arms on a rope bridge in a hurricane, wild beasts at their heels. Instead, Tam became the hurricane, hands flying like wind, lips and tongue like warm rain pelting her skin. She felt like a love song when she touched Tam's soft skin, her feathery hair, her pellet-like nipples that required so little to stand at attention. When Tam took over, though, it was as if Angela was the violin, Tam the bow; Angela the piano, Tam the talented fingers; Angela the drum Tam played with light rhythmic sticks and brushes.

Those were the times Angela surrendered herself, let herself be played, left Tam to find her own release. She was only part of this phenomenon that was Tam impassioned. What Tam did to her excited them both. When Tam finally entered her with those strong, swift, seeking fingers, Angela's body relaxed as if it had been longing for just that, and she opened wider. Orgasm was a long note of unearthly pleasure.

Her tears had stopped. She huddled in a corner of the couch, exhausted and not yet ready to go to Tam.

"I'll see you after dinner tomorrow," Tam had said, moving swiftly through the living room. Before Angela could say or ask anything, Tam had been gone, an old airline bag in one hand, a shopping bag of gifts for the Thorpes in the other, and the scent of frigid air blowing into the apartment. Angela did not rise from the couch for hours that night. The Thorpes, she thought, would be triumphant to have Tam, obviously upset, spend the night. It wasn't until she got into bed by herself that she went icy with the question: did Tam really go to her parents' home?

As she walked through the park in the cold light of Christmas afternoon, a flock of crows grew raucous in the taller trees. She realized that she'd just replayed the whole miserable argument yet again. She still did not know where Tam spent last night. Twice before she'd stayed away all night, but she'd called and said she had so much work to do at the library that she was sleeping on the teacher's couch again, the teacher who had taken her in during a snow storm one night last year.

Cannon Street was utterly deserted. She shivered. The day wasn't raw, but it wasn't warm either. Every shop was as familiar as her face in the mirror. The books in the window of the rental library always looked so enticing. The mock wedding cake at the baker's made her long for the wedding she'd denied her mother. Would life have been easier in this rough time with Tam if they'd been blessed instead of shunned? She envisioned her dapper, boyish Tam, hair cut to a perfection of wave and d.a., in a black tux, that sullen, too good-looking face above a bowtie and stiff white collar. And herself, all in satiny white, a delicate lacy cap atop her multitude of tiny curls, arm in arm with Tam.

The mock wedding cake in the bakery window, she noticed, needed dusting. Down the street her family's candy store, closed today, looked forlorn without the newest generation of brats hitting one another, or slurping cherry Cokes, the current neighborhood rage, through straws. She stood in the middle of the sidewalk feeling bereft. Five years ago, love had transformed the world. The grass had looked greener, the river bluer, the birds had sounded as excited as she'd felt.

Tam was as delicately handsome as ever, but being touched or touching her seemed forced when they had this anger between them. And at them. It wasn't that she thought of Mommy crying or Daddy's hurt, puzzled face every time she kissed Tam, or of the railroad station cleaner who still leered at her after catching her all those years ago with her first lover, Jefferson, making out in what they'd thought was a deserted hallway. It wasn't that she thought, when they made love, about what Tam had lost by coming to her, or that she dwelt on the fear of what would happen if her customers knew what she was. The bed got awfully crowded, though, with all of them hovering, bound and determined to have their disapproval heard.

She dreaded returning to the empty flat. They would be sitting down to dinner at Aunt Rosa's. Someone would ask who was saying grace. Bald Uncle Bert would cheerily cry out, "Grace!" His ever-scowling brother Martin would fold his hands and say an earnest blessing, then pandemonium would take over with the passing of too many dishes at once, one of the uncles pulling out a flask and pouring a shot into Grandma's tea, and some little cousin spilling cider on the good holiday tablecloth. She was thirsty. Her feet were cold. Her lower back ached. And she felt alone, as if Tam was never coming home.

She turned toward Aunt Rosa's. The cold had seeped through her car coat and into the gaps left between its barrel buttons. The river smelled fetid right here, where the factory disgorged its waste. She needed some sort of family, didn't she?

The playground lay between Cannon Street and Aunt Rosa's. As she approached, hands in her pockets, knuckles against the bristles of the hairbrush she always carried, fingers curled around the cold metal cylinder of her lipstick, collar turned up and buttoned against a rising wind, she could hear the sound of someone slapping a pink spaldeen against the handball court wall. Tam loved handball. She'd beaten the boys in school enough times that they wouldn't risk certain humiliation.

The cold wind was making her eyes tear. She walked on, regretting her need to go to Aunt Rosa's. She felt, despite Tam's decision, like she was betraying Tam, and herself, because this was wrong, this denial of their little family of two. The sound of the ball got louder. The players were really smashing it around the court. Kids, whacking the heck out of new balls they got for the holiday.

Had Tam spent the night with her family? Was she seeing someone in the city? She had a whole life at school that was separate and probably filled with temptations: girls who were more educated than Angela, older women who would find Tam irresistible, bars where she could meet other lesbians. She laughed at herself; what else did she want to worry about on Christmas Day?

The handball players were on the other side of the court, behind the concrete wall. Aunt Rosa's was just beyond. Should she turn back? No, she wanted to see the kids enjoying their new spaldeens. It would be a kind of Christmas celebration for her, sharing that little joy. Then she wouldn't need to join her family. She'd go home, make some hot chocolate, and be there when Tam arrived, a light dinner awaiting her after the holiday meal. She'd walked off her loneliness and felt good. Everybody had conflicts around holidays, theirs were just a little more complex than some.

An old airline bag leaned against the fence, a shopping bag filled with wrapped gifts beside it. That Christmas paper looked familiar. She knew the bag too. What was Tam doing here, not with some college girl, not with the Thorpes?

Tam kept playing as she walked onto the court. "I thought you were at your aunt's," Tam called.

"I almost gave in, but then I saw you," Angela said. "What're you doing here, Tam?"

"Waiting to catch you on your way home from your aunt's. I, ah, stopped by the house. You weren't there, so I figured—"

She felt a smile take over her face. Tam had known she'd give in and go to her family. "Oh, Tam," she said, moving forward into her arms.

Tam whispered to her, "I told my family it wasn't right, tearing us away from each other on the holidays. I gave them a choice: both or neither. I left their presents there and came home."

She asked, "Then what are these?"

"Gifts I didn't give them. I think there's enough here for your family. I thought you could run in with them."

They had stepped away from each other, conscious as always of the windows lining the streets to either side of them, of the danger that the wrong person would be looking out a window at the wrong time. The automatic jolt of fear was there, as usual, but Tam's announcement that she'd stood up to her family, stood up for being with her lover, seeped into her like heat.

Her teeth stopped chattering. For the first time in a long while, she wanted nothing more than to go home and pull Tam into the bedroom, onto the bed, and bury her mouth between Tam's legs till the bed rattled with their passion. Tam's round eyes, with a slant to them that increased with her smile, went all soft the way they did when she wanted to make love.

"First," Angela told Tam, "first, we're going to Aunt Rosa's. You're going to give them their gifts. If they don't insist we stay today, they'll regret it for a year. What do you bet we get asked for cherry pie on Washington's Birthday?"

"Wait a minute," Tam objected, laughing. "What about champagne on New Year's Eve?"

"Hot dogs for the Fourth?"

"Spaghetti on Columbus Day?"

Angela stopped at the steps to Aunt Rosa's and straightened Tam's collar, handed her hairbrush to her. "I've missed you, my darling Tam," she said.

"I thought we were going to split up," Tam told her, eyes filling with tears.

She shook her head no. "Let's go break the ice—not us—shall we?"

Tam pulled her lips between her teeth the way she did when she was nervous.

"You can do this," she told Tam. She pictured the long-legged, heavy heron that had lifted itself to flight before her eyes. "I love you for doing this." She followed as Tam took the stairs to Aunt Rosa's two at a time.

ALI VALI lives right outside New Orleans with her partner of many years. As a writer, she couldn't ask for a better more beautiful place, so full of real-life characters to fuel the imagination. When she isn't writing, working in the yard, cheering for the LSU Tigers, or riding her bicycle, Ali makes a living in the nonprofit sector.

Ali has written *The Devil Inside*, *Carly's Sound*, *The Devil Unleashed*, *Second Season*, *Deal With the Devil*, and the forthcoming *Calling the Dead* (available in November 2008).

ROMANTIC DEVIL
ALI VALI

Emma Casey stood at her front door and kissed her son Hayden good-bye as he left for school. Her younger child Hannah was somewhere behind her, making the household staff earn their pay by trying to keep both her and everything within reach of her small hands in one piece.

The routine of school, child care, and taking care of her partner Cain kept her busier than any full-time job, but it was something Emma cherished after her self-imposed exile. Acceptance of her life and the woman she shared it with had come only after she'd walked alone for too long. Derby Cain Casey was the love everyone dreamed to find, but she was also the head of one of New Orleans's crime families. To Emma she could've been the devil incarnate and it wouldn't have mattered. Emma had found her place and it was at Cain's side. Now she had to only work to prove herself to Cain so that they could move on from her mistakes to share a better relationship than they'd had.

Close by Emma heard Hannah let out a shriek followed by giggles, and that could only mean Cain had found her and tossed her in the air. To the outside world Cain was a mobster, but here she was just head playmate to her children and loving spouse. It was two roles she did well.

"If she throws up egg all over that great suit, don't come crying to me," Emma told Cain when she found her with Hannah lifted over her head. The tease made Cain cradle Hannah in her arms and tickle her. "What's on your agenda for today?"

"I've got a few meetings with our new partners this morning, then I thought I'd ask my wife to lunch." Cain put Hannah down after she kissed her forehead. "Unless she's busy," Cain said, and kissed Emma next.

"I'll squeeze you in, but only because I like you so much." Emma rested her chin on Cain's chest so she could look up at the face that dominated her dreams from the day they'd met. "Thanks for asking, since I've hardly seen you in the last couple of weeks."

"Considering you asked for ID when I came to bed last night, I thought it was time to forget about business for a little while and concentrate on the important things." Cain combed Emma's hair back and ran her fingers along the blond eyebrows. "I've missed you for a lot of reasons, but mostly for all the small things like lunch."

Emma peeked over her shoulder to make sure Hannah wasn't about to stick something into an electric socket and smiled when she saw their housekeeper carrying her toward the kitchen. "I was thinking the same thing, and I don't know why. It's funny that I'd miss you this much since I spend all night with you, but I do."

"We have a lot to catch up on as a family, but there's even more to rediscover as a couple."

"God, I thought I was being selfish for thinking that way," Emma said as she wrapped her arms more tightly around Cain's waist. "I love you and the family we have, but I miss us."

Cain cupped the side of Emma's neck and lowered her head to kiss her. "Sounds like you're as ready to be romanced as I am to romance you."

"You romance me every day," Emma said, but it felt good to hear Cain say it. "Don't think you're neglectful in that area, and don't feel that I don't love being mama."

"How about you get dressed and meet me downtown at noon? I'll call with the details later."

Cain kissed her again, but it wasn't long enough for Emma, who watched her until the door closed behind her.

"Chill, Emma, or you're going to freak her out," Emma whispered to herself, but she wasn't lying about missing Cain and the heat they generated as a couple.

By noon they were seated next to each other at a table in the corner of Antoine's in the French Quarter with a bottle of wine on the table. Cain sat back, relaxed, and studied the expression on Emma's face. Because of their history together, Cain knew her wife was daydreaming, which she did herself on occasion, but not usually during lunch and not when the subject of most of her fantasies was sitting across from her.

"What are you thinking about?" Cain asked.

"The first time you asked me out." The chilled light white wine was one of Emma's favorites, and Cain refilled her glass after Emma took another sip. "Are you trying to make me lower my defenses?"

"Absolutely, though thankfully that's gotten easier over the years."

"I never did have any defense against you, so stop telling tall tales, mobster." Emma placed her hand in the one Cain was offering and leaned in. "Tell me another story and I'll see if you remember all the particulars."

❖

"Do I want to go out with you tomorrow night?"

Cain sat on a bar stool in her pub, the Erin Go Braugh, in the Quarter and tried not to laugh out loud. "I'm taking into consideration that I don't date much, at least not in the conventional sense, but I'm fairly sure the answer to that question is yes or no." Emma hadn't lost that deer in the headlights appearance, so she went on. "If the rules of engagement have changed, and now you're supposed to repeat every word I say, that'll get annoying fast."

"I'm sorry, it's that I'm shocked you'd ask me anything after last night." Emma was wiping her hands with a bar towel as if she'd gotten nuclear waste on them.

"A little spilled beer never did anything but make an Irishman cry. So how about it?"

"What'd you have in mind?" Emma asked, still rubbing her fingers with the towel.

A few feet away Cain could hear her brother Billy laugh, most probably at her expense. Getting a woman to go out with her was never this difficult. "You want a complete itinerary?"

"No, I just want to know what to wear." Emma threw her towel on the bar only to have it land in Cain's half-full glass. "Oh jeez." She moved to yank it out and knocked one of the other waiters into Cain. When she looked again, her boss was dripping with spilt beer.

"I don't know about you," Cain said, "but I'm wearing a rain coat."

❖

Emma laughed and tapped her wineglass against Cain's. "I'd forgotten about that."

"Mighty convenient of you, Mrs. Casey," Cain said as she removed the last of the oysters Rockefeller they'd ordered as an appetizer from its shell and fed it to Emma.

"I couldn't help it back then, honey, you made me nervous," Emma said after she swallowed. "Besides, if I hadn't been such a bumpkin, you wouldn't have such a good story to embarrass me with."

Cain filled their glasses again and pushed Emma's closer as an encouragement to take a sip. "I don't tell that story to embarrass you. Every once in a while I love thinking about that shy farmer's daughter because it makes me realize what a lucky bastard I am. You started off shy but you've come into your own, and the results are beautiful."

"I hope you know how much I love it when you talk to me like this, but you can relax if you want. You're getting lucky even if it's downhill from here."

The waiters came out with two trout almandine dishes, but Cain never let go of Emma's hand as they were served. Their first date hadn't been very different from this one, and in a way, it was as if Cain had gone out of her way to re-create it.

"Are we going out for coffee and beignets after this?" Emma asked, because that's what they'd done after that first date. Emma had momentarily panicked when Cain had asked for the check, not caring to hear the dessert specials. She'd started breathing again when Cain held her hand all the way to Café Du Monde and ordered their famous café au lait and beignets.

"I had something else in mind this time, but if you want, we can stay here and try their famous baked Alaska." Cain placed her hand on Emma's forearm and stroked the soft cashmere fabric. It was like she couldn't help but admire Emma's choice of outfit again.

The temperatures in the city were cool, but nothing like the cold they'd encountered in Wisconsin while they visited Emma's father, so Emma had picked a fairly short skirt, tight sweater, and pumps. When she'd purchased them the salesman had given her more than a few compliments on how well the clothes fit, but nothing came close to letting Emma know how she looked than the unveiled want in Cain's eyes.

Before they'd met, Emma had considered herself one of those women who wouldn't ever consider dressing to attract someone, but then she'd met Cain, and while her partner had never asked anything of her when it came to her wardrobe, Emma could see the small laugh lines around her eyes when she smiled at something she really liked. Those little lines were the only way to tell that Cain's smile was genuine, and seeing them when Cain looked at her never made Emma feel like a plaything Cain wanted to show off.

Right now Cain had that look, and it had nothing to do with flaming ice cream or small sugary square donuts. She'd had it since that morning, when Emma had been only a frazzled mom trying to get her kids ready for the day and not anyone remotely sexy.

"Maybe the next time we come we can try something from their dessert menu, but right now I'm thinking that I'll take you up on your offer," she said to Cain.

"Mighty trusting of you, lass."

"The way I look at it, the first time I took you up on your offer of something different, it worked out really well for me, so why would I want to buck that adventurous side of me now?"

"Some would say thinking like that is where you went wrong." Cain's voice cracked uncharacteristically when Emma ran her nails up the inside of her thigh.

"Probably." Emma pushed her half-eaten lunch aside and leaned closer to Cain. "Everyone else wanted me to pick some corn-fed boy who would've spent his days talking about cows and what to feed them, but the choice I made makes me want to not waste any of my time sleeping on the off chance I might miss something. I don't think it's wrong to want to share my life with someone who fills my life with love, passion, and fun."

"You make me sound like a vacation destination."

"If I were to do that, I'd make sure the advertisements mentioned the fantastic rides that leave you breathless. I'm just glad I'm tall enough to ride."

Cain laughed and lifted Emma's hand to her lips. "I've missed you, lass." She pointed to Emma's plate. "Are you finished?"

"Lead on," Emma said as she entwined their fingers.

One of Cain's guys stayed behind and paid the bill, and only Lou got behind the driver's side when they got outside. As always, the FBI surveillance was close by, but for once Emma almost forgot they were there as Cain opened the back door for her and helped her inside. Emma had no clue what Cain had in mind, but she gladly pressed up against her and returned the kiss Cain initiated when she got in behind her.

When the car finally stopped they were at the Lakefront Airport in New Orleans east and the private jet Cain had arranged was ready to go. Emma watched the city recede in the small window before she finally turned to Cain.

"Where are we going?"

"You said you were willing to try something new, and I really want to get something sweet, so the only hint I'm giving is that we'll both get what we want." Cain sounded playful as she stroked Emma's hair.

"What about the kids?"

"Muriel," Cain said, talking about her cousin, "promised they'll be fine until we get back. It'll do her some good since it'll convince her one way or another on the question of wanting kids."

"I'm in the mood for whatever you have in mind, and you've taken care of everything I would've worried about, so I'll sit back and enjoy the ride. The other encouraging sign is that we're alone on this plane."

The small light over the pilot door went off, so Cain went to the refrigerator and took out a bottle of champagne. "Desserts are usually enjoyed more if it's not a group activity."

"True, baby. So does that mean that Merrick, Lou, and a host of other armed people aren't in a plane twenty feet behind us?"

"It's just you and me, and the guy behind that door. Once we land, though, he's not coming with us, so you think you can stand it if it's just you and me?"

Emma accepted the glass and patted the seat next her. "That wasn't a serious question, was it?" She kicked off her shoes and brought her feet up beneath her. "Asking me if I want to be alone with you is like asking Hannah if she's up for ice cream. Believe me, no matter what else is going on in our daughter's life, she's up for ice cream."

"Then here's to you and me, and whatever sweet things are in store for us."

They tapped glasses and drank, but this time Cain didn't bother with her refilling duties. When the glasses were empty she set them aside and pulled Emma into her lap. For the duration of the flight she kissed and touched enough to excite but never enough to send Emma over the edge. Emma almost screamed when Cain sat her back in her seat and got up to put the drinks away when the light came back on and a slight ding signaled that they were about to land. They'd been so busy Emma didn't have a clue as to how long they'd been airborne, and when she looked out the window the landscape didn't appear familiar.

"What are you up to, mobster?" she whispered, but she was so excited she had goose bumps.

❖

Miguel Flores, the manager of Carly's Sound waited a few feet from the steps of the plane with a jeep. Sitting next to him was a Venezuelan customs agent ready to inspect the passports in Cain's hands so they could get into the helicopter Miguel had waiting at the other side of the tarmac.

"Welcome," Miguel said in his accented English as he drove them. "I hope you had a pleasant flight."

"It was wonderful, and if I knew where I was I'd be great," Emma said. The hangar they were heading toward had a logo painted on the front, and while the guitar leaning on the palm tree seemed familiar, she hadn't placed it yet.

"You should think of it this way, señorita." Miguel stepped out of the jeep and waited for Cain to help Emma out. "There are surprises you should fear, like the tax man coming to your house and holding his hand out for more money." He frowned, which made Emma laugh. "And then there are surprises that you spend time thinking about, hoping they will happen to you again, they are so wonderful." He held open the door to the helicopter and helped them with the seat belts. "I can promise you one thing."

"What's that?" Emma wished now that she'd gone with cotton that morning instead of cashmere.

"I am not the tax man, but your spouse, she looks like someone you spend a lot of time thinking how wonderful she is. No?"

"Yes, sir," Emma said louder as the helicopter started up.

"Then you got nothing to worry about."

Cain laughed as Emma pointed from one side to the other every time she spotted things in the water on their short hop to Carly's Sound.

"Poppy called ahead and made all the arrangements, Cain, but please let me know if you need anything else," Miguel said as he drove them to their destination at the secluded resort.

"Thanks, but after hearing her talk about you, I'm sure everything's fine." Cain shook hands with him and led Emma to the last bungalow at the end. Now it was used for Valente extended family and friends, but it had been originally built for a very special woman who gave the island its name.

"Poppy?" Emma asked.

"An old friend," Cain said and took her hand again.

"This place is beautiful," Emma said as they took the steps up to the porch.

"I'll tell you all about it, but why don't you go inside and change and I'll wait for you out here."

"Aren't you coming?"

"Just a few more surprises and then you'll get sick of having me around."

Emma found her luggage in the second bedroom and her clothes hanging in the closet. Either they'd already been on the plane or Cain had shipped them ahead. How they got there didn't matter, but there was a simple sundress laid out across the bed, so she stripped and put it on. She walked out barefoot since there were no shoes and she figured that wasn't a mistake.

Outside Cain had changed as well into white drawstring pants and a loose-fitting shirt. In her bare feet, she looked different. More relaxed than Emma had ever seen her. They didn't exchange a word as Cain led them to a spot from which they watched the sun make its rapid descent into the water.

As they strolled back to the bungalow, Emma noticed that the stretch of beach wasn't empty anymore. She tilted her head in the direction of the table and chairs that had been set out. "You're ready for dessert, I take it?"

"I think it's a little more than that." Cain pulled Emma's chair out for her and popped the cork on the bottle of champagne that was sitting in the bucket of ice. Two barefoot waiters served a light dinner.

"Are we celebrating something?" Emma felt as if she'd fallen through a cloud and into one of her fantasies.

"My mother always told me that even in the worst moments of your life, there is something worth celebrating." When the waiters disappeared, she handed Emma a glass and dropped to her knees next to her. "If that's true, then imagine all there is to celebrate when things are as close to perfect as they get."

Emma was glad that the food they'd been served was a selection of fruit, cheese, and bread. It would hold. "Are you really hungry right at this moment?"

"Famished, but not for mango." Cain put her glass down and scooped Emma off her seat, but headed in the opposite direction from the bungalow.

"I'm sure if you carry me that way," Emma pointed toward their rooms, "you'll find there's a great bed in there."

"I think there's a great bed out here as well." Cain walked to the point where they'd watched the sunset. Under the palm trees was her last surprise of the day.

The staff had draped a canopy bed with white linens that billowed in the wind and placed a few candles in lanterns nearby.

Cain gently lowered Emma to her feet and kissed her until Emma wrapped her hands in the material of her shirt. As slowly as she could, Cain lifted her dress up and off, leaving Emma in just her panties. Before she could take care of those, Emma stopped her with a hand on her chest.

"Let me see you," she told Cain and started on the buttons of her shirt. The pants were easier and after a slight tug on the tie, they pooled at Cain's ankles. Since their reunion they'd made love more than enough times to ease the ache of loss, but this still felt like the first time they'd been together. Only this time, Emma didn't feel the slightest hesitation.

Cain might have been feared by many, but she belonged body and soul to Emma. Every moan, every touch of her lips, and every caress of her fingers belonged to Emma, and the only way they wouldn't was if Emma gave them away. But that would never happen again in this lifetime, or in what came beyond it. In Cain's arms she'd found not only acceptance but a home, and she gave thanks to any higher power listening that when she'd found it again, the door was open and waiting for her.

Emma pressed Cain down on the bed and straddled her hips, wanting to give Cain all that in return. Cain slid her hands under the sides of Emma's underwear and Emma leaned back so Cain could see all of her. "If you want me—"

Before Emma could finish, the fabric gave way when Cain seemed to lose patience with the barrier between them. But Emma wouldn't roll over when Cain tried to guide her in that direction. "I'll give you whatever you want, but not yet," she told Cain, and reached behind her to place the flat of her hand on Cain's sex.

Emma smiled when Cain bucked her hips slightly. "You've taught me so much about love." She leaned down so her nipples were just barely touching Cain's chest. "Don't pout," she said, since getting this close to Cain's lips meant she'd had to move her hand, but it was her lips Emma wanted right now.

As soon as they kissed, Cain's tongue went into her mouth and Cain squeezed her breasts, making Emma's hips jerk down against her. Emma pulled back. "Be good."

"I'm trying to be," Cain said and again tried to roll her over.

"Ah ah." Emma held Cain's hands to the bed so she could give her one more kiss. She didn't have anything to prove, she just wanted to touch Cain first and show her exactly how she felt. Her nipples dragged along Cain's body as she took her time moving down. "Like I said, you taught me about love, but when we're together like this I'm so glad you taught me about passion." Emma spread her open, placed her index and middle finger along Cain's hard clit, and squeezed.

"Please, lass," Cain said, sounding desperate.

Emma let go and reached up, palms open, in a silent request to be held. When Cain clasped her hands, Emma lowered her head and sucked her in. No matter how much Cain moved her hips, she didn't let go until Cain groaned her name as the orgasm took hold.

Cain pulled Emma up and embraced her. "Thank you, but I wanted to—"

Emma kissed her to get her to stop talking. "I had to do something to show you how much I loved my surprises. I don't know why you went through all this trouble, but you outdid yourself today."

This time Emma went willingly when Cain rolled her over "My friend Poppy told me that it was the most beautiful place to watch a sunset."

"It was beautiful."

"You're right, it was, but that's not why we're really here." Cain stroked Emma's throat to the middle of her chest. "There is that old saying that if you love something, set it free. You left, and while it hurt like nothing ever has in my life, I set you free. But now you're back. You came back to me, and if the rest of the saying is true, then you belong to me."

"Oh, my darling, you've got to have known that from the first moment you saw me. But if you didn't, then I'll be happy to spend the rest of my life proving it to you."

"You have nothing to prove, lass. Since you belong to me, then I wanted to give you a beautiful sunset as a gift. You can think back on this one and know that all the ones that come after it, until the end of my life, will be spent with you." Cain kissed the spot on Emma's chest over her heart and reached up to wipe the tears that had spilled from Emma's eyes. Cain repeated the words she'd heard her mother say to her father at every one of their anniversaries. "My love is fierce, my heart is true, and the whole of who I am is yours."

"Thank you," Emma said, her words ending in a hiss when Cain bit down gently on one of her nipples. "Now make love to me, you romantic devil."

It was a command that Cain gladly obeyed, and their laughter as well as their desire echoed off the waves until the sun started to rise. Cain had grown up immersed in tradition, and she was blessed to be starting her own with Emma.

RADCLYFFE is a retired surgeon and full time award-winning author-publisher with over thirty lesbian novels and anthologies in print, including the Lambda Literary winners *Erotic Interludes 2: Stolen Moments* ed. with Stacia Seaman and *Distant Shores, Silent Thunder*. Her novels *Justice Served, Turn Back Time*, and *When Dreams Tremble* were Lambda Literary award finalists. She has selections in multiple anthologies including *Wild Nights, Fantasy, Best Lesbian Erotica 2006, 2007*, and *2008, After Midnight, Caught Looking: Erotic Tales of Voyeurs and Exhibitionists, First-Timers, Ultimate Undies: Erotic Stories About Lingerie and Underwear, Hide and Seek, A is for Amour, H is for Hardcore, L is for Leather*, and *Rubber Sex*. She is the recipient of the 2003 and 2004 Alice B. Readers' award for her body of work and is also the president of Bold Strokes Books, one of the world's largest independent LGBT publishing companies.

ANYONE BUT YOU
RADCLYFFE

The apartment door eased open and a sharply etched wedge of light penetrated almost as far as the couch before the door shut silently, leaving the room in inky blackness once again. At 3 a.m., the intermittent rumble of traffic on the street below, the thin wail of distant sirens, and the occasional shout of late-night bar patrons had the muted quality of a receding dream.

I smelled her perfume at the same instant she stumbled against some object and gave a muffled curse.

"Turn the light on," I said from the couch where I lay. "I'm awake."

"Jesus, Marks! Scare me to death, why don't you! What are you doing out here?"

The light snapped on and I blinked against a rush of tears. The harsh glare accomplished what nothing else could, not even when I stared into the dark for hours, torturing myself with mental pictures of Olivia fucking her latest boy toy. Tears wouldn't change who we were. Or what I felt. "Sorry. I fell asleep."

I swiped at my eyes and ran my hands through my hair while Liv plopped into the big chair across from the sofa. She kicked off her high-heeled sandals and swung her legs over the broad curved arm, wiggling her bare toes with their bright red nails. Her skirt, some kind of clingy black stuff, rose up her thighs until I could make out the shadow of the valley between her legs. I looked away, but not before I had an image of some large masculine hand violating that sacred space. Although I guess it's not a violation, if it's welcomed.

"How was your date?" I sat up and tugged my rumpled T-shirt down over my ratty sweatpants. Pathetic.

Liv rolled her head back and forth on the arm of the chair while she studied the ceiling. "Same old same old. I didn't mind the bar scene when I was in school, you know? But after all this time it gets old."

Ten years we'd been roommates, since college. There'd been five of us back then, but only Liv and I remained. The others, two guys and a girl, had finished school and gotten their own places or left for new adventures somewhere else. For some reason, even though we could both afford it, Liv and I kept the place. We didn't even have that much in common, not really. I ran a heart-lung machine in the cardiac surgical wing at University Hospital. Liv managed a small, trendy restaurant on South Street. I favored softball and kayaking for recreation, Liz was an avid golfer. I'd been an out lesbian since I was fourteen. Liv preferred men whose dicks were bigger than their brains. I'd been in love with her since the minute she'd moved in. Five girlfriends over the ensuing years hadn't changed my mind. Liv had no idea, and I didn't see any point in letting her know. For the longest time, I made myself believe that being friends with her was better than not being around her at all. Lately, I'd been reconsidering. I couldn't sleep when she wasn't in the apartment.

Her bedroom was across the hall from mine, and we both slept with our doors open. By some unspoken agreement, during the week we didn't date, having settled into a comfortable routine at home. We'd usually end up on the couch sharing popcorn and a movie, or if it was too late for anything else, a glass of wine and a recap of the day's adventures. Then we'd shuffle off to the bathroom to get ready for bed, one after the other, passing each other in the hall with easy smiles. I slept in a sleeveless T-shirt and boxers. Liv wore panties and loose tank tops. She had a dancer's body, loose limbed and lean. Her breasts were small and her nipples surprisingly large in comparison. I knew precisely how big they were as they pushed out against those tank tops.

When we turned out the lights, we'd wish each other pleasant dreams, then I'd lie awake listening to her shift and sigh until she fell asleep. Sometimes I'd think about the way her breasts swayed as she slipped by me in the hall and how it would feel to press my fingertips to the triangle of fabric between her thighs. Sometimes I'd imagine her crossing the great divide between us, crawling under the covers, and curling up in my arms. Her fingers would be soft as they teased over my breasts to my belly, and lower, between my legs. She'd stroke me and I'd get wet for her and come.

I'd come quietly, not moving, not breathing, so as not to disturb her dreams as she slumbered across the hall.

"I've been thinking about getting my own place," I blurted, surprising us both.

Liv bolted upright, her eyes wide. "What? Why?"

Now that I'd said it, I felt lost and, at the same time, determined. Leaving was the right thing to do. Staying here with her, wanting her, was killing me. But the thought of not seeing her every day, not finding her in the kitchen making coffee in the morning or fixing leftovers for a midnight supper, was just as devastating. But, I reminded myself, one of these days Liv was going to hook up with a guy who had more to offer than a mind-blowing orgasm, and she was going to leave me anyhow. The only difference would be the length of time I'd put my life on hold, loving her. More certain now, I said, "A place closer to the hospital would be easier when I get called out at night." That wasn't enough of an argument, I knew, so I added the coup de grace, "And besides, the no sleepover rule is getting to be a problem."

Even though it was just the two of us now, Liv and I had kept the rule the five of us had instituted years ago about not bringing our current romantic interest home for the night. We had all agreed we didn't want to wake up to half-naked strangers in the kitchen, or even worse, in the shower. So Liv didn't bring guys home, and I didn't bring girls.

"Oh," Liv said, sounding almost hurt. "I didn't realize you had anything serious going on."

"Well," I said, not wanting to admit there wasn't anyone and hadn't been anyone for almost a year, "it's…you know…headed that way."

"Oh." Liv curled a strand of red-gold hair around her finger and stared at something on the rug. "We could change the rule, you know. You wouldn't have to move then."

The very idea of watching a man fondle Liv right under my nose, in my own living room, literally made me sick. "Yeah, well, you know. Some girls like privacy. Noise and all."

"Noise." Liv didn't look up, and her voice sounded shaky. "I guess even if we closed our doors it wouldn't help all that much."

I laughed, but it came out sounding strangled. I was pretty sure I'd lose my mind if I had to listen to some guy making Liv come. "I don't think so. Hell, I can hear you snoring."

Liv tried to look put out, but I could tell her heart wasn't in it. "I don't snore."

"The hell you don't," I replied, starting to feel like I really might cry. God, I hated that she looked hurt. But I wanted to put my arms around her, I wanted to kiss the sadness from her eyes. I wanted to hold her, naked and warm against my skin, and that's why I knew I couldn't go on. I stood so suddenly Liv jolted back in the chair. "I'll let you know in plenty of time to find another roommate."

I was almost to the hall leading to our bedrooms when I must have imagined I heard her whisper, "I don't want anyone but you."

Then I reminded myself that wishing doesn't make it so.

❖

"Hey, Marks? Jen?"

"Yeah?" When I went to bed, I didn't think I would be able to fall asleep. But I guess I had, because the room was light enough now for me to see Liv standing in the doorway of my bedroom. I'd dumped my sweats and T-shirt on the floor by the bed earlier, so I pulled the sheet up to my chin. I didn't know why, because she'd seen me naked plenty of times before. This time, I felt exposed.

"Are you sleeping?"

"Not really." I sat up and rubbed my face. "Are you okay?"

"Not really." Liv took two steps into the room and stopped. "Can I come in?"

"Yeah. Sure." I inched over toward the center of the bed, still clutching the sheet. "What's wrong?"

Liz sat tentatively on the side of my bed, facing me. She wore her usual loose white ribbed tank top and bikinis. When she bent one knee up and circled it with her arms, I caught a flash of white at the apex of her thighs and the blood rushed from my head. If I doubted my decision to leave earlier, I didn't now. I couldn't be around her this way any longer.

"What's your girlfriend's name?"

"What?" I asked stupidly.

"Your girlfriend. What's her name?"

Truth or lies—I was going to lose either way, and I wouldn't give up everything for a lie. "She doesn't have a name."

Liv laughed a little, but it didn't sound as if she was happy. "Do you just call her *baby* all the time?"

"I don't call her anything at all." I closed my eyes tightly, searching for the right words, and when I opened them again, Liv was leaning closer with an expression halfway between hope and sorrow on her face. I hated that I'd made her look that way, and I gently stroked her cheek. "I'm sorry. I don't call her anything because there isn't anyone to call. Anything."

"No girlfriend?"

I shook my head. Liv glanced down and I realized I'd dropped the sheet when I'd touched her. But when I made a grab for it, she caught my hand.

"Don't. You're beautiful."

"Jesus, Liv," I groaned, yanking my arm away. I wanted to jump out of bed and run, but she was in the way.

"Why did you tell me you had a girlfriend? I've been going crazy thinking about you with her. Thinking about her making noises while you touched her, while you made her—"

I pressed my fingers to her lips. "Stop. Don't say something you'll regret tomorrow."

She grabbed my arm with both hands and kissed my fingers. I froze. God, she didn't just kiss. She savored. My stomach tightened into a simmering ball of need and my skin flushed hot. When she inched the tip of her tongue into the space between my fingers, one after the other, I started panting.

"Liv. Babe," I croaked.

Liv smiled. "Babe? You call her babe?"

"No. I—"

"Who, then?" Liv half crawled up on the bed and leaned over me, her arms braced on either side of my shoulders. I burrowed back into the pillows, trying not to notice the expanse of bare belly that stretched below the bottom of her tank. "Who, Marks? Who do you call babe?"

"No one." She raised an eyebrow. "I mean, not anyone but you. In my mind. Sometimes. Sometimes in my mind I call you babe."

Liv threw one leg over my hips and crouched above me on all fours. The sheet pulled down farther, to my hips. I gripped it and tugged.

"Don't," Liv repeated, more softly this time. "Don't you want me to see?"

"Liv, you don't understand," I pleaded.

"That's just it," Liv said. "I do. I do understand."

She relaxed her arms a little and her breasts touched mine with only the thin cotton between us. My nipples hardened instantly, and Liv gave a little sigh. The sound slashed through me and I got wet.

"Please, Liv. Please move."

"Do you know how long it's been since I slept with a guy?" Liv asked, her mouth just inches from mine.

I groaned and shook my head.

"Nine months," Liv whispered, her breath streaming into my mouth. Her breasts were full and firm against mine, and as she spoke, she settled her pelvis snugly between my legs. I fought not to whimper. "Nine months, and I kept telling myself the guys just weren't right. Lousy kissers, crappy technique, too rough, not rough enough, too fast, not fast enough. Just not right. None of them."

My head was swimming. It took everything in me not to writhe beneath the weight of her body. The sheet did nothing to blunt her heat, and I felt her between my legs, her fire to my fire.

"Liv, don't do this to me." I clasped her hips as lightly as I could and tried to move her away. "This isn't you."

"This *is* me," Liv said as if she'd just made a miraculous discovery. She kissed the edge of my jaw. "Oh, Marks, this is so me. I don't want you to go."

"I can't stay."

"Why not?"

"Because I don't want anyone but you. I love you, Liv. I've loved you forever."

Liv kissed me, sweetly at first, as if she'd never kissed anyone before. She ran her tongue along the edges of my lips, then darted inside my mouth, laughing when I chased her tongue with mine. Then her hands were in my hair and her body pulsed and rolled over me. She made a hungry sound and kissed me like she knew exactly what a kiss was all about. She left me breathless and trembling and delirious with desire.

"I love you, too," Liv whispered. "I love you, Marks. And I love the way you feel. The way we feel together."

I grasped her shoulders and pushed her away until we were staring into each other's eyes. "I want you too bad to stop if we don't stop right now."

Liv smiled and rocked her hips between my legs. I whimpered and jerked under her and she laughed. "No way are we stopping."

"You're so sexy," I groaned. "I want you so much."

"Does that mean you're not going to be getting naked with anyone else?"

"Not a chance." It was the truth, my truth, and saying it set my heart free no matter what the morning would bring. I cupped the back of her neck and pulled her down so I could kiss her like I had wanted to kiss her for as long as I could remember.

Just before her mouth met mine, she whispered, "I meant what I said about loving you. And I don't plan on doing this—any of this—with anyone but you."

And then she kissed me and I knew what the morning would bring. Us.

Books Available From Bold Strokes Books

Lake Effect Snow by C.P. Rowlands. News correspondent Annie T. Booker and FBI Agent Sarah Moore struggle to stay one step ahead of disaster as Annie's life becomes the war zone she once reported on. Eclipse EBook (978-1-60282-068-5)

Revision of Justice by John Morgan Wilson. Murder shifts into high gear, propelling Benjamin Justice into a raging fire that consumes the Hollywood Hills, burning steadily toward the famous Hollywood Sign—and the identity of a cold-blooded killer. Gay Mystery. (978-1-60282-058-6)

I Dare You by Larkin Rose. Stripper by night, corporate raider by day, Kelsey's only looking for sex and power, until she meets a woman who stirs her heart and her body. (978-1-60282-030-2)

Truth Behind the Mask by Lesley Davis. Erith Baylor is drawn to Sentinel Pagan Osborne's quiet strength, but the secrets between them strain duty and family ties. (978-1-60282-029-6)

Cooper's Deale by KI Thompson. Two would-be lovers and a decidedly inopportune murder spell trouble for Addy Cooper, no matter which way the cards fall. (978-1-60282-028-9)

Romantic Interludes 1: Discovery ed. by Radclyffe and Stacia Seaman. An anthology of sensual, erotic contemporary love stories from the best-selling Bold Strokes authors. (978-1-60282-027-2)

A Guarded Heart by Jennifer Fulton. The last place FBI Special Agent Pat Roussel expects to find herself is assigned to an illicit private security gig baby-sitting a celebrity. (Ebook) (978-1-60282-067-8)

Saving Grace by Jennifer Fulton. Champion swimmer Dawn Beaumont, injured in a car crash she caused, flees to Moon Island, where scientist Grace Ramsay welcomes her. (Ebook) (978-1-60282-066-1)

The Sacred Shore by Jennifer Fulton. Successful tech industry survivor Merris Randall does not believe in love at first sight until she meets Olivia Pearce. (Ebook) (978-1-60282-065-4)

Passion Bay by Jennifer Fulton. Two women from different ends of the earth meet in paradise. Author's expanded edition. (Ebook) (978-1-60282-064-7)

Never Wake by Gabrielle Goldsby. After a brutal attack, Emma Webster becomes a self-sentenced prisoner inside her condo—until the world outside her window goes silent. (Ebook) (978-1-60282-063-0)

The Caretaker's Daughter by Gabrielle Goldsby. Against the backdrop of a nineteenth-century English country estate, two women struggle to find love. (Ebook) (978-1-60282-062-3)

Simple Justice by John Morgan Wilson. When a pretty-boy cokehead is murdered, former LA reporter Benjamin Justice and his reluctant new partner, Alexandra Templeton, must unveil the real killer. (978-1-60282-057-9)

Remember Tomorrow by Gabrielle Goldsby. Cees Bannigan and Arieanna Simon find that a successful relationship rests in remembering the mistakes of the past. (978-1-60282-026-5)

Put Away Wet by Susan Smith. Jocelyn "Joey" Fellows has just been savagely dumped—when she posts an online personal ad, she discovers more than just the great sex she expected. (978-1-60282-025-8)

Homecoming by Nell Stark. Sarah Storm loses everything that matters—family, future dreams, and love—will her new "straight" roommate cause Sarah to take a chance at happiness? (978-1-60282-024-1)

The Three by Meghan O'Brien. A daring, provocative exploration of love and sexuality. Two lovers, Elin and Kael, struggle to survive in a postapocalyptic world. (Ebook) (978-1-60282-056-2)

Falling Star by Gill McKnight. Solley Rayner hopes a few weeks with her family will help heal her shattered dreams, but she hasn't counted on meeting a woman who stirs her heart. (978-1-60282-023-4)

Lethal Affairs by Kim Baldwin and Xenia Alexiou. Elite operative Domino is no stranger to peril, but her investigation of journalist Hayley Ward will test more than her skills. (978-1-60282-022-7)

A Place to Rest by Erin Dutton. Sawyer Drake doesn't know what she wants from life until she meets Jori Diamantina—only trouble is, Jori doesn't seem to share her desire. (978-1-60282-021-0)

Warrior's Valor by Gun Brooke. Dwyn Izsontro and Emeron D'Artansis must put aside personal animosity and unwelcome attraction to defeat an enemy of the Protector of the Realm. (978-1-60282-020-3)

Finding Home by Georgia Beers. Take two polar-opposite women with an attraction for one another they're trying desperately to ignore, throw in a far-too-observant dog, and then sit back and enjoy the romance. (978-1-60282-019-7)

Word of Honor by Radclyffe. All Secret Service Agent Cameron Roberts and First Daughter Blair Powell want is a small intimate wedding, but the paparazzi and a domestic terrorist have other plans. (978-1-60282-018-0)

Hotel Liaison by JLee Meyer. Two women searching through a secret past discover that their brief hotel liaison is only the beginning. Will they risk their careers—and their hearts—to follow through on their desires? (978-1-60282-017-3)

Love on Location by Lisa Girolami. Hollywood film producer Kate Nyland and artist Dawn Brock discover that love doesn't always follow the script. (978-1-60282-016-6)

Edge of Darkness by Jove Belle. Investigator Diana Collins charges at life with an irreverent comment and a right hook, but even those may not protect her heart from a charming villain. (978-1-60282-015-9)

Thirteen Hours by Meghan O'Brien. Workaholic Dana Watts's life takes a sudden turn when an unexpected interruption arrives in the form of the most beautiful breasts she has ever seen—stripper Laurel Stanley's. (978-1-60282-014-2)

In Deep Waters 2 by Radclyffe and Karin Kallmaker. All bets are off when two award winning-authors deal the cards of love and passion... and every hand is a winner. (978-1-60282-013-5)

Pink by Jennifer Harris. An irrepressible heroine frolics, frets, and navigates through the "what ifs" of her life: all the unexpected turns of fortune, fame, and karma. (978-1-60282-043-2)

Deal with the Devil by Ali Vali. New Orleans crime boss Cain Casey brings her fury down on the men who threatened her family, and blood and bullets fly. (978-1-60282-012-8)

Naked Heart by Jennifer Fulton. When a sexy ex-CIA agent sets out to seduce and entrap a powerful CEO, there's more to this plan than meets the eye...or the flogger. (978-1-60282-011-1)

Heart of the Matter by KI Thompson. TV newscaster Kate Foster is Professor Ellen Webster's dream girl, but Kate doesn't know Ellen exists...until an accident changes everything. (978-1-60282-010-4)

Heartland by Julie Cannon. When political strategist Rachel Stanton and dude ranch owner Shivley McCoy collide on an empty country road, fate intervenes. (978-1-60282-009-8)

Shadow of the Knife by Jane Fletcher. Militia Rookie Ellen Mittal has no idea just how complex and dangerous her life is about to become. A Celaeno series adventure romance. (978-1-60282-008-1)

To Protect and Serve by VK Powell. Lieutenant Alex Troy is caught in the paradox of her life—to hold steadfast to her professional oath or to protect the woman she loves. (978-1-60282-007-4)

Deeper by Ronica Black. Former homicide detective Erin McKenzie and her fiancée Elizabeth Adams couldn't be happier—until the not-so-distant past comes knocking at the door. (978-1-60282-006-7)

The Lonely Hearts Club by Radclyffe. Take three friends, add two ex-lovers and several new ones, and the result is a recipe for explosive rivalries and incendiary romance. (978-1-60282-005-0)

Venus Besieged by Andrews & Austin. Teague Richfield heads for Sedona and the sensual arms of psychic astrologer Callie Rivers for a much-needed romantic reunion. (978-1-60282-004-3)

Branded Ann by Merry Shannon. Pirate Branded Ann raids a merchant vessel to obtain a treasure map and gets more than she bargained for with the widow Violet. (978-1-60282-003-6)

American Goth by JD Glass. Trapped by an unsuspected inheritance and guided only by the guardian who holds the secret to her future, Samantha Cray fights to fulfill her destiny. (978-1-60282-002-9)

Learning Curve by Rachel Spangler. Ashton Clarke is perfectly content with her life until she meets the intriguing Professor Carrie Fletcher, who isn't looking for a relationship with anyone. (978-1-60282-001-2)

Place of Exile by Rose Beecham. Sheriff's detective Jude Devine struggles with ghosts of her past and an ex-lover who still haunts her dreams. (978-1-933110-98-1)

Fully Involved by Erin Dutton. A love that has smoldered for years ignites when two women and one little boy come together in the aftermath of tragedy. (978-1-933110-99-8)

Heart 2 Heart by Julie Cannon. Suffering from a devastating personal loss, Kyle Bain meets Lane Connor, and the chance for happiness suddenly seems possible. (978-1-60282-000-5)